WOLF POINT

AN ANDY LARSON MYSTERY

WOLF POINT

MIKE THOMPSON

FIVE STAR

A part of Gale, Cengage Learning

GALE
CENGAGE Learning

Farmington Hills, Mich • San Francisco • New York • Waterville, Maine
Meriden, Conn • Mason, Ohio • Chicago

GALE
CENGAGE Learning®

LIBRARY OF CONGRESS CATALOGING-IN-PUBLICATION DATA

Thompson, Mike, approximately 1942–
    Wolf Point : an Andy Larson mystery / Mike Thompson. —
First edition.
        pages cm
    ISBN 978-1-4328-2930-8 (hardcover) — ISBN 1-4328-2930-0
(hardcover) — ISBN 978-1-4328-2935-3 (ebook) — ISBN 1-4328-
2935-1 (ebook)
    1. Prohibition—Montana—History—Fiction. I. Title.
PS3620.H6839W65 2015
813'.6—dc23   2014031295

First Edition. First Printing: January 2015
Find us on Facebook– https://www.facebook.com/FiveStarCengage
Visit our website– http://www.gale.cengage.com/fivestar/
Contact Five Star™ Publishing at FiveStar@cengage.com

Printed in the United States of America
1 2 3 4 5 6 7 19 18 17 16 15

ACKNOWLEDGMENTS

Thanks to Tiffany Schofield, Hazel Rumney, Tracey Matthews, and Nivette Jackaway, the ladies from Five Star who have been such great help to me with this endeavor.

CHAPTER ONE

Sheriff Andy Larson slowly shook his head as he glanced around the room and down at the dead man he was kneeling beside. *God, I got out of North Dakota to get away from things like this,* he told himself. *Bootleg whiskey and machine-gun deaths. Now, it seems I either brought them along or they followed me.* He lifted his fingers from the dead man's cheek and slid them back into his glove. "Old Man Merkel's face is frozen hard as a block of ice," he commented through a cloud of his breath. "They all sure been dead for a while." He rose to his feet, adjusted his battered black cowboy hat, and looked around the frost-encrusted main room of the barn.

Larson was tall and thin with a drooping salt-and-pepper mustache on an Indian-skinned face that was too hard and lined for his twenty-six years. His eyes were narrow and dark with wrinkles splintering out from the corners. His nose was bent in the middle, initially broken in a bar fight in France during *The War to End All Wars* and broken several more times since then. He had left a police job in North Dakota to take the job of chief deputy sheriff of Roosevelt County, Montana, and had moved up to become sheriff when the previous sheriff, Billy Hollis, had been gunned down two months earlier. Larson could be up for the position of sheriff in the regular election in October, but in his mind, he wasn't sure he wanted to keep the job of Roosevelt County sheriff.

7

Larson's eyes moved quickly over the five men's bodies. Three of the bodies, ripped and torn by gunfire, lay amongst the remains of wooden, lead-chewed whiskey cases and shattered bottles. Spent shell casings littered the entire area. The two Merkel boys, their hands tied behind their backs, lay off to one side, a patch of burned hair and a single bullet hole in the top of their heads.

Chief Deputy Dusty Durbin pulled the unlit cigar out of the corner of his mouth and spit. "The only thing not frozen solid in here is the whiskey left in some of those shot-up bottles," he said. "The place smells like a damned distillery." He chuckled to himself. "Makes me kinda thirsty." Durbin was built like a large beer keg with a bulbous red nose protruding from the red mustache and beard covering most of his face. He was known for his odd sense of humor. "I wonder if there's any bottles escaped the lead storm?" He made a production of pretending to search through the ruined wooden cases. "This is really a shame," he said, lifting a broken bottle and reading from the label. "Someone had the nerve to shoot up good Superior Scotch Whiskey."

The others all chuckled with clouds of cold-weather breath and nodded in agreement. They were uniformed in brown canvas, sheepskin-lined coats with heavy, black bearskin collars and navy-blue wool caps with long earflaps hanging down the sides of their faces. Centered on the front of each cap was a silver shield with **Roosevelt County Sheriff's Department** in bold black letters.

"They sure shot the shit out of this place," Deputy John Mooney said, spitting into a broken whiskey bottle. He pointed a gloved hand across the room and shook his head. "They even shot those four cows over there in their stalls." Mooney was the oldest of the deputies, slightly slumped with age, thin white hair, twinkling blue eyes behind wire-rimmed glasses, and a perpetual smile. One cheek always bulged with a wad of tobacco and he was amazingly accurate with his spitting ability. He pointed at the floor of the haymow over their heads. "Look at that line of bullet holes up there. Why'n the hell'd they shoot up the ceiling?"

"Probably to get someone's attention or emphasize a point. There's no doubt this is meant to be a warning or a lesson to somebody," Larson stated, shaking a Camel cigarette out of a pack, snapping a flame onto a wooden match with his thumbnail, and taking a deep pull of smoke into his lungs. He dropped the match to the dirt floor and ground it with his boot. He noticed the look he got from Durbin and shook his head. "I know I shouldn't be smoking in here, but what the hell . . . ?" He exhaled smoke, dragon-like from his nostrils, and shook his head. "I'll be careful. At least the cold keeps this place from stinking. Think what it'd smell like if it was the middle of July instead of the middle of December."

Deputy Durbin walked over and looked into the stalls at the dead cows. "This's interesting," he said, using his cigar for a pointer. "These critters were each killed with one clean shot to the middle of the head. It looks like those two overripe Merkel boys got it the same way as the cows. From the way their hands are tied, I'd say they were executed. What're their names again?"

"Abner and Leroy," Mooney answered. "And I heard they weren't the sharpest knives in the drawer."

"Old Man Merkel and these two were sure chewed to shit by machine-gun fire," Larson stated, nudging one of the bodies with his boot. "Since they're dressed in suits, ties, hats, and fancy topcoats, I'd guess they aren't from around here. Any of you recognize them? Maybe seen them around town?"

"No," Deputy Mooney snorted and crouched to look closely at one of the top-coated strangers. "There really ain't a lot to recognize on this one after that slug tore off most of his jaw."

Deputy Robert Sullivan, the department photographer, stepped into the room carrying a large camera, flash unit, and canvas bag of flashbulbs. "All right, everybody step back so I can get my damned pictures taken," he said, as he twisted the first bulb into the flash unit. "The sooner we get this crap done and get to a warmer place, the better." Sullivan was tall, thin, and pale. His gray eyes squinted over the tops of his thick glasses and his dark brown hair and droopy mustache were the only color on his face. He was the only deputy who could use a typewriter at a decent speed so he handled most of the paperwork.

"We'll get out of your way, Bob," Larson said. "Let's go up to the house, boys."

Sheriff Larson and Deputies Dusty Durbin, John Mooney, Bernie Ward, Dave Dixon, and Ben Graves stepped outside and lined up, looking across the snow-blanketed yard towards the farmhouse.

"Damn, that sun is bright," Durbin said, holding his hand just above his squinting eyes.

Larson pulled a pair of small, wire-rimmed, dark glasses from a shirt pocket and adjusted them on his nose. "Comfort only costs a quarter at Stillings' Drug, boys. How much fresh snow we got here now, an inch or two?"

"Yeah," Mooney agreed, kicking at the snow. "Enough to give everything a light cover and show off fresh tracks."

"Okay," Larson began. "Let's start trying to put some pieces of this puzzle in place. There were no fresh tire tracks up to the barn when we got here. Today's Monday and it snowed Friday morning. That tells us nobody's been in here since Friday. Dusty, what'd the mail carrier tell you when he called in this morning?"

"Martinson told me he'd put two letters in the Merkels' mailbox last Tuesday, the fourteenth. The Merkels didn't get any more mail until Martinson opened the mailbox today and there were the two letters from last Tuesday. There was no smoke coming from the chimney and no tracks of any kind on the road leading in here. He went back to the Burgess' place and used the phone to call in to us about what he wasn't seeing," Durbin explained.

Larson scratched his chin, took a final drag from his cigarette, and flipped it off into the snow. "Did he say anything about any tire tracks on the fourteenth?"

"Not that I remember, but he left some mail on the thirteenth and it was gone."

Larson closed his eyes as he thought. "Then I can make the assumption that the Merkels and the two strangers were killed on or after the fourteenth. At least they didn't make it to the mailbox on the fourteenth."

"Another thing, there's no extra vehicles here," Mooney said and pointed at a snow-covered truck. "That's Merkel's old, beat-up truck over there so the shooters must've taken the city boys' car when they left 'cause they had to get out of here in something."

Larson pointed at a large, wooden, horse-pulled sled. "From all those tracks it looks like that big thing's had a lotta use before that last snow. Anybody see the horses?"

"They're over in the far corner of the corrals. I saw 'em when I was outside earlier," Durbin answered. "They've got plenty of hay and a spring, so they'll be okay for a while. I was thinking it's funny they didn't get shot. I guess maybe the shooter didn't think they knew anything."

CHAPTER TWO

Sheriff Larson shook his head at Durbin's attempted humor. "Let's go to the house," he said, kicking off into the fresh snow on the path to the ramshackle building. He paused at the shed surrounding the back door of the house, kicked the small ridge of snow away, and pushed it open. "I figured this," he said, pulling his dark glasses off, putting them in his pocket, shoving the door wider, and stepping inside. Half of the room, containing nesting boxes and feeders, was separated by a doored wall of chicken wire. In the summer the birds were kept in an outside coop. "All the chickens are frozen stiff. Nobody to stoke the little stove that keeps them warm in here in the winter. They didn't have a chance in hell."

The men made their way into the kitchen and looked around. There was a metal plate with a tall stack of shriveled, white-grease-covered pancakes sitting on the warming surface of the wood-burning kitchen stove. A large, cast-iron skillet, with the shrunken, black remains of three burned pancakes, sat on the cold cooking surface.

Larson tapped the handle of the skillet with a gloved finger. "It looks like we know the time of day everybody was taken up to the barn," he stated, his breath a cloud in the air. "They didn't even give the cook the chance to take this off the fire. You boys get a quick look through the house and tell me if you find anything that might be a clue for us." He stared blankly at the pile of frozen pancakes and patted his pockets for his Camels.

The house was small and the others quickly returned from their search, shaking their heads.

Larson stood with the unlit cigarette between his lips and his thumbnail poised to snap the head of the match gripped in his fingers. "I've been thinking about those four dead cows," he began, as he snapped the flame onto the match and lit his cigarette. "Why'd they shoot the brothers and the damned cows so clean and butcher the old man?" The end of his cigarette glowed and he blew out the match with a long, smoky breath. He looked around, shrugged, and jammed the match upright in the pile of hard greasy pancakes.

"Do you suppose they'd ask a question an' if they didn't git the answer they wanted, they'd shoot a cow?" Durbin suggested. "Kinda like, no answer an' next time it'll be one of you."

Larson nodded. "Sure, why not? *And* when they ran out of cows, they shot Abner and Leroy, so they had to be questioning the old man. Let's go back to the barn and see if Sullivan's done taking pictures. Look the place over again, carefully. Pick up all the shell casings. We'll see if they've got anything distinctive on them, firing pin marks, ejection scratches, you know what I mean. Something that might tie them to the gunning down of Chief Grubb or Sheriff Hollis. Crooks aren't as smart as they think they are. They've gotta screw up someplace."

"If he's done, we can look for identification on the strangers before they haul 'em off to the crime lab in Helena," Mooney stated.

"Yeah, of course, go ahead," Larson replied. "And be sure to check all their pockets real good."

Durbin pulled out a watch, looked at it, and slid it back out of sight. "Wonder what in the hell's takin' them so long to get something out here to pick up those five stiffs in the barn?" he asked, around the unlit cigar clenched in his teeth. "And when I said stiffs, I *was* speaking of their current condition." He

13

chuckled again at his own humor.

Larson shook his head as he followed the others out the door and pulled it shut. "I'll take one of the cars back to town now. I had a note this morning telling me Dennison wanted to talk to me. You boys go do what you gotta do. Scour the place for anything that might be a clue. Dusty, wait a minute, I wanna talk to you before I go."

Durbin pulled his cigar and spit. "How much longer are you gonna put up with Dennison's shit?"

"I don't know," Larson answered and flipped his cigarette away. "I got a letter back from that town he came from in Illinois and it was the same line of glowing crap the town got with his initial application. He's well covered. All I'm working on is suspicions. Have somebody see if they can tell where that big sled was going and what it might have been used for. Like I said earlier, from all the tracks, it had a lotta use."

CHAPTER THREE

Three Months Earlier
September 1923

Sheriff Billy Hollis and Chief Deputy Andy Larson stood on the sidewalk in front of the Good Shepherd Lutheran Church listening to Assistant Police Chief Mike Goetz. All three men were dressed in black suits and hats. Black ribbons stretched across the centers of the badges pinned on their coats.

Sheriff Hollis glanced around over the tops of his wire-rimmed glasses, spit a cud of tobacco into the gold, leaf-cluttered grass behind him, knuckled his white, tobacco-stained mustache dry, and searched his coat pockets for a plug of fresh chew. Hollis had been the Roosevelt County, Montana, sheriff almost as long as the other two men had been alive. He was a straight, tall, white-haired man with a wrinkled, sun-darkened face. His tipped-back hat revealed a white forehead; the sign of a man who had worn a cowboy hat most of his life. He found his tobacco, peeled back the wrapper, and gnawed off a corner. As he worked the chew around in his mouth, he offered the plug to the other two men, who quickly shook their heads. "Suit yerself," he said, as he smoothed the wrapper and dropped it back into a pocket.

"The mayor and the town council offered me the chief's job after Ed was gunned down three days ago," Goetz said, softly. He was a short, thin man with a pale face and darting brown eyes. "I was seriously considering it. But, Jean and I've been discussing it and I'm going to have to pass. Law enforcement in this town isn't what it used to be. Not when the police chief gets shot to hell in his own car, right on main street at night and no clues as to who or why. There's no apparent reason, just plain cold-blooded murder. No, I'm not taking the job. Matter a fact, I'm looking to see if there're any openings on the force in Helena or Bismarck. Ed Grubb was police chief here in Wolf Point for nearly eighteen years and they were pretty easy. No real crime to speak of, but now we seem to be making up for all those years of peace." He glanced at the sheriff, then Larson, and smiled slightly. "Why don't you apply for it, Andy? It pays better than a deputy sheriff."

Larson shook his head, dropped the butt of his cigarette to the sidewalk, and ground it under his boot. "No, I like working for ol' Billy here and being able to do my job out in the country. There's almost twenty-four-hundred square miles in Roosevelt County and I can be a little more . . . ah, easy with my interpretation of the laws. Most of the men *and* women out there straighten up with a little scolding, a threat or two, and maybe a slap on the wrist. I like working out there in the wide open spaces."

Sheriff Hollis snorted his derision and spit across the sidewalk.

Mike Goetz nodded. "I can understand. Guess now they'll advertise outside for someone with law enforcement leadership qualifications. None of the other cops in Wolf Point have the experience or inclination to take the chief's job. Besides, these boys are used to the way police work's been here for years and years. A few parking tickets, a little shoplifting, kid puts a rock through a window; wrestle a drunk once in a while, fights, burglary, stolen car, man slaps his wife. All the usual small-town crime. They don't want to investigate things like someone being chewed to dog food by a damned machine-gun-toting assassin.

A couple of them got sick when they saw the chief's body. His coffin's gonna be on the light side today."

"Yep, things've gone pretty damned soft here over the years," Hollis agreed and spit again. "Hell, the last lynchin' in the county was over . . ." He put his fingers to his forehead and closed his eyes. "Lemme think . . . It's back at the turn of the century. I'd been back from the war 'bout two years. I know I told y'all those stories 'bout ridin' with Colonel Roosevelt. Damn fine man an' a damned fine president, old Teddy was. Anyway it was the year after I beat Dave Daniels in the election for sheriff. I's 'bout thirty-five years old . . ." He stopped, opened his eyes, shook his head, and looked over his glasses at the others. "Sorry, I seem to've developed a tendency to ramble."

Larson smiled and chuckled. "That's all right, Billy, I enjoy your tales about driving cattle up here from Texas and ranching, and I especially like those Teddy Roosevelt stories."

The doors of the church being pushed open and Pastor Teslow stepping out onto the steps interrupted Larson. The pastor was followed closely by four men carrying a casket draped with the Montana state flag; alongside them was a black-veiled woman walking with one gloved hand on the flag and the other pushing a handkerchief to her covered face.

"I'd best get to my car so I can lead the funeral procession," Goetz said, turning and walking towards his automobile. "I'll see you at the cemetery."

CHAPTER FOUR

October 1923

Sheriff Billy Hollis walked out the door of his living quarters on the main floor of the Roosevelt County Jail, stretched, and shoved the door shut with the heel of his boot. He spit a cud of soggy tobacco into a nearby bush and patted his vest pockets for the plug of fresh chew. He brought the block of tobacco out and leaned into the light coming from the window to examine it. *Should keep this stuff in the damned wrapper.* He flicked several specks of lint and lighter-colored particles of unidentified material off the dark plug before sticking it between his teeth and gnawing off a goodly portion. He dropped the tobacco into his pocket, tipped his hat back, and admired the quarter moon rising from the trees. *Damn, beautiful night,* he told himself as he chewed, spit a glob off into the bushes, and thumbed his mustache dry. *But it is kinda warm for this time of year. This warm fall could lead to a damned hard-ass winter.*

A man stepped from behind a large cottonwood tree a short distance away. "Sheriff Billy Hollis?" he called, softly.

Hollis pulled his hat down and squinted towards the outline of the man. "Yeah . . ."

The shadowy figure swung something up from his side and the night air became lit with a string of bright flashes and the staccato chatter of gunfire.

The slugs from the Thompson machine gun slammed Billy Hollis back against the heavy wooden door and tobacco juice

18

ran from his lips to mix with the blood gushing from the bullet wound in his throat. The impact of the slugs tearing through his torso kept him standing against the door as his eyes rolled up and he died.

The machine gun clicked on an empty receiver and the night was suddenly as silent as it had been when Sheriff Hollis was admiring the weather. The little man holding the smoking weapon watched the sheriff slide down to the steps, leaving a trail of blood on the bullet-riddled wood of the door. He worked the action to check it, swung it up onto his shoulder, turned, and disappeared into the darkness of the trees.

Sheriff Hollis' body jerked in a series of spasms and tipped so his sightless eyes were reflected in the growing pool of blood. The old cowboy-soldier-lawman wouldn't be telling any more stories about cattle drives and fighting in a war with Colonel Teddy Roosevelt.

Chief Deputy Andy Larson and acting Police Chief Mike Goetz, their badges again draped in black ribbons, stood under a leafless oak tree and watched the family of Sheriff Billy Hollis getting into cars to return to the church for the traditional after-funeral luncheon.

"Looks like there's gonna be a big feed . . . again," Goetz commented, as Mayor George Hauger joined them and shook out a cigarette.

"Yeah, too damned soon," Larson agreed, as he thumb-nailed a flame onto a stick match, held it to the mayor, and then lit his own. "Too many empty saddles . . ." he muttered through a cloud of smoke.

"Did the County Commission offer you Billy's job?" Goetz asked.

Larson nodded as he slid the Camels into his coat pocket and broke the match between his fingers. "They did and I'm gonna take it. Billy was a good friend and I want the bastard who gunned him down. What's your situation these days?"

Goetz shrugged and pointed at the mayor. "Well, how's the search going, George?"

The mayor took a deep drag on his cigarette. "It's been almost a month now and they've only had one application for the chief's job. A fella named, ah . . . , Parker Dennison. People aren't willing to come out here for the amount of pay we're offering. That and the damned weather this time of year."

Larson nodded. "That's an impressive handle. Sounds like a money man with a name like that."

"Yeah," Goetz agreed. "I've read his packet over a few times and it is impressive. It's from a town outside of Chicago name of Downers Grove. The mayor back there sounded like he doesn't really want to lose him. The way I understand it from the packet, the son-of-a-bitch can walk on water, shoot a gun with either hand, arrest the bad guys, and slap the cuffs on them, all at the same time."

Larson chuckled. "Why in the hell'd he want to come to Wolf Point, of all places?"

"I got the impression he's crossed up the local criminal element back there and they're helping him hide by letting him come out here. It might be a Chicago mob after him. I really don't know."

Larson laughed derisively. "Wolf Point is a hell of a good place to hide out."

"Yeah, and I've got a job in Helena as soon as he gets here, so I wish he'd hurry," Goetz added.

"So, you think this . . . What'd you say his name was, has got the job sewed up?" Larson asked.

Goetz nodded. "Dennison. Parker Dennison and there's no doubt in my mind. The next police chief here in Wolf Point is going to be Parker Dennison."

CHAPTER FIVE

December 1923

Sheriff Andy Larson unbuttoned his coat, tipped his cowboy hat back on his head, and thumbed his mustache. "This is it," he muttered to himself as he rapped firmly on the door marked:

PARKER DENNISON
Chief of Police
Wolf Point, Montana

"Come in."

Larson pushed the door open and walked into the office.

Chief Parker Dennison, sitting at a large, neatly organized desk, waved him in without standing. Behind his desk to his right, the American flag hung neatly on a gold, eagle-topped oak staff and the Montana state flag, on a matching staff, to his left. A large, gold, gilt-framed photo of a stern-faced President Calvin Coolidge was centered between the two flags directly above Dennison's head.

What a wonderful damn picture, Larson told himself as he heeled the door shut.

Parker Dennison was an example of sartorial splendor. His gray, wool, pinstriped suit jacket fit impeccably across his broad shoulders. Expensive gold cufflinks showed against his blue shirt and his red and blue diagonally striped tie hung centered with the help of a gold tie chain. His well-oiled hair was parted

21

perfectly down the center and his pencil-thin mustache was neatly trimmed.

"I understand you've had another shooting out in the county," Dennison said, as he grimaced and pointed to a chair across from his desk.

Larson nodded, spun the chair around, straddled it, and hung his arms over the top. "Yup, Old Man Merkel and his boys, Abner and Leroy. There's two city fellas out there with them. All five are frozen solid as a day-old cow pie this time of year."

Chief Dennison, nodded, steepled his fingers, and touched them to his chin, as he thought he should, to show deep concentration on Larson's words. "Tell me more about it. Is there anything I can do to help?"

The corner of Larson's mouth twitched up under his heavy mustache. *You phony little asshole. You're probably the best-dressed man this side of Minneapolis. The concerned look on your face is enough to make me puke.* He shook his head. "No, they're gonna ship the bodies to Helena to do the medical examinations. Right now my men are out there going over the crime scene."

"Do your people have the expertise to do that kind of work?" Dennison asked.

"Probably as much as the men on your force," Larson answered, sarcastically. *Now let's see the little bastard puff up.*

Chief Dennison's face reddened and he lowered his hands to the desk. "For now I'm working with what's been given me here," he stated. "I'm looking into bringing a couple of my former officers from Downers Grove out to work for me. With the proper personnel it won't take me long to get the law problems in Wolf Point shaped up. These shootings are definite signs we need a stronger police force."

Larson's eyes narrowed. *I think that was supposed to be a cheap shot at me, but I'm not gonna give him the satisfaction of biting. It looks like my guess was right and now he's gonna try to set up his own police system here in Wolf Point. I'll be watching closely, Parker, I'll be watching.*

The natural color of Dennison's face returned and he smiled. "So what have you deduced about the crime so far?"

Here we go. "We know they were killed sometime between the fourteenth and today."

"How do you know that?"

"The mailman told us that the mail he remembered delivering on the fourteenth was still in the box today. He didn't see any smoke coming from the chimney so he thought there may be a problem and he called it in."

"And you found?"

"The three Merkels and two city fellas, out in their barn. Three of 'em pretty well chewed up by machine-gun fire. One odd thing is four cows and the Merkel boys were all shot in the head. Probably by a pistol."

"What makes you think two of them are, as you call them, *city fellas?*"

"They're dressed almost as good as you and I've always considered you a city fella."

Dennison's eyes narrowed and he straightened in his chair. "You just won't give it up, will you," he hissed. "Why don't we clear the air? Get everything off your chest that's been bothering you, *Sheriff.*"

Larson shrugged. *I've been waiting for this, so now it's balls to the wall, all the cards on the table.* "I just call 'em the way I see 'em," he answered and smiled. "You wanna know my thoughts on this whole situation? Old Police Chief Ed Grubb gets gunned down and nobody on the force seems to want his job. All of a sudden it's a dangerous position and these boys here are used to the way police work in Wolf Point's been done forever. It's got the usual small-town crime, so it's an easy job, and if you play it right, with a little power. They like the work, but none of 'em wants to be in charge. Too *damned* dangerous to be the top dog. So the town council puts out the word they're looking for a new police chief and you're the applicant with the best glowing, walk-on-water credentials. Nobody with any real police leadership experience wanted to come out here and freeze their ass off in a town this size for the money they offered. I'll be damned; you are the only one to apply for the job."

Chief Parker Dennison nodded slightly, rolled his jaw, and rubbed a thumb on his pencil-thin mustache. Without taking his eyes from Larson's, he opened an ornate silver box, lifted out a cigarette, lit it with a matching silver desk lighter, and took a long pull of smoke. "Okay, so now I know what's been burning at you all this time. I could sense you didn't like me from the first week I was here. I'm a man with true enforcement experience and background and that put a knot in your tail. Did I get the job you wanted? Is that it? You decided it was time to come into town and live a little easier. Your charming wife wanted you closer when she needed you? Is that it? So, what are you going to do?" he asked, with smoky words and a slight smile. "What *can* you do about it? Have you got a *plan* for my overthrow? You've got all these assumptions, but can you prove them?"

Larson smiled, pulled a pack of Camels from his shirt pocket, shook one up, and pulled it free with his teeth. *Now he's getting pissed.* He tipped his chair forward enough to reach Dennison's lighter. *Let's see how far I can push him before he loses it.* He clicked flame onto it, lit his cigarette, slid the lighter back, settled the chair on all four legs, and shook his head. "Parker, if you bring my wife into any of these conversations again, I'm gonna drag you across that fancy desk and beat the dog shit out of you," he said, softly. "And if I had a plan, I sure as hell wouldn't tell you about it. I know you consider me just some backwoods hick with a badge and I really don't give a shit. I don't want to be the Roosevelt County sheriff, but it was *offered* to me and I want to get Billy Hollis' killer. I figure when he was gunned down a couple of months ago it was supposed to open a door for someone else, *like you*, to appear and take his place. I just screwed up the master plan by taking the job, didn't I, *Parker*?"

Dennison shook his head, took a deep drag from his cigarette, and blew a series of smoke rings. "First, I apologize for what I said about your wife, Larson, but she is very charming. Maybe I've underestimated you. With your vivid imagination, you should have been a writer. You certainly seem to have the ability to see, imagine, and embellish things that don't really exist."

Larson rocked his chair back on two legs and chuckled. "I've been trying to figure out what you'd gain by controlling the law in the area. This is a town of twenty-five-hundred people, counting men, women, and children. Now the railroad's closed the roundhouse here, so there aren't any railroad crews staying overnight. That means I can eliminate prostitution from the list of possibilities. To me it leaves only one thing: bootleg booze. If you had a cooperative sheriff, you could run a lotta liquor through here, couldn't you? Roosevelt County has almost twenty-four-hundred square miles of territory in it. I'm not sure exactly how many miles of road there are, and I sure as hell can't patrol all of them with six deputies, can I? Then we've got the railroad coming through with all those full coal cars and locked boxcars, but I don't have the authority to check them without a warrant. With the right connections and the proper setup, someone could run a whole helluva lotta illegal alcohol through Wolf Point and Roosevelt County, couldn't they?" Larson leaned forward, ground out his cigarette in Dennison's heavy, glass ashtray, stood, twirled his chair back into place, and squared his cowboy hat. "I hate to cut this conversation short, *Parker*, but I've got murders to investigate. I'm glad we had this little talk and now you understand where I stand on law enforcement here in Roosevelt County."

CHAPTER SIX

Sheriff Larson paused with his hand on the doorknob and turned to face Chief Dennison. "A question comes to mind just now."

"And that is?"

"Which of your fine, *current* police officers are you going to get rid of to let you bring in that new big-city experience from back east? I know the town council only authorizes you a force of five and right now all those slots are filled."

Dennison smiled. "I've been looking at the personnel files and see both Rusk and Townsend are long overdue for retirement. I'm sure Wolf Point has a retirement fund and can come up with the money to buy each of them a nice, new gold watch with a message on the back thanking them for all their years of dedicated service."

Larson pulled the door open. "I'll be watching . . ."

His statement was interrupted by a long, staccato burst of muffled gunfire.

"What the hell was that?" Dennison shouted as he leaped to his feet. His head was still at the same level as it had been when he was sitting at his desk. Chief Parker Dennison was *only* five feet, two inches tall. He yanked open a desk drawer, drew out a large, chrome-plated automatic pistol, and with one smooth motion worked the action to chamber a round. He reached back in, brought out a packet of extra clips, and stuffed them into a suit coat pocket.

Damn, that was a well-practiced move, Larson told himself as his hand dropped to the Colt six-shooter holstered on his belt. *Parker sure as hell knows how to work that fancy automatic pistol.* "From the sound and the speed, I'd say that was a Thompson," he answered as he drew his pistol and stepped out into the hall. "It's hard to tell in here where the sound came from, but I'd guess it's probably the bank. Let's go," he called over his shoulder. *Now's when I should have my Thompson.*

Dennison nodded and darted towards the door.

The side door to the squad room flew open and Assistant Chief Harvey Brenner, pistol in hand, and Sergeant Levi Rusk, carrying a short, pump shotgun, burst out and rushed ahead of Larson and Dennison into the short hall towards the front doors.

The glass in the doors of the police station suddenly shattered and the air was filled with flashes of light, the sound of falling glass, the snap of bullets flying, and the chatter of machine-gun fire. The weapon was being fired by a man leaning out the back window of a car moving very slowly past the front of the station. The smoke from the fusillade quickly obscured everything but the flashes from the barrel.

Brenner and Rusk were stopped and thrown backward by the impact of slugs tearing through their bodies. Both men were dead before they flopped onto the floor.

Larson and Dennison dropped and rolled to the walls.

Another burst of gunfire dug grooves in the floor and slugs hummed as they ricocheted on down the hall. The gunman sent another burst back and forth across the walls of the hall, cutting dusty grooves and throwing chunks of plaster to litter the floor.

Dennison rolled back onto his belly and elbows and raised his silver pistol with both hands. "The sons-a-bitches are shooting the shit outta the place!" he shouted as his pistol bucked with a roar and flashes of light as he quickly fired seven shots through the ruined doorway. He thumbed the empty magazine out and fumbled in his coat pocket for the extra magazines.

Larson rose to his knees and fired four quick shots from his Colt into the cloud of gun smoke that shrouded the car in the street.

A scream came from outside over the roar of the car engine as it swerved down the slippery, snowy street. "It sounds like someone out there took a hit," Larson said as he slowly rose to his feet.

"Yeah," Dennison agreed as he stood and dusted the plaster chunks and dust from the front of his suit with his free hand. "One of us hit somebody out there."

CHAPTER SEVEN

"I'll give you the credit. This is your station. The shot was yours," Larson stated as he walked towards the doors, fanning smoke from in front of him with his hand.

Dennison nodded as he walked slowly behind him, glancing down and continuing to brush at the front of his suit.

The street was suddenly filling with people.

"They've robbed the bank!" someone shouted.

"Look at the police car," another yelled.

". . . shot the hell out of it."

". . . front of the police station's all shot up."

". . . dead man laying over there."

"Hey, Sheriff, where's the cops?"

Larson waved them back. "There's nothing you wanna see, folks," he called, as he strode to the dead man crumpled across the snowbank. "Please, just stay back."

"You heard the sheriff!" Dennison roared, swinging his silver pistol in the air above his head as he walked across the sidewalk. "Get back, please, people, get back."

Way to take charge, Chief, Larson thought, glancing at the dead man staring blankly up at the sky. The bottom half of his face was covered with a purple silk scarf.

Dennison stopped and stared down at the body. "He must be part of that bunch they're calling *The Purple Gang*. It looks like one shot in the middle of his chest," he said, looking up at Larson. "He must have taken that slug and flopped out the car window onto the street."

Larson nodded and nudged the dead man's arm with his boot. "He's sure as hell dead. Nice shot."

Dennison glanced at him questioningly and nodded.

Larson holstered his pistol, lifted the steaming machine gun from the snow, and worked the action. A loaded shell spun through the air and disappeared into the snow. He repeated the action and found the chamber empty. "Looks like he was about out of ammo when you shot him, Chief," he called loud enough to be heard by the closer people. *Now, you've got credit for the kill. You've defended the people of Wolf Point, Dennison. Hell, I may have just made you a hero. You've shot the man who killed two of your policemen.*

A pair of sheriff's department cars turned the corner and stopped. Deputy Durbin was the first man out. "What the hell happened here?" he asked as he joined Larson. "This place looks like a damned battlefield."

"Yeah, here take this," Larson said, and handed Durbin the machine gun. "Put it someplace safe and have the boys keep the crowd back. There's nothing for them to see over here. Did you see any traffic on River Road coming back to town?"

Durbin hefted the weapon, glanced down, and shook his head. "Nothing. Looks like that Purple Gang has finally made it up here. You shoot him?" he asked, pointing at the body sprawled on the snow.

"Dennison gets credit for it."

Durbin nodded. "Uh-huh, that means you shot him."

Loud voices from across the street got their attention and they saw Dennison and another man in a very loud, animated conversation.

"It's Grimms, from the bank," Larson said. "He's probably filling Dennison in on the bank robbery. There was a hell of a lot of gunfire here in town for a few minutes."

Durbin looked at the machine gun and worked the action.

"I already checked it," Larson stated. "It had one round left in it. That's a fifty-shot drum so they put a lot of lead in the air pretty fast."

"Are you gonna go over there?" Durbin asked, and pointed at the two shouting men.

Larson's face was expressionless. "No, it happened in town an' we've got enough of our own problems right now. Dennison was pretty damn calm under fire, so he can handle a yelling banker. I was impressed and I'm sure that wasn't his first gun battle." He nodded down at the dead man by their feet. "Have somebody cover this guy up."

Durbin pulled the cigar out of his mouth and emitted a screaming whistle. "Hey, Bernie," he shouted. "Get something to put over this one."

Deputy Bernie Ward nodded, pulled a blanket from the back seat, and, without a word, flipped it over the dead man, turned, and joined the other deputies.

Suddenly there was a flash of light and the shot-up police car burst into flame.

"I was afraid of that," Andy stated and pointed at the firehouse doors in the same building as the police station. "But at least we won't have to go far for a fire truck."

CHAPTER EIGHT

"Andy, Andy!"

Larson looked up to see his wife, Becky, running towards them.

"You want us to go an' try to catch the shooters?" Durbin asked, watching the woman rapidly approaching. "Or get the truck an' fight the fire?"

"Don't waste your time trying to catch those guys. You'd never catch 'em in those old piles of junk we drive." Larson watched the deputies stopping and shooing back the curious people. "They were in some big, fancy roadster, so they'll be miles away from here by now. They hit the bank an' then shot this place all to hell. The only thing we can do now is make phone calls. See what you can do about the fire."

Becky Larson slid to a stop in front of her husband and looked him up and down. "Are you all right?" she asked, breathlessly, as she threw her arms around his waist and pulled him tightly to her.

Larson gave her a kiss on the top of the head and pushed her back so he could look at her face. "I'm fine, Becky. Everything's gonna be all right. We've had a hell of a time here in Wolf Point today, but it'll all work out."

Becky stepped back, dabbed at her eyes, and looked him up and down again. "All right, Andy, but, I *was* worried when I heard all the shooting."

Durbin tucked the machine gun under his arm, pulled the

unlit cigar out of this mouth, touched his fingertips to the brim of his hat, nodded to the lady, and grinned. "Miss Becky. I'm sure if anybody can handle this shi . . . ah, trouble, it's Andy."

Becky smiled weakly. "Thank you, Dusty. I appreciate your confidence in him."

Durbin swung the machine gun from under his arm and pointed it at the burning, bullet-riddled police car. "We'll see what we can do about that. Hey, look," he said, pointing to two men opening the fire station doors. "Here come Stillings an' Jensen. They can handle that part of all this shi . . . ah, mess. Where'n the hell's the rest of the police force? Dennison the only cop on duty today?"

"Brenner and Rusk were working. Their bodies are back there in the hall. They took the first burst of lead through the door and were probably dead when they hit the floor. Who's the other three? Midland, Labre, and . . ."

"Townsend," Durbin finished. "Dennison rotates 'em. He says it makes it hard for the criminal element, his words, not mine, the criminal element to know who or when or how many cops are on duty. Wants to show his big-city police background, I guess."

Larson sighed. "Yeah, like the Wolf Point *criminal element* is a real problem."

Durbin nodded. "You mean you don't think the people who did this today are part of the *local* criminal element? Here comes Dennison."

Chief Dennison brushed at the front of his pinstriped suit as he sauntered back across the street. "Mrs. Larson," he said, proffering his hand to Becky.

"Chief Dennison," Becky said, giving his hand a quick, polite shake and then pointing around the street. "I'm sure you weren't expecting this type of action when you decided to take the chief's job here in Wolf Point, Montana."

"Indeed, I was not. I had hoped to be leaving this type of brutal activity behind me in Illinois," Dennison answered, shaking his head. "Even though this is a small town, with gangs like the one that just shot up the place, my experience with big-city crime may well come in handy."

"We were very lucky when the city council chose you, Chief Dennison," Becky stated. "It would appear at this time you are the ideal man for the job."

Dennison seemed to puff out his chest as he turned his attention to the sheriff. "Mister Grimms tells me they didn't get away with much, because the bank didn't have much to get away *with*. He said he was at his desk when he noticed a big roadster pull up in front. Three men got out, and one man stayed behind the wheel while they stood with their backs to the bank and talked a bit. Then they adjusted their coats, turned, and came into the bank. They were wearing wide-brimmed hats and kept their heads down until they got inside. They straightened up to show their purple masks and pulled machine guns from inside their coats. Edna Bloom, the teller, took one look, gasped, and hit the floor, out cold. Dawn Begley just put her head down on her desk and bawled. They made Grimms help one of them load a canvas bag from the cash drawers and the safe. One thing he's so pissed off about is that they took the bank's only loan record book. If they don't get it back, the debts of a hell of a lot of people are erased. He's sure nobody's going to come forward and demand to pay up."

"Damn," Durbin said, and chuckled. "I knew I shoulda bought that car last week." He quickly lowered his eyes when Dennison scowled at him. "I shoulda," he repeated softly.

"And, he's not very happy about the damage they did to his building with their machine guns on the way out," Dennison continued. "There's no doubt the Purple Gang has finally made it to Wolf Point. They've been hitting small-town banks all over on both sides of the border, but with the slim pickings they got today, and at least one of them dead, I doubt they'll be back. Grimms locked up and sent the ladies home. I told him to get his facts and figures together and come see me later."

Durbin cleared his throat. "Nice shot, Chief," he said around his cigar, pointing down at the shrouded body by their feet.

Dennison glanced at Larson, smiled modestly, and seemed to stand a little taller. "It was something I had to do. With two of my men lying dead, or at least badly wounded, it was the least I could do. Try to avenge their shootings."

Larson glanced at Becky and rolled his eyes upward. *Now the shit's gonna get deep.* "Dusty, go see if you can find the rest of the police force. They should get in here to help the chief. We've got our own mess . . . ah, murders to investigate."

Dennison raised his hand. "I'll go back into my office and take care of it, Sheriff. I'd appreciate it if you'd have your men block the doors shut and cover the bodies. My men will take care of the rest of it when they get here."

Durbin pulled the cigar from his mouth and gave a mock salute. "You got it, Chief. We'll take care of it." He shoved the cigar back into place and winked at Becky.

Dennison nodded, turned, and walked through the shot-up doorway and back up the hall towards his office. The silver pistol glinted as it swung by his side as his other hand brushed at the front of his coat.

Larson, Becky, and Durbin watched him until he turned into his door and disappeared.

"Funny thing," Larson said softly. "Not more than five minutes before all this happened, Dennison told me he was bringing in a couple of his old cops from Illinois to help straighten out the town. I didn't realize we had that many problems. A few speakeasies, but what the heck, every town's got a few of 'em, don't they? I know he's got all the men the

city will pay for, so I asked how he was gonna get the authoriza-
tion for two new men. He told me he planned on retiring
Townsend and Rusk so he'd have the openings."

Durbin nodded. "You don't suppose he set this thing up, do
you? This incident today was sure as hell a convenient way to
get a couple of spaces on his force."

Larson scratched his chin and shook his head. "No, I think
he just lucked out. There was too damned much hot lead in the
air . . . If he'd have set this thing up, he would've known about
the machine-gun fire and not have charged out the way he did.
But, now it'll work out to his advantage. What I see here is
someone trying to scare the hell out of the people of Wolf Point,
or give someone a lesson, or make an example of something. I
don't have a damned clue, but I know the living conditions
around here have sure as hell changed."

"Yeah," Durbin agreed. "Being a lawman here in this town
ain't very healthy anymore. I don't think Dennison is gonna
have to retire any of his men. They'll be throwin' handfuls of
retirement papers on his desk by morning."

Larson nodded his agreement. "Dusty, what about you boys?
Are you gonna stay here in town for this kinda wild activity?"

Durbin laughed softly. "Shit, Andy, we're just a bunch of ol',
uneducated country boys that like a steady income. We ain't
gonna scare off easy. 'Sides that, there's still a lot of old-time
cowboy left in us an' we ain't gonna be scared off by some city
dudes with heavy fire power."

"Yeah, I figure I'm about the same way," Larson said. "You
and the others do what Dennison wanted done and then come
back to the jail. I wanna report on what you found out at Merkel's place. Take that Thompson down the hall and give it to
him. It's part of his damned murder investigation now, but tell
him to keep it around in case we find a way to tie it into our
murder investigations."

Durbin gave another of his mock salutes. "I think you'll find what we got out at the Merkel place today very interesting," he said and marched in through the doors, swinging the machine gun at his side, from time to time pulling it up and making shooting sounds as he continued down the hall.

Andy chuckled and shook his head. "Sometimes I really wonder about that man. At least there's rarely a dull moment when he's around. C'mon, Becky, let's walk back to the jail. I've got a couple of things to do before they all get there."

As Larson and his wife rounded a corner of the second block, Becky stopped and bent down. "Go ahead, Andy, I've got to re-tie my shoe. I'll catch up."

Larson took several steps, stopped, and turned around. "I'll wait."

Becky glanced up as he turned. "Andy, you've got a small tear in the back of your jacket and another one in your pant leg."

Larson put his hand on the back of his jacket, moved it until he felt the torn fabric, and nodded. "I figured as much," he said, as he twisted and looked down at the back of his pant leg.

Becky quickly tied her shoe, stood, and ran to her husband. "Let me look at that."

He felt her run a finger on the torn cloth.

"This is from a bullet," she stated.

He reached back and managed to put a fingertip in the hole. "Damn, ruined a good coat. Well, I guess a little hole in the back isn't exactly ruined. I know you can sew it up good."

"There's another one below that in your coat and there's a hole in the brim of your hat I can stick a finger through, Andy," Becky stated, softly. "Do you know how close you came to making me a widow?"

Larson gathered her in his arms and felt her begin to shake. "I'm sorry, Becky. You knew this was part of the job when you married me. I don't understand all this sudden violence and I don't want you to be in the middle of it. If Wolf Point is gonna turn into some sort of a shooting gallery, I want to send you back to North Dakota to stay with your family."

Becky broke free of his arms and stepped back, hands on her hips and a grim look on her face. "I'm not leaving you here by yourself because of a little shooting, Andy Larson," she stated and stamped her foot. "Remember for better or worse? Well, this may be the worse part, but it'll get better." She threw her arms around his neck, pulled his head down, and gave him a long, hard kiss. "Let's go to the jail; you've got work to do and I've got to sew up your damned coat."

Larson took her hand and felt her strong grip as they began to walk. Out of the corner of his eye he could see her dab a knuckle at the corners of her eyes. *Damn, I am one lucky man.*

CHAPTER NINE

Deputy Dusty Durbin, followed by the other five deputies, walked into Sheriff Larson's office to find him standing at the head of his large conference table, a finger poked through a hole in his hat. "Make yourselves comfortable." He pointed to a small table by the door. "That's fresh coffee, so help yourselves before we get started." He pulled his finger free, shook his head, and sailed the hat to land on top of the coatrack by the door. "There's a damned bullet hole in the brim of my favorite hat."

"Is it some of yours, or did Miss Becky make it?" Sullivan asked, holding up the coffee pot.

"Becky made it."

"Then, it'll be drinkable," Deputy Ward said. "I'll have a cup."

When everyone was seated, Larson cleared his throat. "Before Dusty gives me a report on your findings out at the Merkel place, I want to tell you something about today's bank robbery an' all the shooting. I doubt it was the so-called Purple Gang. As a matter of fact, I'd lay money on it."

"Why's that, Andy?" Sullivan asked.

"I've read all the information we've gotten on the Purple Gang an' they don't shoot up things. They're a burglarize-the-vault-and-run kinda gang. They send someone into the town to look it over before they hit the bank. It's usually a man pretending to be a deaf mute selling pencils on the streets in the vicinity of the bank. Once they've got the town sized up and satisfied it's worth the work, they hit the bank late at night or early in the morning. They cut the telephone an' telegraph lines into town just before they start. Once they're inside, they try to get in the main vault. When they're in there, they clean out the cash an' then go for the safety deposit boxes with drills, torches, crowbars, or nitro. By all reports they've been getting pretty good hauls in cash, bonds, jewelry, and other valuables. Lots of people have stuff in their safety deposit boxes they don't wanna report, so a few things stolen go unreported."

"Okay, then," Durbin said, "What's the idea behind the purple masks? Think they were trying to transfer the blame to the Purple Gang?"

Larson nodded. "That'd be my guess. I go past the bank at least twice a day and I've never seen anyone selling pencils or any crap like that, so no one was checking the place out ahead of time. Besides, we'd notice a stranger in a minute, no matter what he was doing. Somebody robbed the bank today, but it wasn't the Purple Gang."

"Is there something here we should be seeing?" Mooney asked.

"I think someone is trying to put a fear factor into the law enforcement system here in Wolf Point," Larson stated. "No, I'm *sure* someone wants to make it look like wearing a badge here in this town is damned dangerous work."

"Do you think Dennison's behind this, Andy?" Durbin asked.

"There's no doubt in my mind. When I confronted him about it a little while ago, he wouldn't exactly deny it. He kinda challenged me as to what I was going to do about it."

"So, what are you gonna do about it?" Deputy Ward asked.

"For the time being, nothing. I don't have anything but suspicions an' theories. I'd say it has to do with the movement of bootleg booze through Roosevelt County, but there's nothing concrete to go on. I'll have to wait until Dennison or whoever he's working with or for, makes a mistake."

"Remember what happened to Billy Hollis," Durbin said. "Machine guns seem to have suddenly become the weapon of choice here in Wolf Point. Maybe we should be gettin' a couple for us."

"We already . . . I have one put away in my quarters," Larson stated. "It's time for me to bring it out into the open and teach you men how to shoot it. I'll see about the county buying us another one. We want 'em to know we're well-armed and we know there's no second place in a gunfight."

Durbin raised his hand. "Hey, Andy, do you suppose Dennison'd loan us the one you got off the street this morning?"

CHAPTER TEN

Larson shook his head and tried to keep from smiling at Durbin's question. "All right, Smart Ass, tell me what you found out at Merkel's this morning." Durbin nodded, stood, lifted his coat and made a production of pulling a small roll of cloth out of a pocket and laying it on the table. From another pocket he brought what was obviously a pistol wrapped in a bandana and set it beside the bundle. He looked at the others and grinned.

"Well, what've you got there?" Larson asked. "Besides a pistol of some kind."

Durbin carefully unrolled the cloth and used a pencil to spread several empty shell casings. "Forty-fives from at least two different weapons," he began, pushing them into a group. "These are also nine millimeter casings from a Luger." He unfolded the bandana from the pistol. "And, this, I am guessing, is the Luger that these casings were processed through."

"Where'd the Luger come from?" Larson asked.

Durbin pointed his finger at Mooney, who cleared his throat and spoke. "When I was going through the clothes of one of those shot-up city men, I found a German military holster strapped up under his arm. Dixon was picking up casings and pointed out that several of them weren't forty-fives. They were smaller, nine millimeter. We all agreed this man had to have been carrying a Luger. Now where was it? Did they take it or was it around there somewhere?"

"I found it in the hay in the cattle stalls," Dave Dixon announced proudly. "Back in a corner."

"Good work," Larson praised.

Durbin pointed at Deputy Sullivan, who was carefully polishing his thick glasses. "Tell him what you found, Bobby."

Sullivan put his glasses back in place on his nose, stood, and smiled. "Well, like Dusty said, I was done photographing the bodies and looked closely at the Merkel boys. They'd been shot in the top of the head so they were probably kneeling when they were killed and it was smaller than a forty-five."

"Like the Luger," Durbin added.

Sullivan glanced at Durbin and continued. "Closer examination, or as close as I could make out in all that frozen gore, showed me the slugs came out under their jaws. The slugs are probably in that mess on the floor out there, but I sure as hell wasn't going to look for them today."

"Let me break in here," Durbin said. "The cows had been shot in the head with one shot each. After we found the Luger, there were a couple of rounds left in the clip so I decided to do a sample shot into the head of one of the dead cows. It's an identical burn and hole."

"Okay, let's look at this carefully," Larson said. "Abner and Leroy Merkel and the four cows were all killed the same way. Like you said earlier, Dusty, it's like someone'd ask a question and if they didn't get the answer they wanted, they'd kill a cow. I'd say it was Old Man Merkel being questioned because those city boys wouldn't care about someone shooting a damned cow."

"That'd be my guess," Durbin agreed. "Then, when all the cows were dead, they started in on the Merkel boys."

Deputy Mooney raised his hand. "He must've been a thick-headed old bastard if he wouldn't answer when they started shooting his boys."

"Maybe he didn't know the answers," Deputy Graves volunteered. "Or didn't have time to answer before they were shot. The boys, I mean."

"What if they weren't asking him questions?" Deputy Graves suggested. "What if they were making examples of something by the killing?"

"Who killed the two city fellas and what were they doing out there in the first place?" Larson asked. "There's a whole hell of a lot of questions and we don't seem to have any answers."

"Oh, yeah," Mooney said. "The city fellas had Minnesota driver's licenses with Minneapolis addresses. So we know where they're from. One named Frank Morgan an' the other one Horace Turner."

"And there's no doubt from the shell casings there were at least two machine guns," Sullivan said. "At least from a quick examination the shell casings tell us that."

"I suppose the FBI will be coming in to investigate the bank robbery," Durbin said. "Maybe we can get some help or advice from them."

"There've been so many banks hit up here along the border in both Montana and North Dakota that I doubt they'll get here very fast," Larson said.

"One more very important thing, Andy," Durbin said. "We found an area in the hay at the back of the barn that gave us an idea this might have a whole lot more to do with bootleg booze."

"Something beside the cases of booze shot up with the people?" Larson asked.

"Uh-huh," Durbin answered. "We located a place in the big hay storage area on the main floor that had the outlines of boxes or cases. One hell of a lot of 'em."

"Well, tell me," Larson instructed.

"You tell him, Bernie, you found it."

Deputy Ward smiled. "I saw some fresh-tossed hay and looked under it. There was a line of nice square imprints of boxes. It looked like there'd been a leak in the roof and water'd dripped down into the hay and froze. When they took up the boxes, they left little, hard-frozen squares in the hay."

"Could you tell how many cases there were?" Larson asked. "Do you think it was the stuff that was shot up?"

Ward shook his head. "We did a count of the shot-up booze and there were six cases. A rough count from the length and height of the frozen hay wall gave us a back row count of about twenty cases. The imprints to the front were at least four cases deep. It could have been deeper, but the ice ran out."

Larson wrote some numbers on the pad in front of him. "Since we don't know how high it was stacked . . ." He glanced at the men, wrote more numbers, and grinned. "That means there could have been as many as eighty cases of bootleg liquor!" He wrinkled his brow and wrote again and whistled. "Hooch like that wholesales up in Canada anywhere from thirty-two to fifty dollars for a twelve bottle case. In Denver the good stuff is selling from a hundred to a hundred-ten dollars a case. It gives us a low dollar figure of about twenty-five-hundred dollars and a high figure . . ." He paused and wrote more numbers. "A high figure of about eighty-eight-hundred bucks."

"That's a hell of a bundle of money," Ward stated.

"It looks like someone shot five men an' stole a lot of bootleg booze," Larson stated.

"Don't forget those other six cases of hooch an' four good cows," Durbin added and laughed.

CHAPTER ELEVEN

Sheriff Andy Larson grimaced and shook his head. "Did somebody check on where that sled had been going?"

Mooney raised his hand. "I did, Andy. I followed the tracks to a big meadow about a half mile behind the barn and that's where it'd been going. I found a lot of sets of tracks wider than the sled tracks in the snow and I'm sure they're from an airplane."

"An airplane?" Larson asked. "What in the hell makes you think those tracks are from a plane?"

"They just appear and disappear without leaving the meadow so it had to be a plane. The tracks have a narrow groove down the center and I found a couple of places where I saw a tire-tread mark, so I'd say there might have been a tire set in the middle of the skis. I'd guess that way it could also be landed on a hard surface if it had to. The sled tracks are the only ones coming in or going out of the area. There's a place down at both ends of the meadow with a lot of footprints and signs of activity. It looked to me like the plane landed, was unloaded, and took off again. I found a couple of neat rows of holes about the size of a whiskey case in the snow and a lot of foot traffic going from those to where the sled tracks were."

Larson nodded and smiled. "Well done, John."

"Thanks, Sheriff. Oh, yeah, there were remains of fires on the sides and both ends of the meadow, so obviously the plane came at night and those were the markers," Mooney added.

"Got any idea how many times the plane had been in there?" Larson asked.

"No, there were different sets of tracks, but all pretty close together. I'd say at least four or five trips in and out. More snow piled in some of the tracks so they're older. Definitely a lotta visits."

"So somebody's been using the Merkels' farm to run booze," Larson stated. "That's a pretty slick operation and a good explanation for the shootings. Dusty, go in my office and phone the Burgess' place. Ask 'em what they know about planes in the area. They're a couple of miles away, but I'm sure they'd remember planes coming and going if they heard them. It's not like air traffic at the Helena airport."

Dusty Durbin nodded. "I'll be right back."

"How thoroughly did you search the barn?" Larson asked.

"We really just gave it a quick sweep," Mooney answered. "We figured you'd wanna hear about what we'd found and Sullivan needed to get his pictures developed."

Larson glanced at the clock on the wall. "All right, write up your findings and first thing tomorrow we'll go out there and tear the barn apart looking for more clues. I'm gonna ride out and take a look at that meadow. Hard Times needs the exercise and I need some thinking time."

Durbin returned. "Dan Burgess said they'd heard a plane a couple of nights last week and they'd heard them a few times before that. From the sound of the engine they figured it was landing and taking off over at the Merkel place, but it didn't stay too long."

"Why didn't they mention it to somebody?" Larson asked.

"I asked him that exact question and he told me they didn't want to get involved and besides they didn't get along too good with the Merkels. To quote him, Old Man Merkel was an ornery bastard and Abner and Leroy were about as smart as a pile of horse apples."

"Okay, I'm gonna saddle up and take a ride." Larson stood up. "Get that stuff written up for me. I'll be back in three or four hours."

Chapter Twelve

Wolf Point, Montana, Chief of Police Parker Dennison finished giving instructions for cleanup of the station to the remainder of his police force, Patrolmen Larry Midland, Steve Townsend, and Dennis Labre. He looked seriously at the men standing in front of him in the squad room and shrugged into his topcoat. "Now, men, I know this is a very trying time. Two of your fellow officers have just been brutally gunned down in the hallway of the station. One thing I can assure you is that the men who did the robbery and shootings will not return to Wolf Point. Their *modus operandi* is to hit these small-town banks and make a run for it. They never go back to the places where they didn't get any large amounts of money. Hell, by now they're probably up in Canada someplace licking their wounds. Since I *killed* one of them today, they know better than to come back here. I can understand, at a time like this, you may have a desire to leave law enforcement, but I ask you to seriously reconsider such a plan. I will be putting out word that we are in need of replacement personnel as soon as possible and we should be back to full-force strength very quickly. You will all have to be putting in some long hours, but I can assure you that you'll be well paid for your time. Thank you, men. I'm going to take a walk and think some of these things over and try to clear my head. Carry on." He buttoned his coat, adjusted his hat, walked out the door, down the wrecked hallway, and out through the freshly boarded-up doors.

Larry Midland backed up and sat on the edge of a table. "Damn, that little man can talk some shit when he gits rollin', can't he?"

"Yeah," Dennis Labre agreed. "But, I'll be damned if I'm gonna be puttin' my life on the line in this damned town for a measly thirty bucks a week. It's been a pretty decent way to make a livin' up 'til now. I'm gonna start lookin' for police work in some other town."

Larry Midland looked out the window and watched Chief Dennison stop, look at the still-steaming, shot-up police car in front of the station, shake his head, and amble on up the street. He paused outside the Sherman Hotel, looked both ways, and pushed in through the massive, leaded glass doors. "The chief just went into the Sherman," Midland announced. "I wonder if he's going down to Shorty's blind pig in the basement for a shot a hooch?"

"Ha," Labre snorted. "I doubt he knows about Shorty's. He'd a closed it down by now if he did."

Parker Dennison looked around the deserted lobby, walked quickly to the end phone booth, glanced around again, stepped into it, and pulled the door shut. The booth was immediately lit and he quickly reached up and unscrewed the bulb. He deposited a handful of coins on the shelf, took a final glance over his shoulder, and began dialing. He waited and then began to deposit coins as per the operator's instructions.

"Wally's Meat Plant," a voice answered. "You can't beat our meat."

"That's not funny anymore, Lumpy, this is Dennison."

"Hey, Tack Hammer Parker," Danny "Lumpy" Gilliam, shouted. "How's it hangin'? Close to the floor, I bet." His roar of laughter filled the receiver.

Dennison sighed audibly. "Let me talk to Rossi, you damned idiot."

"Gettin' a little sensitive there, aren't ya, Tack Hammer. Lotta pressure bein' the head of a police department that size? Where are you again? Oh yeah, Wolf Butt, Montana." More laughter.

"Put Rossi on the phone and then go put your head in the toilet. Hopefully somebody just used it and didn't flush, you buffoon."

"Whatever you say, *Tack Hammer.*"

"This is Rossi," a new, gravelly voice announced.

"Tiny, you tell Lumpy that if he calls me Tack Hammer again, I'm going to kick him in the nuts so hard his eyes'll roll like lemons in a slot machine . . ." Dennison sighed. "Oh, never mind, the stupid son-of-a-bitch isn't worth the trouble and knowing him, he might enjoy it."

"Hey, Parker, old force names are hard for some people to shake."

"Okay, I understand, but tell him to lay off."

"I'll have a talk with him. Now, what can I do for you, Parker?" Glenn "Tiny" Rossi asked.

"Do you know anything about someone robbing the bank here in Wolf Point this morning?"

"Well, I can tell you it wasn't us," Rossi answered and chuckled. "Hell, we haven't been outta Downers Grove for almost a month and it'd be one hell of a trick if we could hit your bank and get back here to answer the phone."

"I wasn't saying it was you. I was asking if you knew anything about it. They robbed the bank, shot it up as they were leaving, machine-gunned the hell out of the police station, a police car, and killed two of my men."

"Damn," Rossi said, softly.

"I shot and killed a man wearing a purple mask, but *I* know it's not the Purple Gang from up in Canada because this wasn't their style. Someone's trying to shift the blame. Whoever they are, they're machine-gun-crazy, bloodthirsty bastards. I want to know who did this because it's not part of *my* plan."

Rossi whistled. "Damn, killed two cops. You said you killed one of the shooters?"

"Yes, he was leaning out the back window of the car gunning the hell out of the station with a Thompson when I put one in his chest. He fell into the street and the rest of them got away clean. Put out the word that I want to know who these bastards are."

"It sounds to me like this little fracas opened two positions on your police force."

Dennison fingered the coins on the shelf. "Yes, that's correct. Have you got the paperwork done on everyone, so when the word goes out, they can apply to fill my vacancies?"

"It is and I'm the first man on the list."

"Are all the right people in Downers Grove City Hall set to answer the correspondence when they get it?"

"I saw to it personally. The letters are written and all they have to do is date 'em and put 'em in the mail. Of course, they're not quite as glowing as all of yours were."

Dennison heard him chuckle. "Were there any problems having them written?"

"Naw, I gave them to the proper people, slid some cash under the table with a little fear thrown in over the top for balance, and it made the whole process pretty damned easy. This was a helluva plan you came up with Ta . . . Parker."

"So far it's working out very well. Having two of my men killed here today was a stroke of luck. I was going to have to retire a couple of the locals to make room for you and your people and I wasn't sure how that was going to go over. After today's incident, the others will be lined up at my desk to quit or retire tomorrow. I could see it on their faces when I talked to them a few minutes ago. I'll go before the town council and tell them I know several officers who used to work for me in Downers Grove who might be willing to come over here and work for me again. I'll fill them in on how you've all worked so well on big-city crime and your working here will be a strong influence on the reduction of crime in the area. With my personal recommendation, I should have all of you working for me here within a month. How often can a wide spot in the road like this get five experienced city policemen?"

"Say, wait a minute, is this a safe phone to be talking on?" Rossi asked.

"Yes, I'm using a pay phone at the hotel. The pay phones are the only ones in town that don't go through a central city switchboard. I always call you from one of these because I can be sure no one is listening in locally. One more thing, the new sheriff here is too damned smart for his own good. He's starting to question how and why I got here. He's a little too inquisitive and a little too close to the truth, so I need to have him done away with. That'll put fear in the sheriff's office and maybe it will give me the power I need to have total control of the law here in Wolf Point faster than I had planned."

Rossi glanced at the other men, who all seemed to be concentrating on the card game. He cupped his hand around the mouthpiece and whispered, "Then why don't you just go ahead and do it *yourself*, Parker? Hell, you did a good job on the last sheriff. Oh, yeah, and then there was the last police chief that was gunned down. Seems to me you took his place, didn't you?" Rossi asked, sarcastically. "You should have it down to a science by now." He smiled to himself, reached forward, and thumbed down the receiver hook. *Now let's see what you're gonna do, you little weasel. Go do some of your own dirty work.*

The phone clicked and began to hum in Dennison's ear. He grimaced, hung it up, and scooped up the remaining coins from the shelf. He turned to see if anybody was in sight. "I don't know who in the hell you think you are, Rossi," he muttered to himself as he pushed the door open, stepped out, and adjusted his coat. "But someday you're going to regret hanging up on me. You're not as big and powerful as you may think you are and I've got an alternative plan if you don't work out." He pulled on his gloves and flexed the fingers. *I wonder what would happen if I were to walk downstairs and knock on Shorty's door?* He chuckled as he strode across the hotel lobby and pushed out through the front door.

CHAPTER THIRTEEN

Glenn "Tiny" Rossi hung the receiver back on his candlestick phone and glared at Lumpy Gilliam, sitting on the corner of his desk. "You dumb son-of-a-bitch," he muttered as he struggled to pull his bulk up from his desk chair. "I told you not to answer my phone anymore."

Lumpy shrugged and lowered his eyes. "Sorry, Boss."

Rossi clapped his hands at the men playing cards. "Well, boys, it looks like you'd better be getting your long underwear out. It may be chilly here in Downers Grove, but it's a lot damned colder over in Wolf Point, Montana."

"I'm out," Basil Barqhart muttered and threw his cards to the middle of the table. "Are we all going out there right now?"

"Tack Hammer, shit, I mean Dennison, had a couple of his men gunned down today, so there're at least two immediate vacancies. He figures after today the rest of the force will resign and that'll give all five of us cop jobs again."

"I'll raise it a buck." Tom "Thumb" Peppin threw a bill onto the pile. "I'd better go to the cleaners and pick up those fancy uniforms of ours. He said he wanted us to have uniforms when we got out there."

Bob Lamey snorted and flung his cards across the table. "This game is bullshit! Who's going out there to freeze their ass off first?"

Rossi settled himself on the front edge of his desk. "Well, I'm

56

first on the list. You decide amongst yourselves who's going with me."

The phone rang and Lumpy leaned over as if to answer it, but quickly raised his hands and grinned at Rossi. "Just kiddin', Boss."

Rossi glared at him as he held the receiver to his ear. "This is Rossi," he said and listened. "Gimme a number." He quickly wrote on a tablet. "I'll get back to you in a few minutes."

"Who was that?" Lumpy asked.

"It wasn't for you, so it doesn't matter," Rossi answered, putting the paper in his shirt pocket.

"How do we know we'll all get hired to go to Montana?" Peppin asked, raising the corner of his cards for another look. "I'll raise it a buck." He smiled and flipped a bill onto the pile. "Shit, playin' cards with you guys is easier'n workin'."

"Dennison did a damned good job of planning this whole thing out," Tiny Rossi answered. "Oh, yeah, he doesn't like to be called Tack Hammer, so watch yourself. Lumpy, I'm supposed to chew your ass out for calling him that name. He says he's gonna kick you in the nuts the next time you do it."

"Well, we sure as hell can't call someone that size, *Sledge* Hammer," Lumpy argued. "That was his nickname when he was a lieutenant back here."

"Yeah, but nobody used it to his face after Bennedato. He's a mighty big man when he's got a gun in his hand," Tiny Rossi said. "He didn't get to be where he is because of his size. He's one smart, smooth, suave, son-of-a-bitch an' his temper's nothing to mess with. There's more'n one guy resting in cement in the bottom of Saganashkee Slough because they underestimated him. I'm only gonna tell you this one more time, Lumpy, watch your damned smart mouth unless you wanna concrete mattress."

Lumpy Gilliam nodded and rose to his feet. "Gimme the

damned laundry ticket, Thumb. I'll go get our old uniforms. You gotta make sure yours still fits. You been chewing on a lotta cannolis lately."

"I gotta better idea," Rossi interrupted. "Why don't all of you go? I've got work to do here and I can't concentrate with all that babbling around the card table from a bunch of outta work ex-cops. One more thing, when you get back I want that damned card game moved into the outer office. Got that?"

"Yeah, and I got three fives," Thumb Peppin announced and looked around at the other players.

The others, muttering, threw their cards onto the table and began to pick up their money.

Thumb Peppin laughed and pulled the small pile of bills from the center of the table. "Like I said . . ."

"If ya say it again, I'm gonna bust yer nose," Lumpy Gilliam threatened, waving a fist at him.

Thumb Peppin shrugged and made a production of stacking the bills from the pot. "Yeah, whatever."

CHAPTER FOURTEEN

When Rossi was alone, he pulled in the phone, unfolded the paper, dialed, and waited.

"This is Bianci," a voice answered.

"Dominic, Rossi returning your call. This isn't a Minot number, where'n the hell are you?"

"We're holed up in Williston."

"I see. Were you boys by any chance over in Wolf Point today?"

"Yeah, that was us, but we're back here now."

"You stupid sonsabitches!" Rossi screamed. "You were supposed to wait until I gave you the word to go to Wolf Point."

"Hey, Rossi, calm down."

"Calm down, my ass. I got a call awhile ago from Dennison over there and he's pissed. You hit the bank, shot up the town, and killed two cops. That's pretty damned stupid!"

"It was going smooth until somebody opened up on us," Bianci argued. "Geez, two cops dead."

"From what I'm told, you started it by shooting up the bank and then the rest of the town!" Rossi shouted. "What in the hell's wrong with you?"

"All right, first it was Maggadino," Bianci answered. "He has a tendency to be a little heavy with his trigger finger. We were walking out of the bank and he let loose a burst into the air. He said it was a warning to those in the bank."

"Can't you control that idiot?" Rossi demanded, trying to maintain his temper.

"Ah . . . well, I don't know. With him and that Tommy gun . . ."

"What the hell happened at the police station?"

"We got in the car and Semprorio saw the police station down the street. He yells at Maggadino that they oughta shoot up the front of the place when we roll past it. Semprorio's always trying to impress Maggadino with what a badass he is. I didn't believe he was that stupid until Semp's leaning out the back window and blasting the shit out of the front of the building. Zwillman had us moving along at a crawl and the first thing that gets shot up is a cop car."

"What's Maggadino doing?"

"He's sitting on the other side of the back seat with a shit-eating grin on his face, watching Semprorio fire away."

"Couldn't you stop Semprorio?"

"It was all so fast . . ."

"Bullshit. You were enjoying it yourself, weren't you?"

"Ah . . . yeah, I guess I was," Bianci answered. "I mean, what the hell? Shoot up a small-town police station and it'll keep 'em from following us too soon."

"I told you to stay the hell away from Wolf Point!" Rossi shouted. "You left two dead cops and one of our guys laying in the street over there. What in the hell were you thinking?"

"Yeah, that's Semprorio back there in the street. I think he took one square in the middle of his chest before he flopped out the window. Alzado's got a groove on the top of his head from a slug. It's a good thing he's got that thick Italian skull. It woulda killed anybody else. When Semprorio dropped out the window, I punched Zwillman in the shoulder and told him to floor the damned car and get outta town quick," Bianci said and laughed. "Pretty clever of us to throw the blame on those Canadian jerks, wasn't it? They got no idea it was us."

"Hey, asshole, this isn't funny. That was a damned weak attempt to put the blame on the Purple Gang, and the law in Wolf Point is smart enough to know that isn't the way those guys work. You didn't check things like that, did you?"

"What d'ya mean? Bank robbers are bank robbers," Bianci argued.

Rossi snorted in derision. "Those Purple Mask Gang boys sneak into town early, check everything out, and hit the banks at night. They don't turn a bank job into a damned bloodbath! Can't any of you fools read a newspaper? Why in the hell did you go over there anyway? I told you to stay in Minot."

"We were over there a couple days ago and thought it looked like an easy touch so we went back to see if we could pick up some money," Bianci answered.

"Oh, my aching ass," Rossi interrupted. "That's one damned weak excuse. Knowing you guys, you did it for some action. Anyway, Dennison knows that's not how the Purple Gang works, but they're getting the blame for the killings. He's still got the big master plan to control the law in the city and county. Hell, he thinks his plan'll control most of the state by the time he gets it all in motion. But now there are things happening there he doesn't understand and he doesn't like it." Rossi opened a large humidor, lifted out a fat cigar, ran it under his nose, and smiled. "He doesn't have a clue about what we're doing. He still thinks he's the big nuts of the organization. It's going to be a hell of a surprise when he's looking down the barrel of a chopper and we control the law and all the booze running *instead* of him."

Bianci laughed.

"Now, what in the hell were you doing over there a couple days ago," Rossi demanded.

"We followed a couple of Boticello's boys over to a farm north of Wolf Point."

"What?"

61

"Zwillman spotted a big Studebaker with Canadian plates at the hotel here in Williston. It was riding high in the back from overload springs. He checked it out and found there was no back seat, so figured it had to be a booze runner car. I guess they weren't smart enough to put sandbags in the back end so the car wasn't so noticeable when it was empty. Dumb bastards. Anyway, we decided to see where it was going."

"How do you know they were Boticello's people?"

"Waxey Gordon knew one of the guys named Turner, who was a hot driver for Boticello when they'd both worked for him a couple of years ago in Regina. We just took it for granted he was still driving for Boticello."

"Okay, so what happened?"

"We followed it over to Wolf Point and through town to a farm."

"Who was with you?" Rossi asked, lighting an expensive cigar.

"That time it was me, Longy Zwillman, Waxey Gordon, and Nino Maggadino. When we went back the second time we had Joey Alzado and Benny Semprorio with us too. Benny's still over there."

Rossi sighed and blew a smoke ring. "Yeah, yeah, no shit. Tell me about the first trip."

"We followed them out to that farm, parked a ways off, walked up, and watched from the trees while the two from Canada bossed three farmers hauling cases of booze out of the barn and putting them in the trunk and back seat of the car. They were all in the barn for a while, so we moved up to see if we could find out what was going on. We heard three well-spaced shots and slipped up to peek in the windows. One of the Canadian boys, with a smoking gun in his hand, was standing by some stalls with three dead cows in 'em and one of 'em was still kicking her feet."

"Three dead cows?" Rossi asked through a cloud of smoke.

"Yeah, and the old man was standing by a stack of whiskey cases."

"Where were the other two farmers?"

"They were on their knees off to one side. I could see their hands tied behind 'em. Anyway, the other guy, waving a Thompson around, shouted something about booze to the old man, who kept shaking his head. The guy standing over by the stalls, cool as could be, swung his pistol over and popped the last cow in the head. It fell over like a tree and lay there twitching just like the other one."

"Damn," Rossi muttered. "Could you hear what they were arguing about?"

"Yeah, they were arguing about how much booze they were supposed to be taking to Helena. The trunk of the car was full and so was most of the back seat. The old farmer was yelling and banging his hands on the stack of cases in front of him. He said they were supposed to get four of 'em for their work. The other two farmers were crying and carrying on something terrible when the guy who'd shot the cows walked over and, *bam, bam,* shot 'em both in the top of the head. Let me tell ya, he's one mean bastard."

"Son-of-a-bitch," Rossi said softly and knocked the ash off his cigar into an ashtray. "He just shot them in the top of the head?"

"Like someone shooting rats."

"Then what happened?"

"We got our guns out and busted through the side door. Maggadino fired a burst from his Tommy gun through the ceiling. He's always gotta be so damned dramatic."

"And stupid," Rossi added, pushing the ashtray across the desk.

"Exactly," Bianci agreed. "The other guy with the machine gun dropped down behind the stack of whiskey cases and let loose a wild burst in our direction. The boys and I dived for cover, but Nino just started burning off ammo. He had a fifty-shot drum on that gat and it was like he didn't want to keep any of it. That thing was spitting fire and smoke while he waved it back and forth, cutting down the old farmer and the other hood and then he kept blasting away at that stack of cases. There was booze and wood and glass flying through the air until his gun clicked on an empty cylinder."

"Jesus."

"It seems like my ears are still ringing. The air was full of gun smoke and whiskey smell. It all happened so damned fast. The other boys and I are standing there with our mouths hanging open while Nino reloads and walks around nudging bodies with his toe. It was like he was hoping one of 'em was still alive. He's one cold, crazy son-of-a-bitch, he is."

"So, you've got five dead men and a car loaded with whiskey. Where's the whiskey now?"

"Wait, I ain't done. There were thirty-six cases already loaded in the car. We started snooping around and found another stash of thirty-six cases hidden under some hay in a corner of the barn."

"Thirty-six more cases?"

"Yeah, now we got one car loaded with liquor and enough to fill another booze wagon. We managed to put four more cases in the first car and then another twenty in our car. The springs in the rear of ours weren't strong enough to carry any more. Our back bumper was barely clearing the road the way it was. Zwillman and Gordon headed out for Williston, with us right behind them."

"That leaves twelve cases of liquor back in the barn."

"Yeah, we hauled those up into the haymow and hid them under the hay. We'll go get them when we have time. Right now,

Wolf Point ain't a good place for strangers, if you know what I mean."

"Where's all this other stuff now?"

"I rented a garage from a guy here in Williston and the car and the booze are in it."

"How much whiskey did you get total? Sixty cases?"

"That's right, sixty cases. Actually, there's fifty-nine left in the garage. We took one with us for ourselves."

Rossi sighed. "Of course you did. Is the car safe where it's locked up?"

"Yeah, the garage is behind a fence."

"All right, leave it there and get to that address I gave you in Minot; I'll get hold of you when it's time to show up in Wolf Point."

"But . . ."

"Don't argue with me. Get your asses over to Minot and wait."

Rossi slammed the receiver in the hook and sat back in his chair. "Damn," he mumbled and ground out his cigar.

CHAPTER FIFTEEN

Sheriff Andy Larson ground out his cigarette, slowly closed the file in front of him, and sat back in his chair. "Hey, Dusty, you still out there?" he shouted at the open door.

"Yeah, but it's about time to get the hell out of here. It's starting to snow and I don't wanna get stuck here all night," was the yelled reply.

"Anybody else left out there?"

"Nope, they've all gone home."

"Wanna go out to Booger Red's for a beer inspection? Your brother probably misses you anyway."

"You're kidding . . . aren't you?"

"No, he hasn't been hit with a surprise check for over a week now."

Larson could hear his chief deputy laugh. "Is this gonna be official?"

"Yeah, we'll wear our badges and guns. That'll make it official. We'll take my truck. It's got better tires and a decent heater. Besides, people see a department vehicle in the parking lot, they won't stop. We don't wanna cost your brother any business." He looked up to see Dusty Durbin standing in the door of his office, the obligatory stub of an unlit cigar clamped in the corner of his mouth. "Plus both headlights work and it's getting dark fast."

"Let's go."

"Well, I'll give Becky a call, but I don't plan on getting snowed in out there with you boys."

Sheriff Larson pulled his truck in beside four other old, beat-up cars and trucks parked in the leeward side of the ramshackle building with the hand-painted sign, **BOOGER RED'S,** hanging under the lone bulb over the door. Larson stepped out, looked at the sign, and grinned.

Deputy Durbin pulled his badged fur hat down lower on his forehead and squinted into the blowing snow. "From the looks of the snow piled in the tire tracks and on top of these machines, I'd say the usual group's been here for a few hours." He chuckled. "I shouldn't have any trouble getting a ride home if I don't get snowed in."

Larson bent his head so his cowboy hat sheltered part of his face against the wind. "From the snow banked up against Harvey Lyman's heap of rust, I'd say it was froze up and spent the night here . . . again. Well, let's get on in there and see if we make anybody nervous."

The two men walked to the front door. Larson tried the knob and found it locked. "Do you remember the secret word to get us in?" he joked.

Durbin nodded, reached across Larson, and pounded his fist on the door several times. The cover of the little, dime-sized peephole in the center of it swung up and an eye examined them.

"Open the damned door, Harley," Larson ordered and put his thumb over the hole in the door. "It's cold out here."

They heard muffled voices inside.

"How'd you know that was Harley?" Durbin asked.

"He's got those distinctive road-map eyes," Larson answered. "And I'm about to get a little impatient standing out here in this cold."

They heard the lock work, the door bar slide, and the door swung open to reveal Joshua Durbin, Dusty's identical twin brother, known to his friends as Booger Red, grinning at them.

"Well, damn, look who's here. What brings you out on a night like this, *Sheriff* Larson? Don't tell me it's because my dear brother Dusty missed me?" he asked and winked at Dusty.

Larson and Deputy Durbin stepped past him into the warm interior of the blind pig and Durbin made a production of jamming his elbow into his brother's chest and quickly raising his hand to block the punch thrown at him.

They presented a mirrored image as they stood back, grinned, and pointed at each other.

"C'mon, boys, break it up. We're here to check your beer, Josh," Larson stated as he unbuttoned his coat to reveal his gun belt and badge. He looked slowly around the room at the assortment of men studying him and the deputy. "We heard in town that you might be selling some of that twelve percent Canadian beer out here."

Joshua nodded, locked up, and strode to his usual place behind the bar. The oblong room was much better looking than the outside of the building. It was dimly lit by several single-bulbed wall sconces and a large electric chandelier with half of the bulbs burned out. A bar with a full-length mirror and hand-carved, almost life-sized, naked women on the ends, took up most of the narrow side of the room to the left of the door. A tall player piano stood silent against the opposite wall. The loud, off-tune sounds of it would eventually fill the room when someone got up the energy to sit on the bench and pump the foot pedals. A kerosene lamp on the top of the piano did a poor job of lighting a life-sized painting of a naked, coyly reclining woman on the wall above it. Joshua Durbin often bragged that his bar, the chandelier, and the painting had all come out of one of the fanciest whorehouses in Virginia City. The room was warmed by a large, room-centered, glowing potbelly stove and cluttered with an assortment of tables and mismatched chairs and the smells of stale beer, unbathed men, and the smoke from cigars, cigarettes, pipes, kerosene, and burning wood.

Two bearded men, wearing vests, bandanas, and battered, dirty, cowboy hats, returned their attention to their game of checkers. One of them took a drink of beer and belched. "Yer move, Harley, but it ain't gonna do ya no good, 'cause I got ya trapped. I guess yer payin' fer the next beer."

The other player slid a checker forward with a gnarled finger. "In yer ass," he muttered, not taking his finger from the red circle of wood. "How'd I know ya didn't move a coupla my checkers when I's up checkin' the door, huh?" He glanced around at the others in the room as if looking for support to his question. "Ah, hell," he said, lifting his finger and reaching for his beer. "Game ain't over yet."

Three other men, dressed in the same style, sat around the potbelly stove, their chairs balanced on the back legs, their feet resting on the high pipe railing surrounding it. The only one not watching the door had his hat pulled down over his eyes, his hands wrapped around an empty beer mug balanced on his stomach, and he appeared to be asleep. One of them glanced down, leaned, spit into a dirty brass spittoon, and wiped a hand across his beard. The third continued to study the newcomers over the tops of his glasses, finally nodded, and returned his gaze to his nearly empty mug.

Deputy Durbin opened his coat as they walked to the bar, also revealing his gun belt and badge.

Joshua Durbin combed fingers through his thick red beard and studied the two lawmen across from him. "I don't stock anything in here but three-two temperance beer; you know that, Sheriff."

"Well, I guess you've answered all my official inspection questions, Josh," Larson said and thumbed his hat back. "Now, your brother and I need a beer and I don't want you to flip the lever and pour us any of that three-two moose piss you pass off on the government inspectors and strangers as drinkable liquor. We want the good, strong Canadian beer." He snapped a silver dollar down on the bar. "Matter a fact; give everybody a *good* beer on me. With my deputy's official family discount, that buck should cover it."

The men quickly turned their mugs up, laughing, and moved to the bar.

"Damn, Sheriff, ya gotta do that every time ya come out here?" one asked.

"Yeah," another chimed in. "We should know by now that you an' Booger's brother ain't gonna do anything anyway. Anything but drink a few beers with us, that is."

The man asleep by the stove stirred, lost his balance, and, arms flapping, toppled back to crash onto the floor. He sat up looking foolishly at those laughing and pointing at him. "Damn, that's a hell of a way fer a man to wake up," he muttered when he finally managed to get to his feet, waving his empty beer mug. "But ya notice I didn't drop my mug, did I?"

Joshua Durbin arched an eyebrow and a sly grin broke the corners of his mouth as he reached for two clean mugs, slid one under the tap, and pulled down the handle. "The law gets theirs first, boys," he announced. "How could you tell if I were to give you this so-called strong Canadian beer and not temperance beer?" he questioned as he began to fill the first mugful from the golden stream pouring from the tap. He slid it in front of the sheriff. "Well?"

"Believe me, Josh, I can tell after a couple of beers if you're giving me the good stuff or not," Larson answered as he turned up his mug, drained half of it in one long drink, and thumbed the foam off his mustache. "So far it's passed the taste test."

The others laughed as they pushed their empty mugs across the bar for a refill.

"Yeah, Sheriff, why do you do this every time?" one of them asked. "Putting on this act of yers about checking the beer an' makin' us all nervous?"

Larson turned, leaned an elbow back on the bar, took a short swallow, and laughed. "I'll tell you, Harley, it just tickles the hell out of me the way you boys always look at me to see if I'm serious or not."

CHAPTER SIXTEEN

Chief Deputy Dusty Durbin pulled the cigar from the corner of his mouth, took a swallow of beer, wiped his mustache, and grinned. "The looks on your faces are always something to behold," he said, with a chuckle. He took another swallow and pushed the cigar back in his mouth. "Something to behold, even your ugly kisser, Brother."

"Oh, bullshit, Dusty. I know you're not serious when you come out here. Even with the Sheriff."

"You wanna play some cards, Sheriff?" Levi Lyman asked.

"No, thanks, Harvey. I'm just gonna sit around, have a couple beers, and head home." Larson tabled his beer, shrugged off his coat, unbuckled his gun belt, and hung them on a row of hooks behind the door. He stretched, sat down, and took a long swallow of beer.

Deputy Durbin aped his actions and joined him at the table. "Sounds like the wind's dying down out there. We might not get stuck here all night after all."

"That's not all bad. I can still make it home then. If I told Becky I was snowed in out here at your brother's blind pig, she'd only be understanding up to a certain point and I don't think that'd be too good."

A loud pounding on the door caused all eyes to turn to it.

Harley nodded, walked to the door, and flipped the cover on the peephole. "Yeah?"

"Open the door!" a muffled voice ordered from outside.

"Treasury Department!"

Harley quickly backed away from the door. "There's a fella in a suit an' tie out there an' he's holding a blue an' gold shield up to the hole. I could read prohibition service on it. Let's go, boys, let's git the hell outta here!" he said as he grabbed his coat, rushed to the piano, set the kerosene lamp on the floor, put his shoulder to it, and rolled the heavy musical instrument away from the wall.

The others turned up their beers, scooped up their coats and hats, and scampered to join him as he disappeared from sight.

Joshua Durbin rounded the bar and stood by the piano. "You two gonna join 'em?" he asked, pointing at the dark space in the wall. "It's kinda cold down there. I keep meaning to get an outside door dug for that cellar."

Larson shook his head, pulled the badge from his vest, and dropped it into a pocket. "No, I think we'll just hang around and see how these Feds do a raid." He lit a cigarette and pointed at Dusty Durbin's badge, which quickly disappeared.

Joshua Durbin shrugged, shoved the piano back into place, put the lamp back in place, and dusted his hands together. "You don't often see those boys move that fast," he stated and chuckled. "Sure as hell not when you come around, Andy."

"I will have another beer as long as we're hanging around," Larson said, as he drained his beer, scooped up Dusty's mug, unbuttoned his vest, strode behind the bar, and began filling the mugs. "These are probably free because we stayed around to help," he said and grinned at the Durbin brothers.

"If you don't open this damned door, we're going to drive a car through it!" the voice from outside threatened.

Joshua Durbin shrugged, walked to the door, slid the bar back, worked the lock, pulled the door open, and quickly raised his hands.

A large man pushed the barrel of a Thompson into Durbin's

73

chest and backed him into the room. Three other men, two carrying handguns and one with a short, trench shotgun, walked in and the last man closed the door and slid the bar in place. Durbin, hands raised high, appeared to be badly shaken and hesitantly staggered back until he was standing with his back against the corner of the piano.

Why'n the hell'd he go all the way over there? Larson asked himself. *He's sure as hell not stupid enough to try to get out that door.*

Dusty Durbin raised his hands and slowly got to his feet.

"You the bartender?" the first man, obviously the leader, asked in a heavy Irish accent, pointing the machine gun at Larson, who turned off the beer tap, raised his hands, and nodded.

"Yeah, as a matter a fact I am. Are you guys really the Feds?"

The four new men in the room looked at each other and laughed.

"No, we just got these damned badges to make it easier to get into places like this," the first man answered.

Again the men with him laughed.

"Are you the owner?"

Larson glanced at Joshua Durbin through a column of smoke rising from the cigarette in the corner of his mouth and shook his head. "No, the guy who owns the place is in Billings for a week. I'm just the bartender."

"What's yer name, bartender?"

"Andy, Andy Larson."

"All right, Andy Larson, me name is Clarence O'Farrell an' these are me merry men. Where d'ya git yer beer?"

"Oh, I just pull down that handle and it pours out."

O'Farrell's eyes narrowed and he lowered the barrel to point at Larson. "Don't be gittin' smart with me, Bucko. Don't be fergittin' what I got here in me hand."

Larson nodded. "We buy it from government-approved

sources. It's only three-two beer. All legal."

O'Farrell cocked his head and squinted at Larson. "Ya wouldn't be bull-shittin' me now, would ya, Bucko?"

Larson shook his head.

"Pour me a mug a that weak beer," O'Farrell ordered. "I wanna see what that *temperance* stuff tastes like."

Larson shrugged, lifted a fresh mug from a stack, filled it, and slid it across the bar.

The Irishman rested the butt of the machine gun on his hip, took a long swallow, belched, and set the mug on the bar. "Ah, beer's beer to me. Would ya be havin' any whiskey in here?"

Larson shook his head. "Nope, only temperance beer."

"Where's everybody else?" one of the other men, also with an Irish accent, questioned.

Larson wrinkled his brow. "Who else?"

"There's three of ya in here an' at least five cars outside. Now granted, these two boys're big," he said, pointing at the Durbin brothers. "But I don't think they needed two cars each to git out here."

"Some of those wouldn't start last night so they left 'em here."

The man shook his head, raised a long-barreled Mauser pistol, and fired a shot that shattered an empty beer mug on a nearby table.

Everyone in the room jumped.

"Dammit, Boyle!" O'Farrell shouted and turned to glare at the man with the smoking gun. "I warned ya 'bout doin' that kinda thing. I almost shit me pants."

"Sorry, Clarence, I didn't mean ta scare ya, but it'd appear to me," he said as he moved the barrel of the weapon slowly around the room as if in search of a fresh target. "That the man's doin' a piss-poor job a cleanin' up around here an' maybe more of a mess'd clear his mind a bit. Like this." To accentuate his statement, the pistol flashed and another beer mug disintegrated.

"*Dammit,* Boyle!" O'Farrell shouted again, turning and lowering the barrel of the machine gun. "I'm gonna take that fancy pistol o' yers an' stick it up yer ass if ya fire it in here again. D'ya understand me?"

Boyle glared at the leader defiantly and then nodded.

CHAPTER SEVENTEEN

It looks like we're about to have a test of wills here. Larson waved his hands. "All right, all right," he shouted. "The boss's gone and I been drinking and not doing all I should be doing. I'll have it cleaned up before he gets back. Look at the damned mess on the floor now. *Shit!*"

O'Farrell turned his attention back to Larson, nodded, finished the mug in one long swallow, belched, and set it on the bar. "I want ya to give yer boss a message from Tommy Fitzgerald. Tell 'im he'll be gettin' two barrels a bottled, twelve percent Canadian beer every two weeks. That's one hundred and forty-four bottles per trip. His cost is twenty dollars a barrel an' that breaks down to about twenty-eight cents a bottle. He can sell it for whatever he wants, but most places sell it for fifty to sixty cents. His profit margin's up to him. An' when it's delivered, he'll be givin' the deliveryman forty dollars cash. Got that, *Bucko*?"

Larson pursed his lips, scratched his chin, dropped his cigarette to hiss in a partial mug of beer, and nodded. "I guess you work for Tommy Fitzgerald. Well, Daniel O'Farrell, am I to understand the Irish are taking over the beer business in this part of Montana?"

"Exactly. The Guineas are gonna be losin' the beer business around here an' the Micks are takin' it over."

"Is this some sort of a business agreement between you people and the Italians?"

"No, not exactly. Tommy Fitzgerald's decided he can do a better job with the beer an' he's movin' in."

Larson made a production of slowly patting his vest pockets. "Can I have another smoke?"

O'Farrell nodded and shifted the butt of the machine gun on his hip.

Larson shook a cigarette up and continued to pat pockets as if in search for matches. "Here's a bit of news for you, Daniel, and I want you to pass it back up to Mister Fitzgerald. There'll be *no* bottled Canadian beer sold in Roosevelt County, Montana."

O'Farrell glanced over his shoulder at his men and they all laughed. "That beer ya poured me must've affected me hearin'," he said as he turned back to Larson with a grim look on his face. "I's sure ya said we wouldn't be deliverin' no beer here. Is that what ya said now?"

Larson nodded. "Exactly." He noticed Dusty Durbin had taken another step closer to the wall rack where the guns were hidden under their coats. *Don't do anything foolish,* he mentally told him as he gave a slight shake of his head and glanced around the room to see where everyone was standing. While they had all been watching O'Farrell and Boyle trying each other, Joshua Durbin had shifted the piano out from the wall and was now holding something down along his leg in the shadows. *My god, he's got a shotgun. He must've had it hidden behind the piano. Boyle is the most dangerous right now because of that Mauser of his. O'Farrell's blocking any good shots at me by those other two. We'll see how fast Dusty can get to his gun.*

O'Farrell nodded. "Now, what were ya sayin' about no beer?"

"What was that . . . ? Oh, yeah, no bottled beer in Roosevelt County . . ." He patted his vest and nodded. "Here's my matches, in my shirt pocket." His hand slid into his vest and suddenly reappeared with a Colt forty-five automatic that roared, flamed, and bucked as it cleared the fabric. The slug hit Boyle in the center of his chest and the Mauser in his hand fired into the floor as his body crashed over a table and flopped to the floor. Larson swung the pistol to point at O'Farrell and shook his head.

Joshua Durbin leaped forward, threw his arm around O'Farrell's neck in a chokehold, and jammed the short barrel of the shotgun against the back of his head. "You assholes make a move an' his brains'll be all over the ceiling!" he shouted as he turned the man's body to use for cover.

The other two men looked at each other and quickly dropped their weapons onto a table. "We ain't gunners!" one of them cried out, as both of them waved their hands wildly in the air.

"Are you sure?" Dusty Durbin asked, standing with a pistol in each hand. "C'mon, at least one of you must be a shooter. C'mon, go for one of those guns on the table," he taunted.

Both of the men dropped to their knees and flopped onto the floor on their stomachs with their hands clutched on the back of their heads.

O'Farrell's eyes were locked with Larson's. "I'll be puttin' down me machine gun now," he said as he raised it carefully from his hip and held it out to his side. "Here, one a you boys be takin' it." Everything had happened so fast he hadn't had a chance to even lift it to a firing position.

Joshua Durbin reached around him and took the weapon. "Sit down," he ordered, pushing him towards a chair. "And put your hands behind your head where I can see 'em."

Larson lowered the hammer on his pistol and slid it back into his shoulder holster as he walked around the bar and surveyed the room. "You boys get up off the floor and sit at that table with him." He stepped over, knelt beside Boyle's body, and worked the broomhandle Mauser free from his death grip. "Dusty, you'd better get those boys out of the cellar. I'm sure they're probably pretty damned cold by now." He lowered the hammer on the Mauser, laying it beside the shotgun and other pistol on the table.

Minutes later the five men from the cellar stood around the stove holding their hands towards it, looking curiously at the three men sitting with their hands clasped behind their heads and Boyle's rug-covered body.

Larson prodded O'Farrell with the barrel of his machine gun. "All right, you two get the body and bring it outside. Move!"

The headlights of the blue Cadillac reflected out across the snow and the engine sent a large cloud of exhaust drifting upward in the cold, clear night air. O'Farrell glared at Larson with the machine gun resting on his shoulder, while Dusty Durbin supervised the men loading Boyle's body in the trunk.

"C'mere," Larson ordered and O'Farrell followed him off a ways from the others. "It's up to *you* to get rid of that body. I don't care how you do it, and I sure as hell don't want to find it down the road a ways when the snow melts in the spring." He opened his coat and the headlights reflected off the badge he had again pinned on his vest. "I never got around to mentioning it in there, but *I'm* the sheriff of Roosevelt County and if I ever see you around here again, Danny O'Farrell, I'll shoot and ask questions later." He lowered the machine gun and tapped it against O'Farrell's chest for emphasis. "I run a fairly clean county, but I can be one, mean cold-hearted son-of-a-bitch when it's necessary. I like beer, so I have a tendency to look the other way when it comes to beer, but I *will not* be buffaloed or intimidated by any damned criminal element, no matter what nationality. Now I don't wanna go through all the paperwork that's entailed in writing up this incident tonight, *so* it looks like it never happened. If you decide you want to come back and press charges, just remember I've got a whole room full of locals who'll back up my story and you're an out-of-state booze run-ner. Now, be smart and get the hell outta my county and don't come back. Go on, *git!*"

O'Farrell glared at Larson and nodded. "We'll be goin', Sheriff, but rest assured, ya ain't seen the last a me. Ya can put money on it."

Larson smiled, raised his hand into the shape of a gun, cocked his thumb back, pointed at the glaring man's face, and snapped his thumb forward. "Bang."

O'Farrell joined the others and spoke briefly. They loaded in the car and it pulled out onto the snow-banked road. The glow of the headlights disappeared as it rounded a curve in the distance.

Sheriff Larson walked back into the building, strode to the bar, lifted the last remaining mug of beer, took a long swallow, and leaned back against the bar. "Whew, this has sure turned into one hell of a night. I just came out here for a beer and look what's happened. There's no need for me to tell you men that a lot of shit's taken place here tonight. My advice to all of you is that you never saw anything and don't know anything about any of this. What we had here tonight was an attempt by the Irish to take over the beer business in Roosevelt County and I'm sure this is far from over. Josh, I'll advise you to close this place up for a couple of weeks, until we see what's gonna happen. Dusty, let's gather up these extra guns and head back to town. Josh, I want to thank you for what you did here tonight and if you need anything I can help with, just let me know." He snapped a silver dollar on the bar. "Buy these boys one last *good* beer before you lock the place up. G'night, boys."

CHAPTER EIGHTEEN

It was seven o'clock in the morning and still dark when Police Chief Parker Dennison stood with his gloved hand on the doorknob of the bullet-riddled door of the Wolf Point Police Station and stared thoughtfully at the unpainted raw lumber now replacing the lettered glass. He shook his head, inhaled deeply, released a cloud of steamy breath, and squared his shoulders. *This should be an interesting day.* He turned the knob and pushed on the door. It did not move. He stepped back, looked the door up and down, and rattled the knob. *This isn't supposed to be locked.* He raised his fist and pounded on the wood. "Hey, someone inside!" he shouted and beat his fist harder. "Open this damned door!" He put his eye to a crack between the new boards and tried to make out any sign of movement in the darkened inside hall.

The squad room door opened and a square of light lit the wall across from it. A shadow appeared on the light and Dennison could see the shape of a man as he stretched and stepped out into the hallway.

"Hold on," the man called, stretching and walking to the door. "Just hold yer damned horses. I'm comin'."

Dennison stepped back and waited as the inside bolt rattled and the door swung open.

Corporal Larry Midland straightened when he saw the man outside. "Sorry, Chief," he muttered, as he cleared his throat, stepped back, and motioned Dennison in. "Sorry, Chief, I guess

I didn't hear you."

Dennison could smell the liquor on Midland's breath as he shouldered past him. "Why'n the hell is this door locked?"

"After yesterday, anything's possible around here," Midland answered, as he leaned out into the street for a quick look around, hocked up a gob of phlegm, and spit it out into the darkness before he pushed the door shut. "I wasn't gonna take a chance on somebody comin' in here an' shootin' the place up again."

This man is really on edge. I wonder if the other two are the same way? "Oh, bullshit, that's not going to happen again," Dennison responded as he unbuttoned his coat. "Are you the only man on duty?"

Midland nodded and cleared his throat again. "I'm the only one here right now. Labre patrolled some on the streets last night and went home to git some rest so he can come in at eight. Townsend was on duty 'til midnight when I came on. He'll be in about the same time. I guess I'm the rankin' man on the force now, huh, Chief?"

Dennison nodded. "Yes, Corporal Midland, I guess you are. You'll probably be promoted now. Do you have coffee made?"

"It's been in the pot for a long time an' stronger'n hell, but it is coffee." Midland looked down at his shoes and then quickly back up at Dennison. "Ah . . . We'd like to have a quick meeting with you when the others get in, Chief. You want I should bring you a cup?"

"That would be fine, Corporal," Dennison answered as he walked down the hall towards his office. He opened the door, snapped on the lights, looked back at Midland, and motioned with his hand up and down the hall. "You men did a good job of cleaning this up yesterday. It was one hell of a mess when it was all over. Come see me when you're ready." He stepped inside and closed the door. *I bet I'll be making my phone call for some new policemen today, probably before noon.*

The chief heard voices in the hall. He glanced up at the clock on the far wall. *Almost eight-thirty, let's see if I'm as intuitive as I think I am.* He quickly returned his attention to the report he had written and rewritten on yesterday's shootings. *I want to make this sound bad enough so these men are well within their rights to resign from the police force, but not bad enough to require outside assistance from the state or federal government. I'm sure the men on the town council have heard the story and it's been well embellished by now. The fact that two of my officers were gunned down in their own building will certainly add fuel to the fire.* He sat back, chuckled, and tapped his fingers on the report. *I personally feel it wouldn't be right for me to try to stop these men from doing what they feel is best for themselves and their families,* he practiced for his speech to the town council. *These officers I plan to bring in from the east have a great deal of knowledge and experience in dealing with the type of crime that has now come to Wolf Point.* He looked up from the papers on his desk at the sound of the knock on his office door, checked his necktie, squared his shoulders, and quickly put a concerned look on his face. "Come in."

Officers Midland, Townsend, and Labre, the remains of his current police force, walked in and lined up at attention in front of his desk. He noticed Midland had a roll of papers in one hand.

Dennison looked at them questioningly. "Well, men, what can I do for you? Like I told Corporal Midland earlier, you men did a fine job of cleaning up that mess in the hall yesterday."

"Yes, sir, Chief," Midland nodded and answered, "It'll need some carpenter work for the shot-up stuff though. There's some good grooves in the floor an' the walls. But we swept it real good an' hauled all the junk out back. It really was pretty well shot-up."

"The doors'll have to be replaced," Labre added. "They're

chewed up real bad."

"Yeah," Townsend agreed. "That Thompson did a helluva job on 'em."

Dennison sat back in his chair, nodded, and steepled his fingers under his chin. "You said you wanted a meeting with me, men. Again, what can I do for you?"

Midland stepped forward, smoothed out the roll of papers, and laid them on Dennison's desk. "These are resignation papers we made out last night, Chief. We talked this over for a long time an' we all agree that Wolf Point's getting too damned rough for the police. We've all got families an' our wives ain't very happy about the shooting yesterday."

Dennison nodded and fanned out the three handwritten documents Midland had put on his desk. The wording was the same above the individual signatures. He kept his eyes on the documents as he smiled inwardly. *This is all according to my master plan and yesterday just moved it up faster.* He looked up with a stern expression. "Are you men sure about this?"

"Yessir, Chief," Midland answered. "We talked about this for a long time last night."

"And they don't pay us enough to get shot up like Brenner and Rusk yesterday," Labre added.

"What if I were to give each of you a promotion?" Dennison asked.

"Another stripe an' a couple extra dollars a week don't stop a Thompson from chewing us up," Midland answered. "No, sir, Chief, we're resigning."

"Today?" Dennison asked. "You've got to give me at least a week's notice so I can try to find replacements for you."

"Could we please be excused for a minute, Chief?" Midland asked and motioned with his head towards a far corner of the room.

Dennison watched as the three men stepped off and began to

speak softly to each other.

Midland turned. "One week?"

"I'm sure I'll need at least a week. You don't just find qualified policemen standing on street corners these days."

Midland turned back into the huddle and began to gesture and talk again.

Dennison shuffled the papers on his desk and pretended to reread them. *Rossi and his boys should be able to get here in three or four days. Then we start taking control of the liquor moving through here.*

The huddle broke up and the three men returned to the front of Dennison's desk.

"All right, Chief," Midland began. "We agree it's only fair we give you a week. We want that Thompson you got yesterday loaded and kept in the squad room just in case those men decide to come back and finish what they started."

"You don't really think they'll be back, do you?" Dennison argued. "They left one of their own dead in the street, so they know we can be tough if need be." *Easy, don't overdo it. You want them to stay nervous about the possibility of more of that kind of action here.*

"No, Chief, we can see this getting worse instead of better," Midland stated. "First it was Sheriff Hollis and then Chief Grubb. We shoulda seen the handwriting on the wall."

Parker Dennison stood, walked around his desk, and held out his hand to Midland. "I understand, Corporal Midland, I fully understand." He shook hands with the three officers and returned to his chair. "Please carry on with your duties, men. I've got a lot of work to do."

Tiny Rossi opened the door and grinned at the card players. "Pack the uniforms, boys. Wolf Point, Montana, Police Chief Parker Dennison just called and he *needs* a new police force."

CHAPTER NINETEEN

Police Chief Parker Dennison walked out the door of his office buckling the belt of his expensive camel hair topcoat. "Since we're so short of men, I'm going to take a quick drive around town and let a police car be seen on the streets. I should be back within the hour."

Fifteen minutes later he drove up to the gate of the Northern Pacific Railroad guard shack and honked his horn.

Ole Guttormson looked up from his book, peered over the top of his wire-rimmed glasses, smiled a gap-toothed smile, and waved to Chief Dennison. He pushed up from his chair, bundled the neck of his coat, pulled his red and black wool cap tighter over his white hair, opened the door, and gimped out to the gate with his hands pushed deeply in his pockets. "Afternoon, Chief," he called through a cloud of breath as he quickly unhooked the gate, swung it open, and shoved his hands back in his pockets.

Dennison rolled the window down enough to talk and drove up to the old man. "Is it cold enough for you, Ole?"

"Yah, sure it is," Guttormson answered, with his heavy Norwegian accent. "It'd freeze da balls off a . . . off a . . . snowman, if ya know vhat I mean." He cackled as he waved the police car forward.

Dennison chuckled politely. "You can leave that open, Ole, I'll just be a couple of minutes."

Guttormson nodded as he gimped back to the warmth of his office. "Yah, sure, Chief."

Dennison drove down a plowed lane, across a series of track crossings and around the old roundhouse until he saw a lone boxcar sitting at the end of a spur track. He stepped from the car, adjusted his hat, and studied the snow-covered boxcar and the drifted snow around it. He paced around the faded red, metal car, stepping into his old, partially snow-filled footprints. *Of course no one's been here since I was the last time,* he told himself, as he reached under a wheel, pulled out a small wooden ladder, climbed up, and rattled the padlock on the door. *For all practical purposes this yard is almost abandoned and Ole's the only person around. What an ideal setup. I've even got my own private guard.* He carried the ladder around to the other side of the boxcar and checked the lock on that door. Satisfied, he slid the ladder back under the boxcar and returned to his vehicle.

Ten days after Parker Dennison had arrived from the east to take over the job of police chief, a telegram had arrived at the railroad yard telling them to expect a boxcar being delivered and dropped off in Chief Dennison's name. The boxcar had been uncoupled and moved to a spur track behind the old railroad shops. Dennison explained it as the container for his extensive collection of books, furniture, and his mother's large collection of expensive China dishes. "It will all be unloaded and placed in my home once I'm settled. One of these days I'm going to have to learn how to part with some of these things my parents gave me and I've collected and accumulated over the years."

Dennison parked by the gate and trudged through the snow to join Guttormson in the warmth of his guard shack.

"Everyting mit yer furniture an' books all right, Chief?" Guttormson asked, knuckling his great white mustache. "Oh, ya, I forgot to tank ya fer having the city snowplow come out here an' do my road fer me. Da county always leaves a bank across me vhen dey plow da main road. It sure saves me a lotta time an' energy vhen ya do it fer me."

"My furniture and things are fine, Ole, and you're welcome for the plowing. I did it as much for me as for you. I wouldn't want to walk all the way into my boxcar when I come to check it. Could I ask you a couple of personal questions?"

Guttormson peered over the tops of his glasses and nodded. "Yah, sure ya can, Chief."

"Do you like this job?"

"Yah, it's all right."

"Do you work a long day?"

"From seven to seven, six days a veek."

"Does it pay well?"

Guttormson squinted, trying to figure out this line of questions. "Yah, I git tirty bucks a month an' a free place ta live over in the crew bunkhouse. Dey supply me mit coal, some a my food an' all my coffee. Yah, it's pretty damned good fer me."

"Well, here's the reason I'm asking, Ole. I have a new police force coming here to Wolf Point in the next few weeks and they've agreed to help me start moving my books and furniture and all those other things in that boxcar to the garage behind the police station. That way it'll be warmer and safer and I won't have to worry about it while I hunt for a house. It's not that you aren't doing a good job, Ole, but I'd like to be able to start sorting some of it and deciding what to finally get rid of."

"I understand, Chief."

"Good and since most of this will be moved at night when the men get off work, I'm willing to pay you two dollars a night just to compensate you for having to stay up and open the gate."

Guttormson clapped his hands on the counter and grinned.

"Vell, by damn den, I tink dat's great, Chief. Ya let me know vhen ya vant to git started."

"Thanks, Ole, it'll be soon."

Benjamin "The Little Barrel" Boticello leaned back in his desk chair and rolled a cigar between the palm of his hand and his desk as he studied the face of John Johnstone, his chief accountant. "So we haven't heard anything from either Morgan or Turner since they went over to Wolf Point to pick up a load of whiskey and take it to Denver."

Boticello was a man who lived up to his nickname. Impeccably dressed in a vested, custom-tailored suit, he was five feet six inches tall, with a waist of fifty inches, a totally bald head, and a thin mustache, darkened with an eyebrow pencil. Less than a year before he had moved from New Jersey to Canada to develop a new bootleg liquor distribution system for Al Capone. He was an old-style gangster who always hired ruthless men who would work for him and do his bidding without questions. He was a man known for his ability to get things done and someone not to be fooled with.

One Year Earlier

Al Capone knocked the ash of his expensive Cuban cigar into a crystal ashtray and smiled across the table at Benjamin Boticello. He lifted his glass, took a sip, and sighed. "This is the finest Scotch whiskey in the world, Bennie." He laughed uproariously. "I know because I have it brought in from Scotland!"

Boticello grinned, took a sip, and nodded. "Very fine Scotch, indeed, Mister Capone."

"Bennie, call me Al," Capone said and took another sip. "I brought you over here to Chicago to make you a business proposition. I want to set up a new liquor distribution route from Canada down through Montana to Denver and a few points in between. Eventually it'll go in all directions from Denver. There are a few small-time independents that run carloads of booze through there now, but I want to do it in volume. I'm not talking about thirty or forty cases of bootleg liquor in the back end of a Studebaker. I'm talking about fifteen to sixteen hundred cases in a boxcar. By sheer volume we put the small dealers out of business. If necessary, we can always use a little muscle, if you know what I mean."

Boticello nodded enthusiastically. "I understand." He took a small swallow of the amber liquid in his glass and fought the urge to smack his lips. "This *really* is good Scotch, m . . . uh, Al."

"I take it then, you're the right man to handle this operation for me."

"I'm your man."

Capone raised his glass. "To success."

Boticello quickly raised his glass to touch Capone's and grinned. "To success," he echoed.

Both men took a drink and set their glasses on the table. Capone slid an ornate, wooden humidor across to Boticello. "Have one of these, Bennie," he said. "Something else I have imported to make sure I enjoy nothing but the best."

As Boticello prepared to light his cigar, Capone took a drag and blew a series of smoke rings. "All right, I'm sending you up to Estevan, Saskatchewan, to set up the headquarters for this operation. I've already brokered a deal with the Bronfman Brothers in Yorkton to buy liquor from them by the boxcar load. They have a distillery where they make their liquor in thousand-gallon redwood vats, all kinds of liquor. I'm told they brew Scotch using a base of dark-colored Scotch to give it at least a trace of peat smoke taste, 65-overproof alcohol and water. For rum they use straight alcohol and water and add rum caramel and blackstrap molasses. They've got little tricks for gin and whiskey, too. They age it up to a *week* and then bottle it. They've got a machine that can bottle and label around *a thousand bottles an hour.*" Capone stopped, took a sip from his glass, a puff from his cigar, and laughed. "Then by using different labels they can make anywhere from five to ten bucks a case more for the same week-old booze." He took another sip from his drink and laughed again. "That's the reason I get mine shipped in from Scotland. That stuff they sell is one step above goat piss. My people are in the process of setting up all the bank accounts and lines of credit. I'm going to give you one of my best accountants to help with that part of the venture. Mister John Johnstone. He's kind of quiet, but he's smart and knows his numbers. He's been very good for me and I'm sure he'll be good for you." Capone rose to his feet and lifted his glass. "To a very successful financial venture."

Boticello quickly stood, smiled, nodded, and tapped his glass against Capone's. "You can count on me to do a damned good job for both of us, *Al.*"

John Johnstone again nervously shuffled papers and shook his head. "No, Mister Boticello, and it's been over a week now since they headed down there."

"Well, I just got off the phone with the people in Denver and they haven't gotten their shipment of liquor and they're damned mad about it. A good customer gets mad and I get mad, understand?"

Johnstone nodded several times. "Yes, sir, Mister Boticello, I fully understand."

"I hope those two aren't stupid enough to think they can steal a carload of booze from me and get away with it. Hell, even at street value, that's not enough to make a small heist like that worth their while. What's a stripped-down Packard carry, thirty-five to forty cases of booze?" He picked up a pen and wrote numbers on a pad in front of him. "I pay forty-five a case for it up here and get a hundred and ten a case for it in Denver. At the low end of thirty-five cases, I've got an investment of sixteen-hundred that'll turn over to about thirty-eight-hundred bucks in Denver. Hell, it'd be tempting."

Johnstone nodded again. "Yes, sir, they were supposed to move forty cases on this trip and then turn around and make another one right away. Those two trips would have turned a profit of . . ." He stopped and glanced down at the papers in his hand. "Of fifty-two-hundred dollars. But, sir, they've been with you a long time. They've taken bigger shipments and always brought back the money. Remember last year when they took down a caravan of five cars loaded with top-of-the-line Superior Scotch Whiskey? That was two-hundred cases and it was only a hundred dollars a case then and they brought you back every penny of it. I'm sure something's happened to them this time."

CHAPTER TWENTY

Boticello nodded and put down his pen. "I suppose you're right, Johnstone. What's the name of those men who own the farm where Bohlin flies in and drops the whiskey?"

"The name is Merkel," Johnstone answered, looking at a sheet of paper in front of him. "Leo Merkel and his sons, Abner and Leroy."

"Have you talked to them?"

"There's no answer on their phone. I've been calling on a regular basis for five days now and there's no answer."

"How far is it down to that farm?"

"About two-hundred and ten miles by road."

"How far by air?"

"Bohlin told me once that it's about a hundred and forty miles each way."

Boticello nodded, made more notes on the pad, and studied them as he picked up the cigar, snipped off the ends, and pushed it into the corner of his mouth. "I'm going to send Thumper Moran down there to see why the Merkels aren't answering their phone. If anybody can get information, it's him. Also, I want him to see what he can find out about Morgan and Turner. Bohlin's met the Merkels, hasn't he?"

"Yes, he was with us when we set up the airdrops, so he knows them and their farm. Probably better by night than by day, though."

"Good, does he know Moran?"

"I doubt it. You run a varied organization, Mister Boticello." Johnstone chuckled softly. "And I don't think intimidation and air delivery mingle often."

Boticello smiled and spoke around his cigar. "Then it's time they meet. Call them and set it up. They can get to know each other on the way down to the Merkels' farm."

"Yes, sir, Mister Boticello," Johnstone answered, picking up his papers and making almost bowing movements as he backed towards the door. Johnstone was a tall, bent-over, mousy-looking man, with close-cropped gray hair, thick, smudged glasses, and a poor-fitting, wrinkled suit. Everyone's idea of how a book-keeper should look.

Bohlin adjusted the shapeless hat on his head as he sat on the edge of the desk in his hangar office, staring blankly at a row of neatly spaced, sepia-toned photographs from his flying hero days of The Great War. In one he was standing beside a very badly shot-up plane with great tears, rips, neat rows of bullet holes, and smoke marks on the prominent, screaming, war-bonneted Indian head painted on the canvas fuselage behind him. The Indian head was the known, respected, and feared insignia of the Lafayette Escadrille, a flying unit made up entirely of American pilots. Light reflected off the lenses of the goggles pushed up on his leather flight helmet. Pale mask-like circles left by the goggles and his grinning white teeth were a sharp contrast to his soot-blackened face sitting atop his once-white silk scarf. He was holding a bottle of liquor high in a silent toast. *That was the first time I became an ace. A damned proud member of the Lafayette Escadrille.*

In the next photo, he was standing at attention as an unidentified officer pinned a medal on his tunic. *God, I was young.* His eyes slowly moved over to the next picture where a group of grinning young men stood with their arms hung over each other's shoulders. *We were all so young.*

The honking of a car horn outside shattered his reverie. *That must be Thumper Moran.* He opened an inside door and shouted across the hangar to a man in blue coveralls, standing on a wooden box, working inside the engine cowling of a large, brightly colored biplane. "I'll be back late tonight, Charlie, I'm riding with a fella to Wolf Point."

The man, a tuft of gray hair sticking out from under his backward cap, straightened up into sight, wiped a sleeve across his grease-smudged face, and nodded. "I know!" he shouted. "You told me that last night and then again this morning." He thumbed his glasses back up on his pug nose and a grin appeared under his bushy gray mustache. "I *do* remember some things, you know. Have a good trip."

"Thanks," Bohlin muttered as he closed the door and pulled a worn leather flight coat from a rack as he walked across the room. He shrugged into it and buttoned it as he stepped outside into the cold winter air. A cloud of exhaust rose up behind a large, black Buick Roadster. Bohlin gave a quick wave as he tugged the door closed, pulled his hat down tight, and walked slowly to the car.

Thumper Moran tilted his head and looked at the tall, straight man ambling with a slight limp towards him. *So this's the great air hero, "Wild Bill" Bohlin, I've heard so much about. You'd think he was making enough money to buy himself a decent coat. A new hat wouldn't hurt either.*

Bohlin opened the door and slid in as the man sitting behind the wheel stared at him intently.

Moran was dressed in an expensive black pinstriped suit with a properly shaped homburg tipped back, revealing a high forehead. He had the scarred, bent-nosed face of a fighter. He smiled slightly and proffered his right hand. "Wild Bill Bohlin, I'm Thumper Moran."

Bohlin nodded, gave the man's hand a firm shake, reached back, and pulled the door shut. "Damned cold makes my leg ache."

"Yeah, I noticed your limp." Moran turned his eyes to the windshield and pulled the car smoothly into gear. "I've heard a lot about you, Bohlin," he stated as the car made a wide turn back towards the street. "You were big news back a few years ago during the war. Seems you were in the Chicago papers a lot. Kind of a local boy makes good, again and again and again."

Bohlin gave Moran a final glance, smiled slightly, nodded, and turned to the view outside the windshield. "Uh-huh, and I've heard about you too, but it's been recently."

"Nothin' good, I hope," Moran said and chuckled softly.

"You're not a man to be messed with."

"True. So what was your final count?"

"What?"

"How many Kraut planes did you shoot down?"

"Twelve confirmed."

"That's good. You know what we're supposed to be doing?" Moran asked as he pulled out a silver flask and, without looking at it, unscrewed the top with his thumb. The cap fell to swing from a chain as he lifted it to his mouth and took a deep swallow. He smacked his lips and offered the silver container to Bohlin. "Here's some medicine for your achy leg."

Bohlin nodded and took a sip of liquor. "We're going to Wolf Point to visit the Merkels. It's an easy drive if the roads are clear. You stay on this same one all the way to Plentywood, Montana."

"That's what the map told me," Moran agreed and held out his hand for the flask. "The Merkels haven't been answering Mister Boticello's phone calls, a couple of his men are missing, and there's a question as to the whereabouts of a large number of cases of booze the missing men were supposed to be delivering to Denver."

"Yeah, that sums up what I was told," Bohlin answered. "You'll find the Merkel boys are a lotta muscle, but not a lotta brain. Leo, the old man, is the smart one and that's not saying much. I can drive once we get into Montana."

Moran took a sip and handed the flask back to Bohlin. "Yeah, that'd be okay with me. We got plenty of time. How about you telling me how a war hero gets into the booze-flying business, Wild Bill."

CHAPTER TWENTY-ONE

Wild Bill Bohlin sighed and unbuttoned his leather coat. "Seems that a couple of years after a war's over there isn't much demand for heroes anymore." He took a drink, passed the flask back to Moran, felt his shirt pocket, and brought out a pack of Camels and a box of matches. He shook a cigarette free, scratched a match into a flame, lit the cigarette, and inhaled deeply. He blew out the match with a burst of smoky breath, dropped it in the dash ashtray, and stared out the window.

"Okay, so nobody needed a war hero anymore . . ."

"Huh . . . ? Sorry, I was somewhere else for a minute there." Bohlin took another deep drag of smoke and held out his hand for the flask. "I always talk better with a little whiskey in me," he stated as he had another swallow. "When the war started I was already a licensed pilot and was damned hot to go fight in the air over France. The United States wasn't in it yet, but there was an aircraft unit fighting over there called the *Lafayette Escadrille*. At first it was called the *Escadrille Américaine* because it was made up of all American pilots. The Germans filed diplomatic complaints. Why in the hell I don't understand, but they complained so the name was changed to the *Lafayette Escadrille*. I guess the Krauts didn't like the fact that Americans weren't even officially in the war, but were kicking their asses out of the sky anyway. I knew Kiffin Rockwell, one of the original flyers, and he pulled some strings to get me in the unit. I loved it!" Bohlin took a drag from his cigarette and a sip of whiskey. "That was in 1916, then in 1918 we were absorbed in the U.S. forces as the 103rd Pursuit Squadron. Isn't this kinda boring to you?"

"Nope, not at all. We got a long way to go and there's a few more bottles of that good booze under my coat on the back seat, so keep talking."

"See this old leather coat? You'd never know from the looks of it today, but it was new in 1917. Here." He handed the flask to Moran and managed to wiggle and shrug his way out of the coat and hang it over the seat between them. "I had to get outta that thing. It's damned hot in here."

Moran nodded, "Yeah, they got good heaters in these Buicks." He glanced at Bohlin and saw he was dressed in a red and black plaid wool shirt with a blue silk scarf rolled and knotted inside the collar. Military-style jodhpurs were tucked in high, well-polished, brown leather boots with a pair of short-knobbed military spurs strapped onto the heels. "Geez, you wear spurs?"

Bohlin chuckled and smiled wryly. "It's another idiosyncrasy I picked up during the war. I think they complete my old hero *persona*, don't you?" He grabbed an ankle and lifted a foot towards Moran. "Kind of reverting back to the old cavalry days, wouldn't you say?"

Moran shook his head, took a drink, and handed the flask to Bohlin. "Now I'm surprised you're not wearing a gun belt."

Bohlin laughed loudly and dropped his boot to the floor. "I think a saber would be better. Anyway, I was twenty years old, the hottest damn pilot to ever climb aboard a plane, and God's gift to flying." He raised the right sleeve of his leather coat and turned it so Moran could see two rows of three small leather patches spaced evenly up the length of the sleeve. "It was my third day in the air and I was looking for blood, damn, was I looking for blood. I didn't see the bastard in the Fokker when he came down out of the clouds and opened fire on me, a bit above me to my right. It was the flash of his machine guns that I first saw out of the corner of my eye. I turned my head, saw the outline of the plane, and he was already gone below me. He came across under me and climbed back out of sight into the clouds to my left. I knew he was going to come back down and try again. I cut the engine, then pulled the stick hard right, and the plane rolled over like I'd been hit. I let it go into a slow spin and kept watching the clouds rotating above me to see if he was going to follow and try to finish the job. Suddenly, there he was, coming in a dive from my left with his guns blazing! I heard the bullets snap past me through the plane as I kicked out of the spin to stop the vertical rotation, crammed the stick, and rotated into a complete roll. I brought the nose of my Spad up and stitched him from nose to tail as he slid past me. He was on fire when he plowed into the ground. That German was my first kill. I had some mixed feelings right then. Elation for shooting down the plane and sadness for having killed a man. I got over it. When I landed, I found a lot of bullet holes in the plane, six in the sleeve of this coat, but none in me. I was one lucky son-of-a-bitch that day and figured this was my lucky coat. This old coat and I've been through a lot and that's why I still wear it. *For luck.*" Bohlin pretended to take a drink and handed Moran the flask. "No more war stories. So, how'd you get into working for Boticello?"

Moran took a swallow and snorted in derision. "I'm the kinda guy who'll do about anything for a buck. I was a fighter, a boxer, for a while, but it turns out I bleed easy and I got a glass jaw. I ended up as a bouncer in a club that Al Capone owned over in Chicago and he took a liking to me. With my size and looks, not many guys were gonna mess with me. It was the size and looks intimidation factor. I took to carrying a small baseball bat under my coat and that's how I got the nickname 'Thumper.' They said I liked to thump guys on the head. Then one day I thumped the wrong guy. He had connections with some heavy-handed friends. Word went out they were after me and I knew that it was time to get my ass outta town. I took off for Canada and rumor had it I went into hiding in New York. I had a friend who put me in contact with Boticello and he hired me for intimidation and other things that need getting done. I feel safer up here, but I still keep my eyes open."

"Couldn't Capone help you? Maybe watch out for you?"

Moran shook his head and chuckled. "Capone only watches out for Capone."

"Yeah, and do you still carry that bat?"

Moran chuckled. "No, I gotta chrome forty-five auto under each arm. If I have to thump someone now'days, I do it from a distance. Okay, no more of *my* war stories. Tell me how you got into flying booze."

Bohlin lit another cigarette, leaned back, and closed his eyes. "Like I said, there wasn't much call for heroes after the war was over. I read about guys making money barnstorming, so I scraped together enough money to go over to Chicago and buy myself a surplus Curtiss Jenny. I paid two-hundred and twenty dollars for it and I had my money back in less than a year. Folks paid me anywhere from a buck to five for a ride. A buck got them ten minutes and five got them a half hour. You know we're gonna be shit-faced if we keep drinking like this."

Chapter Twenty-Two

"Okay, if you won't tell me war stories, tell me about flying booze. There's gotta be a good story or two behind that."

"I spent some time looking into ways to make good money in the off-season. For the air-show barnstorming, I fly an American De Havilland DH-4 with a 400 horsepower engine, which is plenty for what I do. It has all that power because it was meant to carry two men, four machine guns, ammo, and three-hundred pounds of bombs for the Army. My old Army buddy and chief aircraft mechanic, Charlie Marcum, is still with me. He's my partner and a miracle worker when it comes to planes. If you need it done and it's possible, he'll figure out how to do it and it'll get done." He glanced at Moran and shook his head. "This really doesn't mean anything to you, does it?"

Moran chuckled and shook his head. "No, to be honest with you, it doesn't really mean shit to me, but I guess you're happy as long as you can get the damned thing up in the air."

Bohlin laughed. "Yeah, there's an old saying among pilots, *'It's not the takeoff, it's the landing that'll kill ya.'* At the air shows I'd carry one passenger at a time and do some fancy maneuvers in the air to thrill the crowds. I had her name, *The French Wench*, painted in six-inch letters on both sides of the cockpit. That's kinda racy to some folks, but I really don't care. She's white, with a blue upper wing and a red lower wing. Red, white, and blue vertical stripes on the tail and a three-foot version of the screaming Indian insignia of the Lafayette Escadrille painted on the fuselage. Yessiree, *The French Wench* is a sight to behold when I pull a handle and she gives off a great white smoke trail when I'm coming in, taking off, doing rolls, fancy climbs, dives, and loops. The crowd loves it!"

"I can understand that," Moran agreed.

"Anyway, Charlie and I sat up many days and nights and figured out that with a little work I'd be able to move some *whiskey* with my plane during the off-season. We experimented with weight under the wings and fuselage until we were satisfied as to how much I could safely carry without sticking my plane in the ground and buying the farm. At roughly twenty-eight pounds for a case of whiskey, I can take thirty-six cases of bootleg booze per trip without any problems. We built racks with spaced struts and steel rods for the floor and security, tight under the wings. Then we experimented and built some under the fuselage for balance. I have handles in the cockpit for each side that lift the restraining rod on the back of the racks and let the cases drop into the snow after I land and when I start to take off. Those under the fuselage fall outward, away from the plane, so there's an opening in the center for the tail ski to pass through. At a hundred and ten bucks a case wholesale, I carry almost four-thousand dollars' worth of whiskey per trip."

"It sounds like you did your homework pretty damned good."

"We had the fuel consumption use figured out right down to the thimbleful. The tanks are in the upper wing with gravity feed. I've got a four-hundred mile cruising range, so the trip from Estevan to Wolf Point and back is no problem."

"Damn, isn't it cold in that open cockpit?"

"We'd fixed it so I got hot air blown back into the cockpit from inside the engine cowling. As long as I dress warm and keep my face and hands out of the outside slipstream, I'm plenty warm. Sometimes, actually hot."

"I just thought of something else."

"What?"

"How do you know if you're flying level when you get into fog? I mean, if you can't see anything to indicate being level. You could drag a wing tip in the ground or something like that, couldn't you?"

Bohlin chuckled. "I use a whiskey indicator."

"What the hell's a whiskey indicator?"

"Marcum put a metal bracket on the dash and I keep a half-full pint bottle of whiskey in it."

Moran wrinkled his brow and glanced at Bohlin. "What's that do?"

"As long as the whiskey level is level, I'm level."

Moran started to laugh and shake his head. "That's damned clever, Bohlin. Your buddy Marcum must be quite a guy!"

"*And* I can always get a drink out of it if I need one."

"How'd you get a job with Boticello?" Moran asked.

"Hell, nobody else was flying booze in. I just started snooping around to find a good bootlegger. I had the plan worked out with all the facts and figures in line. I finally got a meeting with Boticello. He listened and was willing to take a chance on me. He'd been working on setting up a distribution point somewhere around Wolf Point for Montana, Denver, and a couple of places over in Wyoming. I showed him that I could fly the stuff in when the roads were snowbound and his booze'd be ready to ship from his distribution point when they were open again. He'd be able to deliver faster than anybody driving the whiskey down there because they'd have to wait for the roads from Canada to be cleared."

"Pretty crafty. How do you make the deliveries? Do they have a runway cleared for you?"

"No. When he had it worked out, he sent me over with a couple of his men to meet the Merkels, the people who owned the farm where I was gonna fly and drop the booze in. They'd already been talked to and made a deal they couldn't pass up. The old man and his boys would pick up the air-delivered booze and store it in their barn until the runners from Helena and other places came to pick it up."

Moran tipped the flask all the way up, took a long drink, and shook the shiny silver vessel. "You're gonna have to crawl into the back seat and get another bottle from under my coat."

"Crack that bottle open," Moran said, minutes later. "Whiskey doesn't get any better with age after it's out of the keg. You said drop the booze? The snow's not that deep. Hell, they wouldn't be able to find the stuff if you dropped it from too high up."

Bohlin laughed as he twisted the cork from the neck of the bottle. "Here comes the good part. I had it set up so I always arrived at the Merkels' farm after dark. I'd check and if the weather was bad, or too windy, I wouldn't make a run. Good weather and I'd make a delivery Wednesday and Saturday."

"How'd you check the weather down there?"

"I'd call the airport in Helena."

"Uh-huh, I see. You said you dumped the stuff in the dark?"

Bohlin held up his hand. "I'm telling the story, so let me explain."

Moran nodded and motioned for the bottle. "Sorry."

Bohlin handed it to him and continued. "There's a long, tree-bordered meadow that runs east and west out behind the Merkels' barn. He and his boys light four big fires on the sides and one at each end to mark it for me in the dark. I come in low for my first pass to take a look at the fires and gauge the ground wind from the flames and the smoke. I can land on either end, taxi to the far end, turn the plane around, and pull the levers to release the wooden cases of liquor. When I rev the engine and start to speed up for takeoff, the cases slide back and drop into the snow. I'm on the ground for less than two minutes and then I'm gone again. The only way the Feds can catch me is if they have their own air force."

Moran laughed. "Obviously you've got skis on *The French Wench.*"

"Yeah, and the wheels come down through the bottom of the skis far enough so I can land on a hard surface like the runway at my hangar in Canada and they don't affect the skis. I've got the same thing on the rear wheel. This way I'm safe."

"You sure as hell seem to think of everything, don't you?"

"Yeah, but I'm not as young and brash as I was back in my hero days. I like life more now and sure as hell don't want to take any unnecessary chances so I plan everything very carefully."

"Boticello pay you good?"

"Two-hundred and fifty bucks a trip and he pays for my gas."

"You gonna fly booze in the summer?"

"Hell, I'd be a fool not to. I can land in that same meadow with wheels. I'll have to do it in the daylight, but that way I can see if anybody like the Feds are around waiting for me. It'll take a little longer to unload, but we'll work that out. I make a lot more money flying booze and don't have anybody puking in the passenger cockpit in front of me."

"That happen a lot?"

"Nah, most of the time we weren't up long enough for them to get sick. We've got to make a border crossing at Regway. What if they find the other bottles back there under your coat? They aren't hidden all that good, you know. And then you've got those pieces under your arms."

Thumper Moran laughed. "A couple of bottles of booze and a few ten spots take away a lot of the curiosity factor at a checkpoint. You understand what I mean, don't you?"

Bohlin chuckled, nodded, pretended to take a swallow, handed Moran the bottle, pulled his hat down over his eyes, and leaned back against the seat. "It's starting to snow again and it's supposed to get worse. Wake me when we get to Regway. I wanna be sure to see your routine. Maybe I'll be able to use it someday. Then I'll drive when we get across the border."

Chapter Twenty-Three

Andy Larson heard the car approaching from behind him and reined Hard Times over to the snow-banked side of the gravel road. "Easy, boy," he said softly, as he leaned forward and patted the big buckskinned horse's neck.

The car slowed and the driver gave a quick wave as he passed the horse and rider.

"Damn, that cowboy looks like somebody I used to know," Bohlin said to Moran who, eyes closed, was slumped against the door.

"Uh-huh," he muttered.

"Damn, that driver looked familiar," Larson said as he looked at the Canadian license of the black Buick Roadster as it sped up and was soon out of sight. "Probably just my imagination." He flapped the reins and clucked his tongue, "Let's go, boy."

Wild Bill Bohlin parked at the front doors of the barn and noted that Thumper Moran staggered and had to lean on the front fender of the car when he finally got out of the car and managed to shrug into his topcoat. *I knew he was putting down a lot more booze than he should have,* he told himself as he squared his hat and pulled on his old leather flight coat. *Boticello might have hooked me up with a damned drunk.* "The sun sure is bright, but it's still damned cold out here."

"Well, should we go inside the barn or back down to the house and see if anybody's home?" Moran asked, squinting and pulling his hat down lower over his eyes.

"There was no smoke coming from the chimney at the house when we passed so I thought nobody's home and that's why I drove up here. There are sure as hell a lot of tire tracks and footprints around here though."

"Yeah," Moran agreed. "Something sure as hell's been happening around here lately."

"That old truck over there with all the snow on it belongs to the Merkels, so I'd say these fresh tracks are from visitors. Let's go into the barn and see if there's anything of interest in there."

Moran lifted the heavy chain and padlock looped loosely through the double-door handles and shrugged. "It isn't going to be all that easy. I may have to shoot this thing off," he said, opening his coat and reaching inside.

"No, no, no," Bohlin said loudly, holding up his hand. "Let's walk around and see if there's some other way to get into the barn. A shot might bring somebody and we don't want any company right now."

"Unless it's the Merkels," Moran added and chuckled. "Let me see if I can pull these things open." He grabbed the handles and managed to pull the doors apart enough to see inside. "Smells like booze in there," he stated, turning his head to try to see more inside the barn. "Kinda dark inside."

That's probably your breath blowing back at you. "Here, lemme look," Bohlin said, tapping the big man on the shoulder.

Moran nodded and stepped back.

Bohlin put his face into the space. "It does smell like booze in there," he agreed. "And I can tell you why. There's a pile of shot-up liquor cases off to the left. Let's go see if we can find another way in to see what that's all about."

Sheriff Andy Larson and Hard Times topped a small hill overlooking the Merkel farm and he saw the black Buick

Roadster parked in front of the barn and two men standing outside the big double-doors talking. *A Canadian car visiting the Merkels. I think I'll wander in and see if I can find out what they're up to. I wonder if they know anything about what's happened in the barn?* He opened his sheepskin coat enough to pull the badge from his shirt and drop it in a pocket. *No sense in going to visit as the law when I can just be a snoopy cowboy.* He dropped his hand to the gun belt under his coat, smiled, and shrugged. *Aw, hell, they probably expect to find a cowboy out here wearing a gun anyway.*

Thumper Moran and Wild Bill Bohlin circled the barn and found a small door in the back.

Moran twisted the knob, shrugged, leaned back, and slammed his shoulder against it. It didn't budge. "Damn door," the big man mumbled, rubbing his shoulder and rattling the knob again. He stepped back several paces, rubbed his hands together, lowered his shoulder, and charged. The door caved inward under his bulk and he fell in to land on his hands and knees on the rough pavement floor. His fancy homburg hit the floor and rolled a ways. "Son-of-a-bitch!" he shouted as he sat back onto his heels, looked at the bloody, scraped palms of his hands, and continued to swear under his breath.

Bill Bohlin stepped into the room and looked at all the clean milking equipment. "You got that damned door that time," he said, fighting to keep a straight face. He stepped over, picked up the hat, made a production out of dusting it, and pushed it onto Moran's head. "Looks okay to me."

Moran pulled himself up the side of the cream separator, adjusted his hat, and shook his head. "Damn," he said, looking down at the torn knee of his pants. "These pants are ruined."

Bohlin nodded in agreement.

"I'm gonna charge Boticello for a new suit for this. Geez, look at that." He bent down, rubbed a finger across the torn cloth, brought it up, and looked at the blood on it. "It isn't bad enough I ruin a pair of pants," he muttered as he wiped his bloody fingers on his pant leg. "I got damned torn-up palms and a bloody knee too. Shit!"

He seems to be sobering up pretty quick. "C'mon, Thumper, let's take a closer look at all that shot-up booze," Bohlin said, and opened a door into the dimly lit main room of the barn. "The place *does* smells like a damned brewery."

As they walked across the room, Moran pulled out a handkerchief and wrapped it around his left hand. "Damn, this one hurts," he grumbled. "The right one's not too bad."

"It looks like somebody might've shot up a few cases of Mister Boticello's missing whiskey," Bohlin stated, pointing to the pile of bullet-chewed wooden cases and shattered bottles.

"What the hell are all these used flashbulbs for?" Moran asked, kicking one of the burned bulbs by his foot.

"Well, that'd explain the chain on the doors," Bohlin answered. "It looks to me like some kind of a police investigation. They always take lots of pictures of a crime scene and I'm sure that's blood all over the dirt and hay by your feet. Funny with all the stuff that's shot up here, there aren't any shell casings. They must've done a pretty thorough collection job on those."

Moran looked down at his feet and instantly jumped aside. "Damn, what kind of a place is this?"

Bohlin shook his head and suddenly something across the room caught his attention. "What the hell is this anyway?" he asked as he walked to the cow stalls and leaned over a rail. "Look here. Four dead cows! Would the cops be investigating the killing of four cows?"

Moran ambled over to join him, carefully watching where he stepped. He looked down at the dead animals. "I don't understand any of this. Shooting up cases of quality booze and killing cows. None of this makes any sense to me."

"I don't see any rhyme or reason to this," Bohlin stated. "I wonder where the Merkels are."

CHAPTER TWENTY-FOUR

Andy Larson reined Hard Times, slid down, and tied the big buckskin to a rail in front of the barn. He looked around, heard voices from inside, and noted the chain was still through the handles of the partially opened doors. He walked over and opened the car door, pulled the keys, dropped them in a coat pocket, and quietly pushed the door shut. He peered into the barn to see the backs of the two men standing at the cattle stalls. *Guess I'll find out how they got in and join them.* He walked around the building, and found the broken door hanging inward on the bottom hinge. *Must be the work of that big fella.* He stepped quietly across the room and paused at the door to the main room. *Okay, cowboy, let's go.* He passed through the door and cleared his throat.

The big man moved very quickly for a man his size and had a forty-five automatic in his hand by the time he was facing Larson.

Larson's hands shot up into the air. "Whoa, easy there, fella," he shouted. "I was just wondering who was in here when I rode up and saw that fancy car parked out front."

Wild Bill Bohlin grimaced and motioned for him to come to them. "C'mere, cowboy," he said.

Larson shook his head as he stepped towards the two men. "Tell the big fella to be careful with that hog leg in his hand."

"Put the gun away, Thumper. This guy looks harmless enough to me," Bohlin said.

Moran shot him a curious look, shrugged, and slid the gun back into his coat pocket.

Suddenly, Bohlin ran forward and threw a high punch at Larson, who ducked and swung a short punch at the man's gut that stopped just short of connecting.

Bohlin and Larson began to laugh uproariously, pound on each other's shoulders, and then grip and shake hands.

Moran, gun again held loosely in his hand, stood looking at the scene the two men had created.

"What the hell . . . ?"

The two men stopped jumping around and turned to face Moran.

"Thumper, I've got to tell you something," Bohlin began. "This is Andy Larson and the first time I saw him, I was lying in a muddy field in France beside a burning airplane that I had just managed to crawl out of. A group of five Germans was moving towards me with their rifles at the ready. My leg hurt like hell and I was trying to get my coat open and get my pistol out. Suddenly, a mud man, with a pistol in each hand, popped up out of a shell hole and ran towards me, firing one of the pistols at the Germans. He was waving the other pistol in the air above his head and shouting something about following him. They opened fire and he dropped to his knees beside me, calmly switched pistols, and started shooting again. I looked over my shoulder and watched as those Krauts fell like metal ducks in a shooting gallery. Damn, he was calm and a helluva shot. He sat back on his heels, never taking his eyes off the downed Krauts on the ground, and grinned a grin that cracked more of the mud covering his face. What a sight! All I could see besides the mud were eyes and teeth. 'Nice of you to drop in on me,' he joked as he reloaded both pistols. 'I was getting a bit lonesome out here all by myself with nobody but those damned Krauts for company.' He slowly stood up, walked over to the dead

Germans, gave each a kick, and came back to where I was lying in the mud with a bullet hole in my calf. 'You don't look all that heavy, so I guess I can carry you for a ways.' He carried me for almost a day."

"Yeah, and it wasn't easy in all that damned mud."

Moran studied Larson and slowly circled the two men. "Is that bulge under your coat a gun?" he asked Larson.

"Matter of fact, it is," Larson answered and patted the concealed weapon.

Moran slowly raised the pistol in his hand. "You the law, Larson?"

Larson shook his head. "Nope."

"Then why you wearing that gun?"

"You can never tell when you might need a gun," Larson answered. "Mountain lions, bears, all kinds of vermin and unfriendly critters out here."

Moran motioned with his pistol. "Open your coat," he ordered.

Larson shrugged and slowly unbuttoned his sheepskin coat.

"Open it so I can see if you're wearing a badge."

Larson opened the coat. "Satisfied?"

"I'll take the pistol," Moran stated and stepped closer to Larson.

"No." Larson shook his head and let his coat fall shut. "Nobody takes my gun from me."

"Yes, I will." Moran started to bring his pistol up.

Larson leaped forward, swung his left hand up, grabbed Moran's wrist, and hit him on the point of the jaw with a hard right uppercut. The big man's eyes rolled up into his head, his knees buckled, and Larson grabbed the pistol from his hand as he flopped over backwards to the floor.

Larson spun to face Bohlin, who quickly raised his hands and chuckled. "He told me he had a glass jaw. I can see he wasn't lying."

Larson glanced at the man on the floor, laughed, checked the safety on the pistol, and dropped it into a coat pocket. "As they say, it looks like he's down for the count." He rubbed his knuckles as he turned to face Bohlin. "He might have a glass jaw, but it's sure as hell a hard one. It's good to see you again after all these years, Bill. They say it's a small world and I guess this proves it. What've you been up to? I see you're still wearing your lucky coat. You flying these days?"

Bohlin tipped his head slightly as he studied Larson's face. "Yeah," he answered slowly. "I'm still flying, barnstorming in the summers under the name, Wild Bill Bohlin. Name makes me sound more like a war hero and draws bigger crowds. What're you doing now, punching cows for a living? I didn't know you were a cowboy." Bohlin chuckled and pointed at the man's inert body on the hay-covered floor. "Maybe punching was a poor choice of words, but I see you do that pretty well, and from the looks of your face, that wasn't the first punch you've thrown."

Larson nodded. "He wasn't expecting me to go against his gun." He smiled and flexed his fingers. "I cowboy whenever I can. Who's the gorilla on the floor? Your bodyguard?"

"What in the hell would I need a bodyguard for?"

"I don't know. Maybe in that snappy outfit parked outside you need a bodyguard. He seemed a bit overprotective."

Bohlin shook his head and pointed at the man on the floor, who was beginning to stir. "I just met Thumper here this morning."

"Thumper?"

"He used to be a bouncer, an enforcer, and carried a baseball bat under his coat to thump people when they didn't agree with him."

"He still got the bat?"

"No, but he's got another forty-five under one of his arms."

Larson knelt, opened Thumper's coat, brought out and checked the pistol, and dropped it into his other outside coat pocket. "You got a gun?" he asked, as he stood up.

Bohlin shook his head and pulled his leather coat open. "I'm a man of peace these days."

"You said you met *Thumper* this morning. Instant friendship?"

"No, more of a working relationship."

Larson looked at him questioningly.

"We came down here from Canada today to talk to the Merkels."

"You know the Merkels?"

Bohlin nodded. "Yeah, I met 'em a couple of months ago. What happened in here?" he asked, waving a hand at the room. "It looks like somebody shot those four cows and a few cases of booze."

Larson glanced down at Moran, who was now up on one elbow, tenderly rotating his jaw with the fingertips of his dirty hand. "Stay down there," Larson ordered. "I've got *my* gun and both of yours. And besides, every time you move you're getting more cow shit on that fancy coat of yours."

Bohlin's eyes moved from Larson to Moran and back up to Larson.

Moran's eyes were mere slits of anger in his face. He raised his bloody, dirty hand and turned his palm to look at it. He raised it to his nose, sniffed it, grimaced, and shook his head. He made a motion as if to wipe it on the front of his coat, shook his head, balled his fist, and gingerly put it down in the straw.

Larson stepped back, brought one of Moran's pistols out of his pocket, and let it hang loosely at his side. "They've got a saying up here in Montana about the man with the gun making the rules, so just do as I say and we'll all be happier."

"He scraped his hands up pretty bad when he busted down that door and fell on 'em," Bohlin volunteered. "I don't think that frozen cow shit he's got on 'em is doing 'em any good."

CHAPTER TWENTY-FIVE

Sheriff Andy Larson nodded and motioned with the pistol. "C'mon, get up, *Thumper*. Go over there and sit on that feed bunk."

Thumper Moran slowly got to his feet and carefully adjusted the handkerchief on his left hand as he walked over and sat on the edge of the wooden feed bunk.

"There's a pump back there in the dairy room," Larson said, pointing at the nearby door. "I don't know if it's frozen up, but you can go back in there and try to get some water to wash your hands. I noticed there was some soap and a few rags on that counter. Go see what you can do for yourself *and* it won't do you any good to try to run because I've got the car keys in my pocket. If you do run, I can shoot you or mount up, drop a loop over you, and drag you behind my horse. I'm as good with a rope as I am with a pistol so that's a fair warning. Now go wash up."

Thumper, head down with dejection, walked into the dairy room and Larson soon heard the splash of water. "Sounds like the pump's working," he said to Bohlin without taking his eyes from the door of the room where the water was running. "I'll bet that water's damned cold."

"Yeah, I imagine it is," Bohlin agreed.

"What do you two want to talk to the Merkels about?" Larson asked.

Again, Bohlin tilted his head slightly as he looked at Larson.

"You're pretty nosy for a cowboy."

"Yeah, I have a tendency to want to know about things that're goin' on around me. So, what're you doing here?"

"Well, to be honest with you, we're here to check on some lost whiskey and a couple of missing men who work for the man we work for."

"I thought you said you were a barnstormer."

"I said I was a barnstormer in the summer. This is winter."

"So you work the whiskey trade in the winter?"

"Yeah, I do because it pays well."

"I thought they hauled whiskey in cars and trucks."

"They do, but a lot of time the roads in this part of the country are snowed in for days and I can get into areas where the roads haven't been cleared. It gives my boss the advantage of weatherproof delivery. How much do you make working as a cowboy?"

"Forty a month and found."

"Found?" Bohlin questioned.

"That means they feed me," Larson answered.

Bohlin scratched his chin and nodded. "I see. Do you know where the Merkels are?"

"Yep, I'm told they're laid out in the cold storage vault behind Hank Bement's place waiting to be sent to Helena any day now for an autopsy. Bement's the undertaker here in Wolf Point."

"Autopsy?"

"Yep, they know what killed them, but an autopsy has to be done for any murder. I guess that's why there's no real rush to get 'em over there."

Thumper Moran stepped out of the dairy room with strips of cloth wrapped around his hands. A large circle of wet material around the torn knee of his pants showed that he'd also washed his scraped knee. "Thanks for letting me do that," he said. "My hands don't look so bad once I got all that blood and shit washed off them." He lifted his hands. "There were a couple of flour sacks in there and I tore one of them up for these bandages."

"We were just discussing the Merkels," Bohlin said. "Andy tells me they're waiting to be shipped to Helena for autopsies. So how'd they die?"

"From what I'm told they got the same ending as those cases of whiskey over there. At least that's the rumor around town," Larson added quickly.

Moran stepped closer. "What about those cows?"

Larson shrugged. "Hell, I don't know. What cows?"

"Those over there," Moran stated, pointing with a wrapped hand.

"Hmm," Larson said as he walked over to look at the frozen carcasses. "Four dead cows. Nobody in town said anything about dead cows."

"Were the Merkels the only people killed here in this barn?" Moran asked.

"I heard tell of a couple of strangers," Larson answered. "City fellas."

"Any names?" Bohlin asked.

Larson shook his head.

"You wanna make some easy money, Andy?" Bohlin asked.

Here it comes. "Doing what?"

Bohlin glanced over at Moran, who glared and shook his head.

Bohlin raised an eyebrow at Moran and smiled slightly. "Now that the Merkels are gone, I need somebody to light some landing fires for me."

"That sounds easy enough." *That also answers my questions about his flying.*

Moran shook his head, shrugged, and walked over to look down at the shattered whiskey cases and shattered glass.

"Have you got a phone, Andy?" Bohlin asked.

"Nope."

"Well, that makes this a little difficult then."

As difficult as I can make it. "What if I can get to a phone and call you?"

"That might work. Have you got a couple of friends that can help you?"

"How many fires do you want me to light?"

"Well, there's a bit of work to be done after the fires are lit."

"Such as?"

"Lifting."

"Lifting?" *Damn, he's slow getting to the subject.*

"Okay. I think I can trust you. I'll be flying in and dropping off thirty-six cases of whiskey. Somebody has to load it onto the sled the Merkels used and haul it here to the barn. I just think that's more lifting than one man should be doing. From the looks of this place and what's happened here recently, I'd say this will probably be one of my last runs in here. I know this is a promised delivery, so the boss must have somebody picking the stuff up. I'll see what the man has to say when I get back up to him."

Larson looked Bohlin up and down. *Stupid of me. I should've kept a closer eye on this place. They don't seem to know anything about the shooting here so I've got no grounds to arrest them. Attempted booze smuggling?* "Who's gonna pick up the whiskey?"

"That's not your problem," Moran growled.

"Then how much and when do I get paid?" Larson asked.

Bohlin's brow wrinkled in thought. "We'll talk more when I get things worked out with the boss, but I can attach the money to one of the cases of booze. How's that?"

"You didn't tell me how much."

"Well, let's see . . . How about two bucks a case? Loaded, moved, and stacked in the barn."

Larson made a production of counting on his fingers. "That's . . . ah . . ."

"Make it an even seventy-five dollars for this trip," Bohlin interrupted. "That's more'n you make in a month working cattle. And that's for three or four hours' work."

Larson glanced at Moran and saw he was now interested in their conversation. "Let's make it five bucks a case."

"I told you how much that'd be. More'n a month of working cattle."

"Yeah, but I can't go to jail for working cattle. And besides that, from the looks of this place, it's damned dangerous work."

"We'll make it three bucks a case and no more," Moran interjected. "Take it or leave it."

Again Larson worked his fingers and mumbled to himself.

"That's more than a hundred bucks a trip!" Moran shouted. "And I'll see about throwing in a case of whiskey."

"That's two and a half months of cowboy pay," Bohlin added. "Think about that, Andy."

Larson nodded and grinned. "Gimme a number an' I'll call you tomorrow to set it all up. I gotta couple of boys who'll work for me for the right money. A buck and a half a case for them . . . each."

"Okay, deal." Bohlin dug out a card. "That's a Canadian number so it'll cost you a little more from a pay phone. Take a lot of quarters and call me tomorrow at about two o'clock."

"Now, gimme my damned guns back," Moran ordered.

Larson's eyes narrowed. "I think maybe I oughta take them to town and give them to the sheriff."

"We're working for the same people now," Moran argued. "Why'd I shoot someone who's working with me?"

"Give him his damned guns, Andy," Bohlin said.

Larson shrugged, dropped the clip from the pistol in his hand, and put it in his pocket. He worked the action and a bullet spun out and dropped into the straw on the floor. He twirled the pistol and lobbed it to Moran. "Here, you can get the clips from me next time we see each other." He dug the second pistol from his pocket, repeated the action, and handed it to Bohlin. "Now you've both got empty guns and I feel a little easier about doing business 'til we get to know each other better."

CHAPTER TWENTY-SIX

Benjamin "Little Barrel" Boticello hung up his phone and pushed down a button on his intercom. "Johnstone, get in here."

There was a soft rap on the door. "Come in!" Boticello shouted. "Geez."

John Johnstone, notebook in hand, entered and carefully closed the door. "Yes, sir, Mister Boticello. You wanted to see me?"

Boticello gave an exasperated snort. "Why in the hell do you think I buzzed you, you *idiot?*"

"Yes, sir." *I see the little asshole's in a good mood again today.*

"I want a hundred and eight cases of Superior Whiskey taken out to Bohlin's hangar. He'll start making deliveries to Wolf Point again in a couple nights. When he gets started again, he'll be flying three nights in a row to make up for what was stolen a couple weeks ago. Hell, make it a hundred and forty-four cases, just in case he can fly a fourth night. The people in Helena and Denver are getting damned low in their supply of the good liquor."

"Then you have confirmed the whiskey was stolen, Mister Boticello?"

"I'd say the fact I'm sending more whiskey confirms that it's gone, doesn't it?" Boticello growled. "Thumper Moran just called me from someplace in Montana and told me he and Bohlin are on their way back right now. They're in one hell of a snowstorm right up by the border, so they're going to spend the night in that town where they called from. They found out the Merkels had been gunned down and a couple of unidentified strangers were shot up with them. They're sure it was Morgan and Turner. He said something I didn't understand about four dead cows. There were some shot-up cases of whiskey in the Merkels' barn, but only a few of them. How many cases should there have been in the barn on that night?"

"Seventy-two cases, Mister Boticello," Johnstone answered quickly. "Morgan and Turner were supposed to have picked up forty of them to take to Denver."

Boticello nodded. "I like a man with quick answers, Johnstone."

"Yes, sir, I know *my* numbers and *your* business."

"Yeah, and some of that makes me nervous." Boticello made a shooing motion with his hand. "Get out there and have them start moving that whiskey. I sure as hell hope Thumper and Bohlin make it back first thing in the morning. This snowstorm works well for *my* deliveries. I'll make one more drop at the Merkels. Bohlin's got someone lined up to handle the fires and the booze pickup. I've got an alternative drop site picked out on the other side of Wolf Point and it'll be ready soon. A little problem like the incident at the Merkels won't slow me down. I always have a secondary plan. Now get out of here."

Johnstone was already making his bowing, backing walk to the door. "Yes, sir, Mister Boticello."

The air in the hotel room was heavy with cigar and cigarette smoke and the slight smell of whiskey. Two men, Longy Zwillman and Waxey Gordon, hats covering their faces, were asleep on the bed, both snoring softly. Nino Maggadino sat in a chair, reading a newspaper; a short cigarette dropped a trail of ash down his vest as it bobbed in the corner of his mouth. Dominic Bianci and Joey Alzado, a thin bandage wrapped around his head, sat at the small table playing a silent game of gin rummy.

The ringing of the telephone startled everyone and Bianci quickly grabbed the receiver and pulled the candlestick phone closer. "Yeah?"

Gordon and Zwillman both muttered curses as they sat up and pushed their hats back on their heads. Maggadino folded his newspaper and ground his cigarette out in the ashtray on the windowsill. Alzado took a quick glance at his cards, snorted, and tossed them facedown onto the table.

"We're just sitting around scratching our asses and picking our noses while we wait for orders from you," Bianci said and grinned at the others. He made notes on a pad in front of him and chuckled. "I got it, Stoney. I *know* this'll work good. We'll take care of everything and I'll talk to you in a few days." He hung up the receiver, made more notes, looked at the other men sitting around the room, and grinned again. "Well, it looks like we're back in the whiskey business. Boticello's putting Bohlin back in the air to the farm in Wolf Point in a couple of days. He had a big truckload of *Superior* sent over to Bohlin's hangar. He's gonna fly that whiskey in for three nights straight and he may go in again for a fourth trip. That's almost twelve grand worth of whiskey we can get our hands on with no cost to us. If he makes that extra trip, we make extra money."

All the men chuckled.

"So what's the plan?" Nino Maggadino asked.

"There's supposed to be a car a night going from Helena to Wolf Point to pick up that night's drop. One more drop at the Merkels' place and then Boticello's got a new drop point on the other side of Wolf Point. We'll get that tomorrow. They haul it back to Helena, take their portion, and the rest continues on to Denver. The Stone Man's gonna call and tell them Boticello's arranged for us to deliver it all to them after the third drop at the new location. It saves them from having to make three runs to Wolf Point."

"Do you think they'll go for that?" Waxey Gordon asked.

"Hey, The Stone Man can be very convincing over the phone," Rossi answered. "*Especially* when he tells them they're getting a fifteen or twenty percent discount because of all the delays so far."

"That Stone Man is one smart, clever son-of-a-bitch," Maggadino said, and everyone laughed.

"Who's this guy, *The Stone Man*?" Alzado interrupted.

"You'll find out when he thinks the time's right," Bianci answered.

Alzado shrugged and nodded his bandaged head. "Okay, I guess. Have you ever met him?"

"Yeah, I talked to him once in person, but I didn't get a good look at him. We met in a parking lot one night, but he stayed in the car and we talked through the window. He had a hat on and a scarf wrapped high on his face so I really couldn't see him. I guess he doesn't want anybody to know him until the time is right."

"If he's in so tight with Boticello," Maggadino said, "isn't he afraid Boticello'll figure out somebody on the inside is doing this?"

"I'd say that's why he stayed in the car," Bianci stated. "He doesn't want anybody to be able to identify him and snitch him to Boticello. He knows the operation and how it runs. It'll be the same buyers; just a different seller. Those people don't give a shit who they buy from as long as they get good delivery of the product at a fair price. He didn't get to where he is today by being stupid. We'll go over there tomorrow and set it up to take the whiskey as it's delivered. We'll let the regular people do it the first time so we know how it's done. When we get it all, we'll use a car and a truck to haul it to a warehouse in Havre. We'll clean out and use the Canadian runner's Studebaker since it's set for a heavy load. Switch plates and gas it up. We'll get there after dark. Bohlin comes around midnight, so we want to be able to watch how they do everything."

"I thought this booze was supposed to go to Helena and Denver," Gordon said.

"So does Boticello," Bianci answered and everyone laughed. "It'll go there in a couple of days. The Stone Man's going to take over Boticello's operation shortly. He's got all the names of the buyers and we can sell it there quick and easy. He said to leave the carload of whiskey we got the other day here and we'll get it moved when we've got time."

"How does the delivery work?" Maggadino asked.

"This Bohlin fella flies in, lands, turns around, drops the whiskey into the snow, and takes off again. He won't even get a look at us, so he won't know we're not the regular people. All we gotta do is light the fires where they were before and wait. We put the truck in the barn, load the liquor in the truck, and wait for the next shipment."

"This whole thing sounds like we're gonna do a helluva lot of waitin'," Joey Alzado noted. "You all better bring a bunch of money, 'cause we're gonna be doin' a lotta card playin'."

"But not with your cards," Gordon added, and several of the others whispered back and forth.

"All right, listen up," Bianci said. "After the whiskey is dropped from the third flight, *we're going to shoot the plane down. Probably blast it as it's taking off again.*"

The room was silent. "Why's that?" Maggadino asked.

"Stone Man says it'll cause confusion," Bianci answered.

"How'n the hell's shooting down a plane going to cause confusion?" Zwillman asked.

"Boticello's going to be out a hundred to a hundred and eight cases of booze. He's trying to get rid of the smaller dealers in the area and now he'll think one of them is making a move to

130

take him out. It'll cause a war and put pressure on Boticello. Nobody'll trust anybody. When the time's right, The Stone Man takes over. Make sure you're all well-armed and we'll take care of any messy business the right way."

CHAPTER TWENTY-SEVEN

Sheriff Andy Larson hung his coat on the rack by the door and took a cup of steaming coffee back to his desk. He sat, tipped his hat back, took a sip of coffee, and slowly looked around at the deputies: Dusty Durbin, Ben Graves, John Mooney, Robert Sullivan, Bernie Ward, and Dave Dixon.

"Well, what the hell's going on?" Durbin demanded around the unlit cigar gripped in the corner of his mouth.

"That call over at the hotel took five dollars' worth of quarters," Larson said.

Several of the deputies snorted in exasperation.

Larson laughed. "Okay, okay. Bohlin's gonna make the delivery tonight, sometime right around midnight. We're to light the fires at eleven-thirty and wait. We'll be able to hear the plane a long way off. He told me his boss is mad because they've fallen behind on their Denver deliveries and he wants to make drops here three nights in a row. There's going to be a car coming in from Helena to haul the booze back there and then part of it goes to Denver. It's supposed to be here about the time of Bohlin's delivery to us and he wants it in and out as fast as possible. The shootings and the missing whiskey from the last time have made his boss nervous. From what Bohlin told me the man's afraid there's someone inside his organization who's a loose cannon and trying to take over."

"Do we have enough room in the jail for this influx of visitors?" Sullivan asked and enjoyed the laughter his question brought.

"Good word, *influx*," Mooney noted. "You can tell who the educated one in the group is."

"I'll have three of you out in the meadow with me. You're gonna gather the cases when they fall off the wings of Bohlin's plane. Let's see . . . Mooney, Ward, and Dixon. I've got plans for the rest of you, too. Dave, you've got the most experience with horses, so you'll be in charge of the sled. The horses are in the pasture not far from the barn. It's a full moon night, so unless clouds move in, it should be easy to see just about everything out there."

Andy Larson glanced at his watch and looked around at his six deputies, shifting and wiggling to fight the cold. "It's a little after eleven. Let's start getting the fires lit," he said, his breath making a small cloud in front of him. "It's damned cold, but there's no wind tonight so he can land on either end, but I want him to make his turn to drop the liquor where we are. We'll make a production of where we're waiting. I'm pretty sure he'll see us and come right in. Okay, we'll go over this whole thing one more time. Dave, is everything ready with the sled?"

"It's in position and everything is set for your signal."

"Great. When we hear his plane, you get to the sled and wait. Dusty, you, Robert, and John'll go to the road by the barn and watch for the pickup people to arrive. You've got the Thompson and if there's any sign of trouble, go ahead and use it. We're not sure what to expect. For all we know this is the same crew that gunned down everyone and stole the booze before. They might just be drivers or they might be some heavy hands sent in to make an impression. With thirty-six cases of liquor, they'll probably have more than one car. Maybe even a truck. The moon's got the area pretty well lit up, so you can see and be seen. Be careful, we don't want to take any chances. Now, go get those fires lit. Light 'em up, boys!"

Wild Bill Bohlin circled high in the air and looked down at the fires burning on the sides and ends of the meadow where he was to deliver the whiskey. *It looks like Andy did exactly what I told him. That's good because Boticello isn't in for any mistakes at this stage of the game.* The airplane descended lower and made a final pass over the meadow. He could see Larson and two men standing and waving by a fire at one end. Off to the side a third man sat on the seat of a heavy sled, holding the reins of two fidgeting draft horses. *It all looks good.* He brought the plane around, touched down onto the snow, and cut the engine speed as he coasted to where Larson and the two men waited. He spun the plane in a tight semicircle on the snow, dropped the engine speed to an idle, pulled the release levers, and heard the restraint bars holding the cases of liquor pop up and open. He gave the engine a long rev, throwing up a cloud of loose snow, and the vibration of the plane caused several cases of whiskey to slide backward and fall into the snow as the plane came to a stop.

Andy Larson trudged through the snow, stepped up on the wheel above the ski, pulled himself up onto the wing, and stepped up to look down at Bohlin.

Bohlin looked up at him and grinned. "Well, Andy, you did a fine job indeed," he shouted over the engine noise. "The canvas bag with your money's nailed on that end case in there."

Larson nodded and pulled his coat open to reveal the silver five-sided star pinned on his vest. "Shut off the engine, Bill, you're under arrest." He waved his arm and Dave Dixon slapped the reins on the back of the horses and they lunged forward, snapping a steel cable up out of the snow. One end of the cable, draped with colored rags, was hooked to the back of the sled and the other end wrapped around a large tree on the opposite side of the meadow. "You can't get past that cable, Bill; it'll tear off your skis and dig the propeller into the ground. *Shut off* the damned engine!"

A look of disbelief clouded over Bohlin's widened eyes and he shook his head. "No, no, no . . ." he muttered as he switched off the engine. "I can't *believe* this shit."

The cold night air was suddenly very still. "Mooney, break open one of those cases and give me a bottle of whatever's in it. Take another bottle and go share a bit of it with Dixon and Ward over there on the sled while Bill and I have a little talk. Just a nip to fight the cold now. We've got to move this liquor up to the barn in a few minutes."

Bernie Ward nodded and gave several kicks at the lid of the nearest wooden whiskey case, catching his heel on the corner and breaking open a space between the lid and the side.

"Careful there, Bernie," Larson warned. "Don't be breaking any of the merchandise. We're not sure who it belongs to."

Ward kicked it again, got his fingers into the space, and with a mighty tug, pulled the top of the case open. "Damn," he said, pulling a bottle out and holding it up to the moonlight. "*Superior.* We're drinking the good stuff tonight, boys." He chuckled as he worked the cork free and took a small swallow before trudging off through the snow to join his fellow deputies.

"C'mon down, Wild Bill," Larson said, jumping off the wing and sitting on a case of whiskey to settle it down into the snow. He pulled a bottle free from the open case, read the label, and began to work on the cork. "C'mon, *Hero.* We'll have a couple of bumps for the good old days and good old friends. Then, we'll discuss the situation here tonight."

Bohlin pulled off his gloves, unbuckled himself, and stood up in the cockpit. "How do you know I don't have a gun," he asked as he swung his legs up and stepped onto the surface of the wing.

"You've been reading too many Al Capone stories in the papers," Larson answered. "Not everyone now'days shoots his way out of a tight spot. Besides, *you* wouldn't shoot *me* anyway."

Bohlin dropped to the ground, sat on a crate, and held out his hand. "Gimme the damned bottle."

Larson chuckled, took a small sip, and handed the bottle to Bohlin. "That look on your face when you saw my badge was priceless."

Bohlin nodded sheepishly, took a swallow, and held the bottle out to Larson, who shook his head. "I'm on duty."

Bohlin shrugged, smiled, and took another drink. "This is *really* getting to be funny."

"I look at it this way, Bill. Maybe I just saved your life again by getting you out of the bootleg business."

Bohlin shrugged and started to raise the bottle to his mouth.

Larson put a restraining hand on his arm. "That's enough for now."

"Hell, if I'm going to jail, I might as well go drunk," Bohlin stated and jerked his arm free.

"Who said you were going to jail?"

CHAPTER TWENTY-EIGHT

Bohlin slowly lowered the bottle to his knee. "What?" he asked, in disbelief.

"Who said you were going to jail?" Larson repeated.

Bohlin leaned forward, rested his elbows on his knees, and looked intently at Andy Larson. "Okay, now what?"

Larson tipped his hat back and patted his pocket for a pack of Camels. "I've put a lot of thought into this, Bill." He shook a cigarette up in the pack and offered it to Bohlin, who nodded and took the cigarette. Larson took out a cigarette and pushed the pack into a pocket.

Bohlin produced a small metal trench lighter, snapped a flame unto it and held it out towards Larson. Larson pulled a bright glow onto the end of his cigarette and nodded. "I even feel a *small* amount of guilt for lying to you a couple of days ago."

Bohlin lit his cigarette and dropped the lighter into his pocket. He blew a stream of smoke into the air, took a small sip from the bottle, and offered it to Larson again. "I won't tell anybody that I saw you taking a drink, *Sheriff.*"

Larson took the bottle, glanced over at the three men sitting on the end of the sled, shrugged, and took a sip. "Don't have too good a time over there," he shouted and stuck the bottle down in the snow. "We still don't know what to expect from the bootleg pickup cars."

Mooney waved the bottle in the air. "We each had a drink and that's it, Andy."

"Like I was saying," Larson began. "I feel a little guilty about lying to and tricking an old friend. Maybe I should've arrested both of you on the spot the other day."

Bohlin shook his head and took a deep drag from his cigarette. "Why do I get the feeling you're peeing on my foot and telling me it's warm rain?"

"No, I'm being honest. I put a lot of thought into this whole operation of yours. I'll tell you that I think it's a *brilliant* way to deliver booze this time of year. I have nothing against a man having a drink or two. I personally prefer beer and drink more than my share even though it's illegal. Hell, I'm the law and I know where to get it when I want it."

"Is this more warm rain?"

"Shut up and listen." Larson took a pull of smoke from his cigarette. "I'm the sheriff in a very big county that's ideally situated to be a drop-off and distribution point for large amounts of booze coming in from Canada on the way to Helena, Denver, and other places to the south. Since drinkable alcohol is currently against the law, it's up to me to do whatever I can to stop it. Booze smuggling is a *rough,* moneymaking business and we have several dead lawmen in Wolf Point to prove that. I recently had a run-in with an Irish gang who wants to take over this territory just for the beer part of it. I have people in town I don't trust as far as I can throw a fresh cow pie. I've finally come to the conclusion that you and your plane are a very minor line on my list of problems. I'll tell you I'm a long way from being a saint, but I'm a damn good, old-fashioned lawman. I *can't* be bought and there're still a hell of a lot of things I do consider a crime."

Bohlin nodded, lifted the bottle, took a sip, and held it out to Larson. "You're talking up a thirst."

Larson shook his head.

Bohlin shrugged, took a drink, and stuck the bottle back in the snow.

Larson studied the bottle, looked up at Bohlin, and smiled weakly. "Unfortunately, I don't consider *drinking* a crime and at times that makes this job pretty damned tough. The men making the big money are the criminals. Guys like Orv Mayer, who hauls a little whiskey and a keg or two of good Canadian beer around here on a packhorse to supply Booger Red, don't bother me. He lost his railroad job and has a family to support. I don't think of him as a criminal, he's just a man making a living in hard times. Now you and your boss are another story." He pointed a thumb at the racks of whiskey cases hanging under the wing and rapped his knuckles on the case he was sitting on. "To me, this is a crime because somebody's getting rich due to the stupidity of the government. Here's where we stand right now. I've got you grounded and a goodly amount of someone else's illegal whiskey is in my custody. So, what's your boss's name?"

"I don't see what difference that makes."

Larson took a deep drag of smoke and let it out slowly. "I just like to know who I'm competing with for control of the booze traffic in Roosevelt County."

CHAPTER TWENTY-NINE

"How much trouble can you handle, Andy?" Bohlin asked.

"I won't know the answer to that until I see how much trouble there is. What should I expect?"

Bohlin shrugged and held out the bottle. "So, what're you going to do with me, now that you've got me grounded?"

Larson shook his head. "Well, by law I'm required to confiscate anything that's used in a felony and running bootleg liquor is sure as hell a felony. Then again, I could drop that cable and let you fly on outta here, couldn't I? Of course, you've got to leave the liquor behind."

Bohlin looked at Larson through narrowed eyes. "You'd really let me go?" He took a sip and pushed the bottle into the snow.

Larson nodded. "That's it, Bill, if you give me your word that you won't fly any more liquor in Roosevelt County, Montana, I'm willing to let you go."

"When I get back to my place, how'll I explain the thirty-six cases of liquor stuck back here in the snow? That liquor's been entrusted to me until I get it delivered. No matter what I tell him, my bootlegger boss is not going to be a happy, understanding person when I go back and inform him that now the law's got his whiskey."

Larson chuckled. "No, Bill. I see that as a great incentive not to go back."

Bohlin sighed. "It seems you've got this all figured right down to the gnat's ass, haven't you?"

Larson shrugged. "It's your call, my friend, but I'd advise you not to go back to Canada."

Bohlin shook his head, stared down at the bottle in the snow, and coughed as he looked up at Larson. "I've got a few things back in my office at the airfield that mean a lot to me, especially a tin box full of money that's under the floorboards. I've also got my partner, Charlie Marcum, back there waiting for me. We have a lot of tools and equipment in the shop to pack up and load on the truck . . ."

"It's your call, Bill."

"How much time have I got?"

"Take all the time you need. It's just a simple yes or no. I'd say with the speed that things happen up in the air, you're a man who can make a quick decision."

Bohlin slapped his knees and stood up. "I'll take you up on the deal, Andy, but I've got to take a little time to think this over. I can sneak back in there tonight and we can get the stuff out of there before they wake up and start to ask questions. I figure I've got until midday tomorrow to get in and get out. Oh, yeah, one more thing. The man I work for, or should I say, I *used* to work for, is named Benjamin Boticello. To his friends he's *The Little Barrel*. He's built like one and he's one mean little bastard who's not to be messed with. And he's got contacts in high places with the bootleg business."

"This Boticello's up in Canada?"

Bohlin nodded. "He's up in Canada. Estevan, Canada."

"Okay." Larson stood up and stuck out his hand. "Good luck, Bill. Stop in and see me again someday. I'm sure it'll be under better conditions. I've got to go join my men watching the road. Leave the whiskey here and go when you're ready." He pointed at the open case lying in the snow. "Hell, if you want it, take a couple of bottles of that good Scotch whiskey with you." He whistled and waved at the men sitting on the sled. "Let him out!"

Dave Dixon nodded and slapped the reins on the backs of the horses. "Let's go, boys!" he shouted, pulling the reins hard to the left and circling the big horses back across the meadow to where the end of the cable was tied to the tree.

Bernie Ward jumped down into the snow, unhooked the cable from the sled, and climbed back aboard. "I guess he'll drop all those cases of liquor when he takes off."

"Yeah. We'd best go up and join the others at the road," Deputy Graves said. "We don't wanna miss out on any of the action. Besides, those boys in the car can load it on the sled. They'll need the exercise when they git here. They've been riding for a while and should loosen up a bit."

"I'll tie up the horses while you get the shotguns," Dixon said and jumped down into the snow.

CHAPTER THIRTY

"It's sure as shit cold out there," Longy Zwillman stated as he drove the long Buick Roadster down the high snow-banked Montana road.

Nino Maggadino sat on the passenger side, tapping an unknown rhythm on the receiver of the Thompson machine gun on his knees and staring absentmindedly out into the eerie blue moonlit night.

Dominic Bianci snored softly as he dozed in the back seat.

Waxey Gordon drove the Canadian whiskey runner's Studebaker a short distance behind. "You got any idea who this guy, The Stone Man, is?" he asked Joey Alzado, rummaging through the glove box.

"Nah, I figured it's none of my business. I got the same answer as you did, so I let it drop."

"What're you looking for?"

"Nothing really, I'm just snooping to see if those Canadian boys had left anything good in here."

"Find anything?"

"There's some English cigarettes, but I tried one once and it tasted like mule shit."

"You got experience smoking mule shit?"

"No, but I'm getting experience riding with some." Alzado laughed hysterically at his own humor. "What do you know about that new guy, Adonis, driving the truck back there?"

"Bianci brings him in this morning and says, this is Ruben

143

Adonis. He'll be driving the truck on this operation. That's all I know about him."

"Yeah, okay. Bianci must've hired him. Maybe he's just that, a driver."

"Who knows?"

"What time is it?" Zwillman asked.

Maggadino dug a watch out and held it close to his face. "It's a couple of minutes after twelve."

"Then we got about a half hour to go. Probably thirty, thirty-five miles."

"Damn, how many cigarettes have you smoked?" Bianci coughed from the back seat. "You could do a ham in here."

"Open your damned window if you don't like it," Zwillman answered. "You been sawing wood back there while I was doing all the damned driving, so I'm entitled to smoke when I want to."

"Yeah, whatever." Bianci turned so he could see out the back window. "Gordon and Alzado are still with us."

"Well, no shit, was I supposed to lose 'em?" Zwillman muttered. "And the truck's still behind them."

"What'd you say?" Bianci demanded.

"Nothing," Zwillman answered. "I was just talking to myself."

"I think you're getting a bit big for your britches there, Zwillman."

Sheriff Andy Larson and three of his deputies trudged down the road to where his other men were keeping watch. The deputies were each carrying a short, trench pump shotgun on their shoulder.

"You think they'll come in easy, Andy?" Graves asked, as he and the others matched stride with the sheriff, their boots making crunching sounds in the cold, hard snow.

"If they're just drivers, they probably will. I don't see any reason for them to be bringing big guns along on something this routine, but after the shootings a few days ago, it's anybody's guess. They might be expecting trouble." They could see the glow of the fire outlining the pickup truck ahead on the side of the road. "We're coming in!" he shouted.

Deputy John Mooney, his cowboy hat tipped forward and shoulders wrapped in a buffalo robe, sat on the tailgate of a pickup truck with his feet swinging. His short shotgun lay beside him in the bed of the truck.

Deputy Robert Sullivan stood close to the fire, the blanket wrapped around his shoulders held in place by the sling of his machine gun. He held his hands down towards the warmth of the blazing wood.

"Where's Dusty?" Larson asked as they joined the men at the fire.

"He's down the road by that big cottonwood," Sullivan answered, pointing up the road. "He'll step out into the road when they've passed and cap the roadblock. We're taking turns down there and coming up here to warm up. The man down there has a Thompson."

"Things are pretty quiet so far, Andy," Mooney said, as he continued to swing his feet.

Larson pulled out a silver pocket watch and turned it toward the moonlight to read it. "It's almost twelve-thirty," he announced. "We can probably be expecting them any time now."

"When's your buddy taking off?" Sullivan asked. "He did take you up on your offer, didn't he?"

"Yeah, he's gonna go. He wants to go back to his hangar in Canada and get some things like money he's got stashed, his partner-mechanic, and some necessary items out of his shop. He knows his big boss, named Boticello, back up there isn't gonna be very happy with what's happened here tonight. Maybe I should've waited until he brought all three loads of booze down and then grabbed him. Oh, well . . ."

"Look, Andy," Mooney said, jumping down and pointing up the road. "Headlights!"

They could see beams of headlights from the approaching vehicles as they topped a low hill a mile away.

"It looks like three of them," Sullivan said, as he lifted a silver whistle to his lips and gave out three long, shrill blasts.

"Let's get ready," Larson said as he lifted a Thompson from the bed of the truck, checked the action, and slammed his fist on the bottom of the ammo drum. "Looks like two cars and a truck. John, get back up on the tailgate and sit the way you were. Give 'em a friendly wave as they get closer. We'll go off and hide in the snow on the sides until they stop. Hopefully, this setup won't look like a roadblock to them and they'll come in not really expecting trouble. Don't anybody show themselves until I call for you. Make sure of any firing angles and safe fields of fire if anything starts. These Thompsons put out a lot of lead in a hurry and I don't want us chewing each other up."

Mooney hopped back on the tailgate and tucked his pump shotgun under the buffalo robe.

Larson took two more small logs from the back of the truck, threw them on the fire, and motioned for the others to move out into the snow. "Get well dug in, boys, it's about to get interesting."

CHAPTER THIRTY-ONE

Longy Zwillman took his foot off the gas and leaned forward, pointing ahead. "What the hell's that all about?"

Nino Maggadino tightened the grip on his Thompson as he bent forward and squinted at the fire burning ahead in the road.

Dominic Bianci hung his arms over the seat. "Careful. I don't know what the hell that is."

"It looks like an old cowboy sitting on the tailgate of that truck," Maggadino stated.

"What the hell's the fire for?" Zwillman asked. "And it looks like he's too far out in the road for me to get past him. Should I make a run for it anyway? Slam him off the road?"

Bianci tapped him on the shoulder. "No, take your time and let's just be careful. These people down here in Montana have got some strange ways about them. Pull up close and let Nino get out and talk to him."

"Okay," Zwillman said, as he slowed the vehicle and brought it to a stop ten feet from the fire.

Waxey Gordon saw the brake lights flash on the car in front of him. "What the hell's going on?" he asked as he pushed in the clutch and stepped on the brake pedal. "Where's the Tommy gun?"

"It's wrapped in a blanket on the floor in back," Joey Alzado answered.

"Well, get the damned thing. We might need it!"

147

"It's about time we stopped," Ruben Adonis muttered as he brought the truck to a stop a short distance behind the Studebaker. He set the hand brake, hopped down, strode quickly around to the back of the truck, unbuttoned his fly, and began to relieve himself. He saw movement out of the corner of his eye and turned to see a big man with an unlit cigar, sticking out of a mass of red beard, walking towards him a short distance away. He carried a machine gun loosely pointed at him and he raised a finger to his lips to signal for silence. Adonis let out an audible sigh, turned his back to the man, and continued to relieve himself. He felt something cold poke into the back of his neck and quickly raised his hands.

"If I's you, friend, I'd reach down and put that thing of yours away before it gits frost bit," a deep voice advised softly. "One hand should be able to do the job."

Adonis nodded, slowly lowered one hand, did the man's bidding, and raised his arm again.

"That's good," Dusty Durbin said, stepping around and looking him up and down. "You got a gun?"

Adonis nodded and pointed down at his armpit.

"Take it out and toss it down by my foot."

Again, the man did as he was told.

"Now lay down on your belly and put your hands behind you."

Adonis felt the ratcheting snap of the handcuffs and a yank to check their security.

"Now you be real quiet," was whispered in his ear and he could see the man's feet as he moved along the back of the truck.

In the lead car Maggadino shifted the machine gun up and pushed off the safety. "I'm ready." He rolled his window down and carefully scanned the moonlit snowbanks to the side of the road. "There's a lot of tracks and trails out there in the snow, but I don't see anybody, so I guess it's okay." Satisfied, he opened the door and stepped out into the road, keeping the machine gun down out of sight from the old cowboy sitting on the tailgate. Once again, he slowly looked over the moonlit snow before turning his attention to the old cowboy.

Andy Larson lay on his back in the snow nest he had quickly dug, machine gun laying across his chest. "Take it easy, John," he whispered.

"What's going on, Old Man?" Maggadino called. "Why'n the hell're you sitting in the road with that fire going?"

"It's to keep me warm," Mooney answered, pulling the buffalo robe up tighter on his neck.

Good answer, Larson told himself.

"That's not what I asked you," Maggadino argued. "Why are you sitting in that damned truck in the middle of the damned road?"

Mooney sighed and shook his head. "This poor old truck won't start. I was hoping somebody'd come along and help me 'fore I ran outta firewood."

Maggadino leaned back down into the car. "Well? Why don't we just push him out of the way?"

"Yeah," Bianci agreed. "We've got things to do. Tell the old man to get down and close the tailgate so we can push it with our car."

"I heard him," Mooney said, glancing down the road where he had just seen Dusty Durbin walking towards the back of the truck. "Keep yer shirt on, I'm gittin' down." He dropped to the road, tossed the buffalo robe off his shoulders, gathered it up with the shotgun inside, and shifted it around until his finger was on the trigger. He coughed to cover the sound of his cocking back the hammer and slowly turned his head to see if he could see Sheriff Larson or any of the others. *Okay, let's do it!*

A ball of flame suddenly burst from under the edge of the

149

buffalo robe and a load of double-ought buckshot destroyed the grill and radiator of the Buick sitting a short distance away. Mooney pumped the action as he dropped to his knees, rolled behind the truck, and sent a second load of shot through the left front tire.

The car instantly settled down onto the rim of the destroyed tire and the air was filled with steam from the torn radiator and gun smoke from the two shotgun blasts.

Maggadino crouched and started to swing the machine gun up and around the door. Suddenly flashes of light and a short, staccato burst of machine-gun fire erupted from the snowbank to his right and a neat row of holes punched across the fender and hood of the fancy automobile. He knew he was at a total disadvantage and there was no way he could turn and fire, so he quickly dropped his right hand away from the trigger and, his left hand holding the weapon by the forearm, slowly raised it above his head.

"Throw it off into the snow behind you," Andy Larson ordered from behind him.

Joey Alzado hung over the seat of the Studebaker, struggling to unwrap the machine gun when the back door burst open and a cold, steel, flash suppressor was jammed into the side of his neck.

"You'll have a real bad headache," Dusty Durbin growled around his cigar.

Alzado dropped the blanket-wrapped weapon, slowly raised his hands, turned, and settled back onto the seat. Out of the corner of his eye he could see Waxey Gordon's fingers pressed against the roof.

Durbin chuckled softly and stepped back from the open door. "Smart boys, now wait for orders."

"All right, everybody out of the cars!" Sheriff Larson shouted, looking around at his deputies kneeling and crouching with their guns pointed at the two cars. "Don't be trying anything stupid. None of you'll get out of the cars alive." To emphasize his statement, he sent another short burst from his machine gun through the steam-clouded hood of the Buick. "Now, put your hands on your heads and get out of the damned cars!"

Bianci heard the chatter of gunfire, the slugs chew through the metal, and cringed. He looked out at the mustached lawman standing in the moonlight with the smoking machine gun resting on his hip. "Do as he says," he ordered as he opened the back door of the Buick, stuck his hands into sight, and stepped out onto the road. *I won't give that crazy bastard an excuse to shoot me.* The other men quickly joined him, put their hands on their heads, and looked around at Sheriff Larson and his heavily armed band of lawmen.

The sputter and then the roar of an airplane engine could be heard in the meadow behind the barn. The engine changed to a higher pitch and, as they watched, *The French Wench,* trailing a show-tail of smoke, cleared the tops of the trees, circled, went into a steep upward climb, and did several barrel rolls, leaving a giant corkscrew of smoke behind it across the face of the moon.

Larson grinned and shook his head. "He's just gotta show me what he can do."

The plane dived back at them, did another roll just above the trees, the smoke stopped, and the pilot waved as the plane climbed and then faded away from the moon.

Sheriff Larson waved his Thompson at the disappearing aircraft. "Good luck, *Hero,*" he called softly.

CHAPTER THIRTY-TWO

Sheriff Andy Larson looked at the six men standing with their hands on their heads. "Who's in charge here?"

The men all glanced at each other, but no one answered.

"Suit yourselves," Larson said. "You're gonna get mighty damned cold standing around out here with your hands on your heads until I get an answer. Form a circle facing outward. I don't want any of you looking or talking to each other."

Muttering, the men formed a loose circle.

"No talking," Larson commanded. "One more time. Who's the big nuts in this group?"

Dominic Bianci slowly raised his hand. "Okay, I'm in charge."

"Now that wasn't so hard, was it?" Larson asked. "What's your name, fella?"

"Dominic Bianci."

"All right, Dominic, we've got a bit of work to do here tonight and it's best for all of you if I get full cooperation. You understand?"

Bianci nodded.

"Good. Now, anybody got any firepower hidden under their coats?"

The men glanced over their shoulders at each other, but no one spoke.

"Okay. One by one my deputies are gonna pat each of you boys down. If they find any guns, it won't be pleasant for whoever has one."

Longy Zwillman raised his hand. "I've got a forty-five under my right arm."

"Me too," Maggadino announced.

"I've got a thirty-eight on my belt," Alzado confessed.

"Now that's cooperation I like," Larson said, smiling. "Dusty, relieve them of their guns."

Durbin quickly walked around the circle, confiscated the guns, stuffed them in his coat pockets, and stepped clear. "That's it, I got 'em all, Andy."

"Now, Bernie, you go around and make sure all these boys've been telling the truth. Open your coats and hold them wide. While he's doing that, Ben, you and Robert go see what you can find in the way of firearms in their vehicles."

Deputy Bernie Ward slowly moved around the circle, carefully patting each of the men down. He finished the last man and stepped back. "They're all clean, Andy."

"Good, now I've got work for you boys to do. There's a few cases of whiskey laying in the snow down in that meadow that need to be loaded on the sled, hauled to the barn, and put away while I decide what we're gonna do with them. You were after the whiskey and now you'll be able to handle it a little. Dusty, take them down there and get going while I talk to Dominic here. Better get moving, the wind from the north is starting to blow pretty good. It's gonna be damned cold before the night's over."

Deputies Ward and Sullivan returned, each carrying a Thompson machine gun.

"Looks like two more for the arsenal," Ward said, holding the weapon high over his head.

"Don't forget the one in the snow over by the Buick," Larson warned. "Be sure to dry it off good. Dave, when they get the sled loaded and you've hauled it to the barn, bring the horses out here and pull this Buick off to the side and clear the road so we can get the truck up to the barn."

Dixon laughed. "I've got an uncle up on the Dakota-Canada border that makes damned good money pulling booze runners' cars out when they get stuck in the back roads' mud. He's got a team of Percherons just like those down there." He pointed off towards the remaining glow of the fires by the meadow. "C'mon, you guys, we got work to do. Move it!"

Larson rapped his knuckles on the Studebaker hood. "Take this and the truck over to the barn and load the booze in them when they get it up there. There should be enough room in the truck for the booze and the prisoners when they get finished doing their chores. Here," he said and handed the Thompson to Durbin. "Come over here and stand by the fire, Dominic, we've got some talking to do."

The two men stood at the fire holding their hands down towards the warmth of the flames.

"So tell me, Dominic, who do you answer to?" Larson asked.

Bianci stared into the fire, kicked a log further into the flames, and shook his head.

"You gonna talk to me, Dominic? I can be a pleasant person, or I can be one mean sumbitch. It's your call, but I'd advise you to stay on my good side. Everybody's gone now, so it's just you and me. I'd hate to have to shoot you in the leg 'cause you tried to jump me." Larson opened his coat and pulled his pistol up in the holster.

Bianci looked at Larson's face, down at his pistol, then back up at his face, and shrugged. "I don't think you'll shoot me, Sheriff. As a matter of fact, I *know* you won't shoot me."

It looks like this tactic won't work with this guy, so I guess I have to try another one. Larson nodded, smiled slightly, and brought out a pack of Camels. "Ask yourself if the consequences are worth thirty-six cases of whiskey." He shook a cigarette up, pulled it free, and offered the pack to Bianci.

Bianci rattled a cigarette loose, handed the pack back, crouched, brought up a piece of glowing wood, lit his cigarette, and handed the wood to Larson.

Larson took a deep drag of smoke and dropped the wood back into the fire. "Well?" he asked and blew trails of smoke from his nose. "What're you gonna tell me?"

The end of Bianci's cigarette glowed briefly; he exhaled a short burst of smoke and shook his head again. "I'm not telling you anything."

"Does the name Boticello mean anything to you?"

Bianci nodded. "Yeah, I've met him. He runs booze out of Estevan. We bought a truckload of whiskey from him a year ago, but his prices were too damned high. We haven't dealt with him since."

"And I've got thirty-six cases of his bootleg booze in the snow here tonight."

Bianci shrugged. "So?"

"And there's supposed to be an equal amount tomorrow night and the same the next night. Right?"

Bianci shook his head. "You're telling the story."

"And you and your boys were gonna steal all of it."

Bianci shrugged again.

There's got to be something that'll trigger this guy's mind into talking to me. Larson dropped his cigarette butt into the fire. "We're really not getting a lot accomplished, are we? Don't you wonder how we knew the plane with all that booze was coming in here tonight? Aren't you curious about how we knew you were coming here? You can tell by the roadblock that you were expected, can't you?"

Bianci took a deep drag on his cigarette, flipping it out into the snow, and his eyes narrowed as he looked at Larson. "What're you trying to tell me, Sheriff?"

"You've been set up, Dominic. You're all here to take the fall for someone. What if I told you we were supposed to gun all of you down when you tried to run the roadblock? Even if you didn't try to run it, we were gonna shoot the shit out of you and say you did."

Bianci's eyes hardened as he studied Larson's face. "So who set us up? Was it Boticello?"

Larson smiled evilly. *I've got you thinking and asking yourself questions. Your mind will now be your own worst enemy.* "You were all supposed to be killed here tonight to prove a point, or better yet to make a show of power."

"What do you mean prove a point?" Fear was now showing in Bianci's voice.

"There's a battle going on here in Wolf Point and Roosevelt County for control of the bootleg liquor running business. There're a few different groups grasping for the brass ring. What a better way to show power than to set up a few people and then have them gunned down?"

"I don't know what you're talking about."

Larson laughed and kicked the end of a log farther into the fire. "You just think about it. I seem to know a lot about your operation and there's a lot of coincidences here tonight, aren't there? The law is waiting for you and the plane. The plane just took off. Why didn't I arrest him? Why haven't I pulled the trigger on you and your men? Maybe I'm waiting for you to do all the work of loading the whiskey and then . . ." Larson raised his hand like a gun, cocked the thumb, and pointed it at Bianci's face. *"Bang."*

CHAPTER THIRTY-THREE

"Wait a minute, wait a minute, wait a minute," Bianci repeated softly. "Lemme think about this."

"You got two minutes." *And now I got you.*

"Okay. You mentioned Boticello. Is he behind this?"

"I'm not saying anything until I get more from you."

"How come you didn't gun us down?"

"You're not out of here yet."

"Like I said, how come you didn't gun us down?"

"I've done enough senseless killing in my life. Besides, my deputies don't know about the orders for the shootings. I was just going to make an excuse to open up and the others would have followed my lead. When it was all over I could have said you fired first and the others would all go along with that."

"What do you mean by . . . ?"

Larson raised his hand and interrupted. "Haven't you figured out by now, you dumb bastard, that I'm on the *inside* of all this? With the law on the inside of the battle to control the liquor flow through Roosevelt County, the whole thing is easier and cleaner." *Let's see where this leads.*

Bianci tipped his head back, studied Larson's poker face, and tried to decide if he was telling the truth. *He does seem to know a hell of a lot about all this. A lot more than a small-town sheriff would know unless he was in . . .* "All right, who do *you* answer to?"

Larson laughed and shook his head. "That's not for you to know at this time, but I'm willing to make you a deal. For the right information, *I'll let you all go.*"

A look of incredulity ran across Bianci's face. "Wh . . . what?"

"You heard me. You give me the information I want and I'll let all of you crowd into that truck or that booze runner Studebaker and shag your asses out of here. I'd recommend you get the hell out of the northern part of the country because the hounds of hell are gonna be after you at a full run when this is all over. You were supposed to be dead and there's gonna be a lotta missing liquor."

"You're shitting me," Bianci said softly. "You'd let us go?"

"I'm a man of my word. You tell me what I need to bring the control of this liquor war over to our side and you'll all go free."

"How do I know you won't let us get down the road a ways and then shoot us to pieces?"

"Because I told you I wouldn't. Hell, I could've shot a couple of you awhile ago to show I want information." Larson pointed his thumb back over his shoulder. "Kinda like somebody did to those men and the cows in that barn over there a few days ago. The men are gone, but the cows are still laying up there with their legs sticking out to the side." He could see the change in Bianci's face. *He knows something about that.* "You wouldn't know anything about that now, would you?"

Bianci shook his head. "No, no, I wouldn't."

He's lying. "All right then, how about giving me some information to help me decide if I'm gonna let you go. Tell me your part in tonight's dealings."

"I don't know . . ."

"I'm not making the offer again. It's either talk or jail . . . or maybe some gunfire. Your choice."

"All right," Bianci said dejectedly. "What do you wanna know?"

"How were you gonna get the booze from all three nights? Wasn't there supposed to be a pickup team coming in from

Helena to get it every night? Were you gonna kill the Helena pickup team?"

Bianci shook his head. "No, somebody on the inside was gonna call the Helena people and tell 'em *they* were going to deliver it all to them after the last shipment. There'd be a twenty percent discount for the delay. Nobody'd turn down discount like that for a little delivery holdup in this business."

"Boticello isn't going to be very pleasant about this, is he? Someone in his organization is working both sides of the fence. Tell me who it is."

"Rossi calls him *The Stone Man,* and he's the one calling the shots." Bianci paused and looked down at the fire. *Hell, I shouldn't have told him that. I know now Boticello was gonna have me killed, but did The Stone Man know about it? Shit, who can I trust now? I'm gonna pay a visit to Boticello when this is all over.* He looked up at Larson staring blankly at him.

"That doesn't tell me much."

Bianci cleared his throat as he stalled for time to think. "Well . . . I've never met him, but Rossi told me he lives up to his name and I'd best not mess with him. He gives me orders over the phone. He's the brains behind all this."

"That doesn't tell me much. Who's Rossi?"

Bianci shook his head.

"You're not cooperating, Dominic. I'm not letting you get out of here for the little bit you've told me. The jail in Wolf Point is mighty small and cold this time of year. It could be a long wait until the Feds come for you." Larson shrugged and let out a long audible sigh. "Then again, I could just shoot you all."

"Rossi's a guy from back east someplace. We got our orders from The Stone Man passed down through him for a while. We don't hear from Rossi anymore. The Stone Man calls me himself now."

"What's Rossi's first name? Have you ever met him?"

"Yeah, I met him once at a meeting in Chicago. His name is Glenn Rossi. They call him Tiny. Probably because he is about six and a half feet tall. He was part of a plan being set up by somebody who wasn't there that day. I think it had to do with crooked cops. Hell, I don't remember . . . There was so much going on."

"What's Rossi look like?"

"Like I said, he's tall with hard narrow eyes that always seemed to be looking through you. Black hair with a little gray, dark skin, narrow mustache, well dressed. You know, like all us wops and dagos."

This is going nowhere, but I'll remember the name Glenn Rossi if it comes up again. "So you were gonna sit around for three nights and collect over a hundred cases of whiskey?"

"Yeah, but it's like you said, it was all set up to start a war. We didn't know we were gonna be caught in the middle and executed in a power play."

"Meaning?"

"When we got the last shipment, we were supposed to shoot down the plane."

Larson's brow wrinkled. *Damn, I wasn't far off when I told him I'd saved his life again.* "Why shoot down the plane?"

"That'd cut off Boticello's air delivery system. He'd be back on the same playing field as we are and we now have an inside track. We have a supply of whiskey we don't have any money invested in, so we can cut prices and start taking his customers."

"And so a war begins," Larson stated.

"And so a war begins," Bianci agreed.

"Let's go to the barn."

CHAPTER THIRTY-FOUR

As Sheriff Andy Larson and Dominic Bianci approached the barn, Deputy Dave Dixon halted the team of horses blowing great clouds of breath out of their noses and waited for them to reach him.

"All the liquor's on the sled in the barn," Dixon said. "I pulled it in there to get it out of the damned cold wind. I'll go tow the Buick off to the side and clear the road enough to bring the truck up to the barn and load it in there. Damn, it's getting cold!"

"Sounds good, Dave," Larson agreed. "You'll probably have to move my pickup off to the side a bit more to get the booze truck past it."

"I'll turn it around and get it out of the way." Dixon flipped the reins on the backs of the horses. "Let's go, boys."

Chief Deputy Dusty Durbin, a Thompson machine gun nestled in the crook of his arm, stood just inside the barn door studying the five glum whiskey runners sitting on the edge of the heavy wooden sled. The main room of the barn was dimly lit by a row of metal-shaded, electric lights hanging down the center of the ceiling, and it was cold enough to see the breath of all the men. Stacked behind them on the sled were several low rows of wooden whiskey cases. Durbin combed his fingers through his red beard and rolled his unlit cigar back and forth between his teeth. *These booze runners have been awfully quiet. I really expected at least a little bit of trouble from them. I don't like it*

161

when they're this quiet.

Deputy Ben Graves leaned against the rails of the stalls with the frozen cattle. His trench shotgun rested on his hip as his eyes moved across the faces of the men on the sled. *They sure gave up easy.*

Deputies Bernie Ward and John Mooney, lost in their own thoughts, stood a short distance away with their shotguns held loosely across their chests.

Deputy Robert Sullivan, softly whistling tunelessly to cover his ragged nerves, sat on an upturned wooden cider keg, a machine gun laid across his knees. *I'm getting too damned old for this stuff.*

The whiskey runners, Zwillman, Gordon, Maggadino, Alzado, and Adonis sat with their eyes moving back and forth among the well-armed deputies. One of them said something softly to the man sitting next to him.

"Shut up!" Durbin shouted. "No talking!"

"This case here's been busted open and there's a few bottles missing," Waxey Gordon called out, tapping his shoe on the side of an open whiskey case. "It's colder'n shit in here so how 'bout we get a drink or two for all the work we just done? It'll warm us up a bit."

"We're gonna close those big doors to keep some of that damned cold wind out of here," Mooney announced as he and Ward pushed the doors shut. "We can open them again when the truck gets here."

"Well, what about a drink?" Gordon demanded.

The deputies exchanged glances and finally all looked at Dusty Durbin to make the decision.

"All right, you can share a bottle," Durbin declared. "Just keep your hands where we can see them and no fast moves. Understand?"

Gordon pulled a bottle from the open case and worked on the cork.

Several of the others slid closer to him and began to whisper.

"Shut the hell up!" Durbin ordered, raising his machine gun. "I told you no talking!"

The room was silent and all eyes were on Gordon working the cork cap with his gloved fingers.

"Take your damned gloves off," Maggadino growled, standing up and moving in front of the others. "Your fingers ain't gonna freeze that damned fast."

John Mooney walked across the barn to join Graves by the stalls. "Looks like the cows haven't moved since we's here last time," he joked. "Son-of-a-bitch is it cold." He worked the sling on his shotgun up onto his shoulder. "I wonder where Andy and that other booze runner are?"

Ward stepped behind the sled and rested his shotgun on the tops of the wooden cases.

Gordon pulled a hand free, twisted out the cork, took a quick drink, passed the bottle to Zwillman, and worked his hand back into his glove.

Zwillman took a long drink, coughed, handed the bottle to Adonis, and wiped his gloved fingers across his suddenly watering eyes. "Damn, that's good stuff," he managed to whisper.

Nino Maggadino stood off to one side with his arms folded, watching the other runners sharing the Superior whiskey. He moved his head slightly, gauging the distance to each of the armed deputies.

"You keep an eye on these guys. I'm gonna go get the truck," Durbin called as he backed to the doors, pushed the space wider, turned in the doorway, and looked out across the moonlit countryside.

Maggadino held out his hand. "Gimme that damned bottle before it's all gone," he growled and snatched the bottle from

Adonis. He tipped the bottle up, appeared to lose his balance, and staggered a short distance towards the door.

Deputy Durbin turned to see who was talking.

With a roar, Maggadino threw the bottle at Durbin and charged.

Durbin's instinctive reaction was to swing the machine gun up to stop or deflect the bottle and the bottle bounced off his hand on the forearm of the weapon.

Maggadino slammed him back to bounce off the door and stumble backward out into the snow.

As the deputy struggled to regain his balance, Maggadino wrenched the Thompson from him and slammed the stock across the side of his face. Unconscious, Durbin toppled off into the snow.

Maggadino dropped the barrel of the machine gun towards Durbin's bloody face, shook his head, spun the weapon up, and laughed hysterically as it roared and bucked, spitting flame, smoke and lead across the wood and through the open door in a quick "Z" pattern, chewing into the whiskey runners and the stacks of wooden cases behind them.

It had all happened so fast that everyone in the barn was momentarily stunned, but the men immediately began to move as the machine gun started to fire.

"What the hell was that?" Larson shouted, as he swung up his machine gun and prodded it into Bianci's back. "C'mon, start running!"

CHAPTER THIRTY-FIVE

The deputies inside the barn dived and ducked for cover as the machine gun outside chattered and chewed holes in the door and slugs snapped through the air.

Sullivan rose shakily to his knees from behind the cider keg and brought the Thompson to his shoulder. *God, I don't dare shoot. What if I hit Dusty?* He lowered the weapon to rest on the keg and glanced around the room for the others.

Ward spun around the stacks of cases with his shotgun raised to his shoulder to find Zwillman, Gordon, and Alzado all slumped in a pile. Whiskey and blood ran across the bed of the sled to drop onto the face of Adonis, his sightless eyes staring up at the ceiling.

"Poor bastards," Ward muttered as he slowly sank back behind the sled.

Mooney and Graves rose to their knees and began to fire and pump their shotguns. The double-ought shot chewed at the doors, sending splinters and balls of hot lead flying out into the night.

"Hold your fire!" Deputy Graves screamed as he bolted across the room to hit the light switch and the room went black. "Dusty's out there! Hold your fire."

Before he could drop to the snow, Maggadino was hit in the shoulder by a ball of buckshot and a large sliver of wood embedded itself just below his eye. His laughter turned to loud curses of pain as he flopped into the snow and looked through all the smoke at the disintegrating door. He rose to his knees and laughed again as he fired a short burst of machine-gun fire into the building. "C'mon out and git me, you bastards," he screamed. He winced as he touched inside the torn cloth on his coat and gingerly gripped the splinter of wood in his cheek. He took a deep breath, pulled it free, and flipped it out into the snow. Muttering a string of curses, he wiped his bloody fingers on his coat, raised the barrel of the Thompson, and fired another short burst into the barn. "C'mon out!"

Dusty Durbin stirred and rose up on his elbows to look with blinking eyes at Maggadino kneeling nearby.

Maggadino saw Durbin move and smiled evilly as he spun the machine gun towards him. "What do you think now, *law dog*?" he asked and wiped at the trickle of blood running down his face. "Not quite so powerful now, are you? Not such a big man, huh?"

Durbin looked at him and beyond to see Andy Larson pushing someone in front of him through the snow. "You've got the gun," he stated. "But, you'd be smart to drop it and put your hands in the air. Sheriff Larson is behind you."

Maggadino tipped his head back and laughed hysterically. "Just how damned stupid do you think I am, *law dog*?"

Durbin sat up, shaking his head, and gingerly slid his fingertips over the growing bruise that was closing his left eye. "You hit me pretty damned hard." He kept watching Larson moving in closer. *I've gotta keep him occupied with me.*

Maggadino laughed and swung the machine gun back and forth. "It's nothing compared to what I'm gonna do to you now."

Inside the barn the deputies heard the talking. There was enough moonlight streaming through the door for them to see each other; they nodded, stood up, and moved silently towards the door.

Sullivan shook his head, sat back on the cider keg, and looked down at the weapon in his shaking hands. *I can't do it.* Tears formed in his eyes as he watched the others moving towards the doors. *I just can't do it.*

Durbin slowly moved his fingers over his swollen, bearded face. *Keep watching my hand,* he thought, as his unseen hand went towards the revolver holstered on his belt. "I think you broke my cheekbone, you bastard," he muttered loud enough for Maggadino to hear.

Maggadino leered at him. "Tough shit."

Andy Larson pushed Bianci down into the snow and put a foot on his back. "Stay here," he whispered and moved off.

John Mooney reached the torn wooden door and raised his hand.

The others all stopped.

Mooney slowly moved his head until he could see outside.

Maggadino rose to his feet, gave a quick glance at the darkened barn, and returned his attention to Durbin. "C'mon, *law dog,* stand up." He motioned towards the barn with his weapon. "Things are too damned quiet in there. We're gonna go in and see what's happened, but you're going first. I can't believe I got all of 'em."

Durbin made a production out of slowly rising up to his feet. As he straightened, he brought his pistol up behind his back.

Andy Larson stopped and raised his machine gun. "Drop the gun!" he shouted. "I've got a chopper pointed at your back and I'll use it. Trust me; I'll shoot you down where you stand."

Maggadino's eyes narrowed and his shoulders tensed as he considered his options. His weapon was pointed directly at Durbin, but he wasn't sure where Larson was behind him.

Durbin swung the pistol out and pointed it at Maggadino. "Do like he says," he ordered and thumbed back the hammer.

John Mooney brought his shotgun up to his shoulder and

stepped out of the barn door to face Maggadino. "You haven't got a chance. We've got you from three sides."

Maggadino took a deep breath and let it out slowly. "Okay. You got me." He lowered the weapon and started to raise his other hand.

"Drop the damned gun!" Durbin shouted and took a step towards him.

Maggadino laughed hysterically, suddenly swung the gun up, and spun towards the man behind him. The gun burst with fire and smoke and lead punched a line of craters in the snow towards Larson.

The three other men all fired at once and Maggadino's Thompson continued to fire a spiral of slugs into the air as he gyrated from the impact of the bullets and finally crumpled into the snow. The smoking weapon clicked on an empty chamber; it was suddenly very quiet and then the hot barrel made a loud hissing sound as it settled into the snow.

CHAPTER THIRTY-SIX

Deputy Dave Dixon tied the team of Percherons to the back bumper of the shot-up Buick they had just dragged off the road and patted their streaming noses. "Good boys," he said through a cloud of breath. He trudged back in knee-deep snow, climbed up into the cab of the International truck that had been brought to transport the whiskey, and started the engine. *Now I'll move Andy's truck while this one warms up.* On the third attempt the engine of Larson's pickup turned over and finally began to run on all four cylinders. With several maneuvers he turned the pickup around facing back towards town and pulled it off to the side enough to get past it with the International. *I'll let this one run to warm up, too.*

Dixon climbed back into the International and began to drive to the barn. Out of the corner of his eye he thought he saw movement off to the side in the distance; he stopped the truck and rolled down the window for a clear view of the moonlit snow. "Damn, I could've sworn I saw somebody out there," he muttered, putting the truck back in gear and continuing towards the barn. Suddenly the area on the front of the barn was lit up by sustained flashes of gunfire. "What the hell's that?" He stamped the gas pedal to the floor and the big truck swerved forward on the snow-packed road. He saw another burst of automatic weapon fire light up the area as he hit the brakes and turned off the engine. *This is just a bigger target if the wrong guys are doing the shooting. How'n the hell'd they get guns?* He dropped to the ground and pulled his pistol from the holster. Gun in hand, he ran in a crouch towards the figures in the moonlight in front of the barn.

Dominic Bianci rose up from the snow and watched Dixon running towards the barn and the noise of the shooting. When he was sure Dixon wouldn't see him, he pushed to his feet and ran towards the exhaust-cloud-encased pickup truck a short distance away. "My god, they *are* executing those men!" he panted as he slid under the steering wheel. "He told me they wouldn't do that." His heart was pounding as the tires spun in the packed snow and the vehicle slewed down the snow-banked road. "He told me they wouldn't do that," he repeated to himself. "I've got to get as far away as possible. I'm the only witness and they'll be after me for sure. I'm going to go get that bastard Boticello." He glanced to his right and saw a trench shotgun leaning up into the corner between the seat and the door. "Now I know how I can get him." He leaned over and lifted the shotgun onto the seat. His mixture of anger and fear made him grip the wheel so tight his knuckles hurt. *I can be there by morning and he'll be at his office.*

Four flashing bursts of gunfire from different directions made Dixon drop to his knees and strain to see what was going on ahead of him. He saw a man spin to the snow and the machine gun in his hands fire upward into the sky and it was suddenly silent. He jumped to his feet and brushed the snow off his pistol. "Andy, is that you?" he shouted.

Two men walked out of the darkened barn and joined the others looking down at the dead man.

Sheriff Larson turned and waved. "C'mon in, Dave; the action here is over."

Dixon trotted up to join the men standing around the bloody, crumpled figure on the snow. "What the hell happened?"

Dusty Durbin nudged the dead man with his foot. "That

bastard was faster'n meaner . . ." he started and his voice trailed off. "I let my guard down . . . and he jumped me."

"Don't let it eat at you, Dusty," Larson consoled. "The man was mean as hell and had a death wish. It could've happened to any of us."

"The other four of his gang inside are all dead," Deputy Ward announced. "This bastard here killed all of 'em."

"I don't think he really cared. He just wanted to kill someone," Mooney added.

Durbin reached down, brought up a handful of snow, and gingerly pressed it against his swollen eye. "Damn, he was mean. There's no doubt the bastard had a death wish. He knew we had him dead to rights, but he chose to do it his way."

Larson looked around. "Where's Sullivan?"

"I saw him in the barn," Ward answered. "I'll go check on him."

"Now what the hell's that?" Graves shouted, pointing down the road at headlight beams as they disappeared over a hill.

"Shit," Dixon mumbled. "I'm afraid that's *your* truck, Andy. I left it running to warm up for you, but, who'n the hell's driving it? Oh, no . . . I remember there's a shotgun in the front seat. I meant to bring it with me."

Andy Larson shook his head, chuckled nervously, and put his machine gun up onto his shoulder. "That's got to be Bianci making a run for it. And now he's armed. Poor bastard probably thinks we're executing everybody."

"Why would he think that?" Durbin asked, putting more snow against his swollen face.

Larson took a deep breath, slowly exhaled a cloud into the cold night air, and shook his head. "I told him I was connected with the booze runners and had the inside track on everything that was going on to try to scare information out of him. I told him we were supposed to shoot him and all his men tonight as a power show for one of the competing bootleg factions, but that I'd let them all go if he cooperated and gave me the information I wanted."

"So now he thinks you went back on your word," Mooney stated.

"Yeah, and now he's gonna un-ass the territory as fast as he can. He won't know who he can trust because he has no idea who I'm supposed to be connected with."

"He'll just keep running," Dixon agreed. "In your truck for quite a ways, I'm afraid. The gas tank was almost full."

"Did you get any information out of him?" Ward asked.

Larson nodded. "A couple of names."

"Hey, Andy," Ward called as he trotted up to them. "I found Sullivan sitting in the barn crying and muttering something about getting killed. I tried to talk to him, but he just kept repeating things about getting killed. I hate to say it, but I'm afraid he's snapped."

Larson looked down at Maggadino's crumpled, bloody body and shook his head. "I guess there are some days that, no matter how hard you try, things are gonna turn to shit." He handed Ward his machine gun and patted his pockets for his cigarettes. "I gotta take a walk and do some serious thinking. You guys know what to do."

CHAPTER THIRTY-SEVEN

Wild Bill Bohlin put *The French Wench* into a slow glide, banked over the airfield, lined up with the runway leading to his well-lit hangar, and gently put the plane down. *I've got a hell of a lot for us to do in a few short hours,* he told himself as he taxied up to the big hangar and shut off the engine. He crawled out of the cockpit, dropped off the wing, walked through the small door set in the large double hangar doors, and flipped on the lights. His boot heels echoed as he strode across the large main room. He opened a door on the far side, snapped on the lights, and the room was lit by a bulb hanging in an enamel shade. "C'mon, Charlie, rise and shine! We've got a lotta stuff to do and not much time to do it."

In a bed on the far side of the room someone stirred and mumbled; a red underwear sheathed arm came out; and a hand felt on the bedside table until it touched a pair of wire-rimmed glasses. Charlie Marcum pushed clear of the quilt, hooked the glasses over his ears, and began to scratch parts of his upper body. "Damn," he muttered, then yawned and stretched. "What the hell time is it anyway?"

"It's about two-thirty. Now shake a leg. We've gotta lot to do. I'll go and make some coffee."

"I'll be there in a few minutes. Geez, two-thirty."

Bohlin was stacking the pictures from his wall in a small cardboard box when Marcum walked into the office, still yawning and scratching. Without speaking, he poured himself a mug

173

of steaming coffee from the pot on the hot plate. He blew on it and took a sip. "Damn, that's hot! Okay, so what in the hell's going on? What's making you get me up in the middle of the night?"

Bohlin picked up his mug of coffee, shook his head, and took a sip. "I got busted on this flight."

"Busted? You mean like arrested?"

"Exactly. Seems my old war buddy, Andy Larson, isn't really a cowboy, like he said. He's the *law* down there in Wolf Point, Montana."

"No shit?" Marcum looked down at his coffee mug and fought the urge to laugh. "The law, huh?"

"Andy Larson is the damned Roosevelt County *sheriff.*"

"So, did you shoot him and escape?" Marcum scowled and tried to keep from laughing.

"It's not all that damned funny," Bohlin stated. "But . . ."

Marcum tipped his head and narrowed his eyes. "So, how'd you get away?"

"He let me go."

"What'n the hell's so bad about that? He just let you go?"

"Yeah, but he's got thirty-six cases of The Little Barrel's whiskey."

Marcum took a sip of coffee and nodded, fighting to keep from grinning. "I can see where that *could* be a problem."

"We're going to pack up and get the hell out of here as fast as we can. I figure I've got 'til about noon before I have to tell him something. He likes to have a report about that time, so we've got about nine hours to get it all done."

"He can't get that pissed off about a measly thirty-six cases of whiskey. Hell, look at all the other stuff you've delivered without a problem."

"He's not the forgiving type. Right now he figures somebody inside his organization is trying to take over and I'm afraid he might think it's me. When he's in this kind of a mood, he's the kind that'd shoot and then ask questions. Don't forget he lost that other big shipment a few days ago. He's not gonna be reasoned with right now. We're going to pack and get out. Today."

"Okay, but first I want to hear the full story on your arrest by your old war buddy."

Five minutes later they both poured a fresh cup of coffee.

Marcum nodded. "Yep, he flat-assed got you, didn't he. Okay, what's your plan?"

"We'll pack all the necessary tools and equipment in the truck. We'll load and fill that fifty gallon tank. I don't want to hit any airports until we're a long way off. I'm sure the word and good reward for my location will go out real fast. Damned fast. We'll leave some maps here in the office with a southerly route marked and we'll head east. I've got a friend in Minnesota where I can hide *The French Wench* until we can repaint her."

"Hell, we can repaint her now and she'll be dry enough to fly out of here about the time you wanna leave."

"No, I don't want to repaint her just yet. I want to be sure she's identifiable later today."

Marcum looked at him questioningly. "Suit yourself. The truck's got new overload springs, so the weight of the tools, the new engine I'm working on, and the gas shouldn't be a problem. I pulled the air-show side panel off the truck when we came up here so all we've got is a Ford delivery truck. What about the coupe?"

"We'll just leave that behind. We can afford to buy another one when we get where we're going. We'll take only the necessities."

"Okay, where *are* we going?"

"I guess we'll know when we get there. I want to give you a

good head start today." He thumped his knuckles on the desk. "We've got over ten-thousand dollars in the strongbox in the hole under this desk. I'll give you five and I'll take five, just in case something happens to one of us. Fair enough?"

"Works for me," Marcum answered with a big smile.

"When you're well on your way, I've got one more delivery to make. About noon, I'd say. We'll load her before you leave. Twelve cases under each wing will do for this drop."

"You're not going to tell me, are you?"

Bohlin shook his head again. "I'll draw up a map of where we're headed. When we meet later to fuel me up, I should have a good story for you. Let's get moving. It'll start getting light by about seven and I want you well on your way."

Wild Bill and Charlie Marcum snapped the last restraining rod on the racks of whiskey cases secured under the wings of *The French Wench,* rattled it to make sure it was secure, and stepped back to admire their work. "Let's turn her around to face the doors and you get on outta here."

Minutes later, they rolled the big hangar doors open enough to let the truck out. Marcum opened the door and stepped up onto the running board.

"Okay, everything's loaded and I'm ready to roll. It's a little after seven, so I'll be heading south into North Dakota. I'll stay on the roads you marked so you'll be able to find me to refuel. You're not gonna tell me, are you?"

Bohlin shook his head, chuckled and pointed outside. "If this thing works the way I think it will, I'll have a hell of a story to tell you. You'll just have to wait. That screaming Indian on the roof of the truck makes it easy for me to spot you from the air. I can catch up pretty fast, even with your four-hour head start. I'm not doing anything until noon anyway."

The men shook hands. Charlie Marcum climbed into the

truck and started the engine. "You sure you don't want to tell me?"

Bohlin shook his head, walked to the big doors, and waited for Marcum to drive out. "Get going, I need to take a nap."

CHAPTER THIRTY-EIGHT

Dominic Bianci drove the snow-banked roads to Williston, North Dakota, before stopping for gas and a quick breakfast at an all-night diner. His initial fear upon escaping turned more and more to anger at the thoughts of his companions being gunned down and executed by the law back at the farm in Montana. *Someone wanted to make an example of us to do a power show in the bootleg business. They set it up for us all to be shot down like rabid dogs. Boticello must be behind this. The sheriff brought his name up first, didn't he? If the sheriff is in on it, he'd know, wouldn't he? The pilot got away. He works for Boticello and he wouldn't do anything to one of his own people.* Bianci's mind was in an anger-fed turmoil. *Damn, I need a drink.*

Bianci drove into the outskirts of Estevan and pulled out his watch to check the time. *Almost six-thirty.* He had made the two-hundred-mile drive on the moonlit, snow-covered roads in less than seven hours. *Boticello won't be at his office before eight. I need some coffee and some whiskey.* He drove until he found a diner, went in, sat at the counter, tipped his hat back, and unbuttoned his topcoat.

An aproned, unshaven fat man in reasonably white clothes came out from the kitchen and stood across the counter from Bianci. "What'll ya have?"

"Coffee. Black."

The man slid a steaming mug of coffee onto the counter in front of Bianci. "Anything else?"

"Yeah, I need a bottle of whiskey."

The man reached up and adjusted the dingy white cap on his head as he studied Bianci. "You ain't from around here, are ya?"

"No, south of here, Williston."

The cook leaned over and looked out at the pickup truck parked in front of the diner. "Them're Montana plates on that truck yer drivin'."

"It belongs to my brother. He lives over in Wolf Point. I borrowed it to drive up to Yorkton."

The cook nodded. "Well, I'm sad to tell ya, Yank, but I run a diner here, not a saloon."

Bianci lifted his cup, blew on the steaming coffee, and looked up at the man. *I wonder what his buy-off price is?* He took a sip from the mug, set it down, and brought a long leather wallet out of an inside coat pocket. He opened it, fanned through the bills, brought out a fifty-dollar bill, and smoothed it on the counter beside his coffee mug. "I'm damned thirsty for something a bit stronger than coffee," he said softly

The cook pursed his lips as he looked at the bill and then up at Bianci's face. "You willin' to pay that much for a bottle of *good* Canadian whiskey, Yank?"

Bianci nodded and pushed the bill towards the cook. "I'm thirsty."

The cook snatched at the bill, but Bianci balled his fist on top of it, shook his head, and glared at him. "I get the whiskey, you get the fifty."

The cook bobbed his head. "I'll be right back." He walked into the back, lifted the receiver off the wall phone, and gave several cranks to the handle on the side. He turned his back, spoke briefly, hung up the receiver, turned with a smile on his face, and walked out to the counter. "You'll have a liter bottle of the finest Canadian whiskey here in a few minutes, Yank," he stated, glancing down at the fifty-dollar bill and then up at the clock on the far wall. "You want some more coffee while we wait?"

Bianci took a swallow of coffee, nodded, and pushed the mug forward. "Sure, go ahead and top it off for me." When the cup was full again, Bianci made a production out of smoothing the bill beside it.

Fifteen minutes later the cook stopped pacing, poured Bianci more coffee, and glanced at the money and the clock. "Damn, where is that kid?" he mumbled as he put the pot back, and began to pace again, constantly looking at the fifty-dollar bill, the clock, and out the front windows.

Suddenly the front door burst open and a small, freckle-faced boy rushed in carrying a wadded burlap sack. "I'm sorry, Mister Beeler, but Pa couldn't get his car started so I had to run all the way down here with this for you," he panted, holding out the wad of burlap in a mitten-covered hand. "He says yer s'posed to gimme cash money for it."

"Did he say how much, Rodney?" Beeler, the cook, asked and smiled.

"Yup, he said twenty-five dollars."

The smile disappeared. "I thought it was twenty."

Danny shook his stocking-capped head. "Nope, Mister Beeler, Pa said twenty-five dollars in my hand or I don't give you this." He held out the burlap bag and then quickly put it behind his back. "That's what my pa said." He glanced over his shoulder and began to back towards the door.

Bianci turned on his stool, leaned his elbows back on the counter, and smiled at the drama unfolding before him. *I like this kid.* His eyes moved back and forth between Beeler and the boy. *I'm betting the kid gets the full twenty-five.*

Beeler began to walk around to the end of the counter and the boy quickly put his hand on the doorknob.

Bianci reached out and carefully set his coffee mug on the bill.

Beeler looked at the mug partially covering the money and then at the boy with his hand on the doorknob. He muttered several curse words under his breath and shrugged. "Okay. Twenty-five it is." He walked to the cash register, cranked the handle on the side, and stopped the drawer with his stomach. He put his hand in it, looked at the boy and the money on the counter, shook his head, and brought out bills. "Here." He fanned a ten and three fives in his hand, folded them, and then held them out towards the boy.

Danny looked as if he wasn't sure he could trust him. He glanced at Bianci, who smiled and nodded.

"Take the money, boy, he isn't going to try to cheat you. Not with me sitting here as a witness."

Danny walked to Beeler with the wad of burlap held in one hand and his other hand open for the money. He snatched the money, tossed the wrapped bottle towards Beeler, spun, and ran to the door.

Bianci jumped to his feet. "Hold on a second there, kid!" he shouted.

The boy already had the door open, but he paused and looked back over his shoulder. "What?"

Bianci held up his hand and motioned for the boy to wait. "Come here, Danny." He reached in his pocket, pulled out a wad of money, and pulled a dollar bill free. "Here," he said, holding out the bill. "This's a little tip for all your work. I admire your spunk and you should be rewarded for it."

The boy's eyes darted from the bill to Bianci's face to Beeler and he shook his head. "I can't take that money, Mister. If Pa ever found out I had a dollar, I'd git a terrible lickin' for it. He'd think I stole it or somethin'."

Bianci looked at the boy and nodded understandingly. "What

about a quarter? Would your old man beat you for a quarter?"

Danny's eyes narrowed as he studied the stranger and thought about his offer. "No, I don't guess he'd gimme a lickin' over a quarter."

"Good," Bianci said and held the bill out to Beeler. "Give me change, quarters and dimes."

Beeler shook his head as he opened the cash register and counted out change for the dollar.

"Give it to the kid," Bianci instructed. "All of it."

Danny looked questioningly at Bianci and then Beeler holding out the handful of coins.

"Take it, kid," Bianci instructed. "Just spread it around and your Pa'll never know."

Danny slowly stepped forward and held out his hand.

As Beeler dropped the coins into the boy's hand, Danny looked at them and broke into a wide gap-toothed grin. He quickly ran to the door and disappeared outside.

Bianci reached down and slid the fifty-dollar bill toward Beeler. "Now give me *my* damned whiskey and don't you ever say anything to the kid's old man about this. Understand?"

CHAPTER THIRTY-NINE

Dominic Bianci unwrapped the burlap bag from the whiskey bottle, looked at the label, and nodded as he began to work the cork out. "I need a fresh cup," he said, glancing at Beeler who was admiring the fifty-dollar bill.

"Huh? Oh, yeah, sure." He reached under the counter and brought up a cup. "You going to be drinking alone, Yank?"

Bianci shrugged, pulled the cork free, poured the cup half-full of whiskey, and glanced up at Beeler. "Why weren't you going to give that kid a tip?"

"He's charging me five dollars more than his old man quoted me," Beeler answered, eyeing the contents of the coffee cup. "I know the old bastard quoted me twenty."

Bianci lifted the cup to his face, sniffed, and took a slow sip. "Damn, that's good stuff."

Beeler nodded and rubbed his mouth.

"Oh, hell, get a cup," Bianci snorted. "It's not good for a man to drink alone."

Beeler's hand came up with a cup. "Let's go sit at that table in the back corner," he said, with a slight smile. "It's about time for some of the regulars to start showing up . . ."

"And you don't wanna share," Bianci interrupted and laughed as he walked across the room, shrugged out of his coat, and sat down.

The two men settled on chairs in the corner and silently enjoyed sipping from their coffee cups.

"You still made twenty-five dollars on this bottle, didn't you?" Bianci asked.

Beeler nodded and set his cup on the table. "Yeah, but I'm sure the kid made five off the deal."

Bianci chuckled. "If the kid was *that good,* he made six bucks."

Beeler smiled and took another sip of his whiskey. "Yeah, I guess yer right, Yank. Where are ya *really* going?"

Bianci brought a leather cigar case out and went through the process of lighting a cigar. "A good drink deserves a good cigar," he stated, and blew a series of concentric smoke rings.

"I asked ya where ya was goin'?"

Bianci blew another cloud of smoke and took a sip from his cup. "I'm gonna kill somebody."

Beeler laughed. "Sure ya are, Yank, but I don't care as long as it ain't me." He glanced out the window. "Here comes the first of my regulars, so I gotta go to work." He tipped up his cup and walked to the counter with it swinging on his finger. "Thanks, Yank," he called from the counter. "If it slows down, I may have to come over for another quick one. Oh, by the way, please keep that bottle out of sight. Like I told ya before, this is a diner, not a saloon."

Bianci nodded. "Whatever you say." He set the bottle on a chair and draped his coat over it.

Dominic Bianci had reached the phase of drunkenness where he was angrier, bigger, and bulletproof, but he knew he could handle himself with the situation he was about to go into. He looked up at the clock. *Eight o'clock. Time to pay a visit to the Boticello Medical Supply Company.* He drained his cup, stood, shrugged into his coat, lifted the bottle, and took a quick look at the contents. *Half a bottle on an empty stomach, that's not good. Oh, hell, go and get it done. You can eat later. Besides, Beeler drank some of it.* He heard a woman gasp and turned to see her sitting with her hand on her mouth, staring at the bottle he held in front of him. "Geez, lady, it isn't going to bite you," he mumbled as he put it in a coat pocket, straightened his hat, and walked carefully towards the door. He stopped and looked at Beeler. "You *should* open a saloon." He chuckled as he walked out to the parking lot, got into Larson's stolen pickup, and started the engine.

CHAPTER FORTY

Dominic Bianci drove aimlessly for a few minutes, getting his bearings until he recognized a street name and turned down it. At the end of the street was a series of warehouses with a small office building in the front of the complex. Across the windows of the office building painted in large gold and black letters were the words: **BENJAMIN BOTICELLO MEDICAL SUPPLY.**

Bianci drove in and circled the snowy parking lot. A long, black Packard Phaeton was parked parallel to the front of the building in a well-shoveled space marked with a reserved sign. *That has to be Boticello's car,* he told himself as he pulled into a "customers only" parking space. His gloved fingers drummed on the top of the steering wheel as he sat studying the front of the building. The lights were on in the front office and he could see the usual file cabinets, a desk, a couch, and several chairs. Garishly framed copies of Old Master's art decorated the walls along with a large painting of Joseph Boticello, gazing thoughtfully across the room. He could see the clock; it was twelve minutes after eight. *I wonder what time everybody gets here?* he asked himself as he reached out and patted the shotgun. *I'd best go get this done before the place is full of people.* He opened the door, reached back in, and pulled the shotgun out. He quickly glanced around, worked the pump enough to see it was loaded, swung the gun so the butt was tucked into his armpit, and pulled his coat shut over it. "Let's go see *The Little Barrel,*" he said firmly, as if to reassure himself of his planned actions. He inhaled deeply and released a cloud of steamy breath. *C'mon, let's get it over with.* He glanced in at the bottle lying on the seat and quickly shook his head. He could feel the adrenalin rush beginning to sober him. *I want to be at my best when I do this.*

Benjamin Boticello sat at his desk, a steaming cup of coffee by his elbow, running his fingers down a column of figures. His secretary, Darla, always prepared the coffee pot before she left at night so he could plug it in and have coffee whenever he came to work. His accountant, John Johnstone, always had the day's business written up and put on his desk before he left for the night. He was now completing most of his in-office morning ritual so he could get on the phone and conduct business with other parts of his bootleg liquor kingdom. He heard someone knocking at the front door and glanced up at the clock. *Who in the hell'd be at the door this time of the morning? John and Darla both have keys.* The knocking persisted. *Damn.* He stood, walked to his door, and looked across the secretary's office to see a man standing outside in the cold. The man smiled and waved. *He looks familiar,* Boticello told himself as he walked across the room and stood at the door. "What can I do for you?" His brow wrinkled. "I know, you don't I?"

Dominic Bianci nodded. "Yes, Mister Boticello, I'm Dominic Bianci; we had some business transactions a few months ago. I'm out of Williston. It's cold out here," he called through the glass.

Boticello nodded, reached down, snapped the lock, and stepped back.

Bianci pushed open the door, pulled his gloves off, stuffed them in his pockets, and proffered his hand to Boticello. "If you remember, I bought a couple truckloads of whiskey from you awhile back. Damn, it's cold, isn't it?" He pushed the door closed with his shoulder. "I'm here to do a little more business with you, Mister Boticello."

Boticello grasped his hand and gave it a perfunctory shake before reaching around him and snapping the lock on the door. "I was sure I recognized you. Let's go into my office. I've got coffee in there. We can have a cup while we're discussing business."

"Lead the way."

Boticello pointed at the coffee pot on a corner table. "Help yourself." He walked around his desk and sat down.

Bianci stepped to the front of the desk and slowly unbuttoned his coat. "I'll pass on the coffee, but I do have something to discuss with you." His hand slid into his coat and suddenly reappeared with the short, trench shotgun. He held it at his hip pointed at Boticello, who quickly raised his hands.

"Wait a minute! Don't do anything stupid . . ."

"Shut up!" Bianci shouted. "The sheriff over in Wolf Point followed your orders and shot down all my men last night."

"What in the hell are you talking about?"

Bianci's eyes narrowed as he stared at Boticello. "Don't be cute with me," he hissed. "You know damned good and well what I'm talking about. Then your pilot got away."

"Wait a minute, wait a minute. What do you mean, my pilot *got away*?"

"That Wolf Point sheriff had all our guns and kept us covered. We were standing there with our hands on our heads when that damned plane roared up into the air, smoke trailing out behind it like it was on fire. He did a couple of fancy rolls and climbs across the moon, then buzzed down at us, climbed up, and disappeared into the night."

Boticello shook his head. "I don't understand any of this. What in the hell were *you* doing over at Wolf Point last night? And what in the hell do you mean the sheriff had you disarmed and covered?"

Tell him you were over there to steal his whiskey and go ahead and shoot him. Bianci moved his thumb back on the hammer of the shotgun. *He's just stalling for time until somebody gets here to cover his ass. There's no sense on dragging this out.*

"I asked you, what *were* you doing over there last night?" Boticello demanded, lowering his hands to his desk.

Bianci's face hardened. *The Stone Man set that all up. What the hell is going on?* "I was there to steal your whiskey."

Boticello looked at him questioningly and nodded as he slid his foot up into a small opening on the underside of his desk. "John, come in," he said, looking past Bianci and motioning with his hand as he rested his toes on the pedal in the opening.

Bianci turned slightly to glance at the door. "Wha . . ." His question was cut short by the blast of the double-barreled shotgun tearing through a thin partition of wood in the front of Boticello's desk. The twin loads of double-ought buckshot lifted his body, slamming it across the room to topple a table and flop on the floor. The wall beside the door was pitted and splattered with blood.

Boticello slowly rose from behind his desk and fanned at the cloud of gun smoke obscuring his view. *I've had that mechanism in my desk for years, but this was my first opportunity to use it.* He stepped over to Bianci's torn body and stood staring down at it. "I've never trusted anyone," he told the bloody corpse. "That's why I had that contraption built into my desk. For just such an occasion." He turned and looked at the jagged, still-smoking hole in the thin panel of wood. "And it worked for the job it was designed to do," he said as he leaned across his desk, lifted his cup of coffee with a shaking hand, and poured it over the smoldering wood. *Damn, that was close. What the hell was he talking about? The sheriff followed my orders and shot all his men? Steal my whiskey . . . ? I don't understand any of this. Maybe Johnstone can give me some answers when he comes in.* He looked around him and shuddered. *Damn, this place is a mess.* He closed the office door, looked down at his trembling hands, and surveyed the carnage. *I've got to keep Darla out of here. Johnstone and Moran can help me take the body out through the back door and get rid of it. He must have a vehicle outside someplace. They can haul him out in that to get rid of him.*

John Johnstone pulled his key from the lock and pushed into the office. "Damn, what smells so bad in here?" he asked softly. "It smells like a combination of wood smoke, gun smoke, and shit."

Benjamin Boticello opened his office door, stepped out into the hallway, and pulled the door closed.

"This place really stinks bad, Mister Boticello," Johnstone repeated, fanning his hand in the air.

"Yeah, leave the door open and we'll see if we can air the place out. Go out and meet Darla and tell her to take the rest of the day . . . , no, make that the rest of the week off. Then get your ass back in here. We've got a lot to do. Moran's due in anytime. Get going."

"There's a couple of big fans in the back room," Johnstone said over his shoulder as he pushed open the door.

CHAPTER FORTY-ONE

Thumper Moran and John Johnstone spread a small tarp over Dominic Bianci's body and tucked in the edges before slamming the tailgate on the truck shut.

Moran hooked his thumb back at the office building. "Let's go and see if Boticello's got anything else he wants done before we get rid of this body."

"Yes, and I could use a cup of coffee and I saw that the pot was on. It's damned cold out here," Johnstone agreed. "And the cleanup is going to be a real pain in the ass. Did you get a good look at that shotgun contraption he had rigged in his desk?"

"Boy, did I. I'm glad I never pissed him off when I was standing across from him in his office."

Both men chuckled as they pushed in through the front doors.

"It still stinks in here," Moran noted.

Boticello walked out, pulling off his gloves. "Damn, things are in one hell of a mess in there."

"A ten gauge up close'll do that," Moran agreed. "We're gonna have a cup of coffee and then head out into the country. Johnstone's going to follow me in his car."

"Do you have any idea who that man was?" Johnstone asked, then wagged his head. "I guess that was a rather stupid question, wasn't it?"

"Yeah, I recognized him at the front door and, like a dumb ass, let him in," Boticello answered. "I knew his face, but didn't have a name until he gave it to me. Dominic Bianci. I'd sold him a couple truckloads of booze awhile back. That's why I remembered him. He'd been in here to pay me."

Johnstone nodded and poured himself a cup of coffee. "I recall that name now."

"He said something I couldn't figure out. He said the sheriff over there in Wolf Point followed *my orders* last night and shot down all his men after he'd taken their guns away. He told me he was there to steal my whiskey. How'n the hell did he know about the whiskey shipment? Have you got any idea what he was talking about?"

Moran and Johnstone both shook their heads.

"He told me Bohlin gave them some sort of a damned air show when he took off. I don't understand a lot of this; as a matter of fact, I don't understand any of this. Where in the hell is Bohlin? He better be able to shed some light on this. I want to hear his version of all this crap!"

Moran looked questioningly at Johnstone as he filled his coffee cup. "Beats the shit out of me. You understand any of that, John?"

Johnstone's brow wrinkled and he shook his head. "I have no idea what happened."

Boticello scowled at Johnstone. "Son-of-a-bitch!" he exploded. "You did get hold of Winslow over there in Helena to do the pickup, didn't you?"

"Yes, sir, yes, sir, Mister Boticello. Of . . . of . . . of course, I did *exactly* what you told me, sir," Johnstone stuttered. "I always follow your orders to the letter. You know that, Mister Boticello."

Moran put his coffee cup up in front of his face to cover his smile. *You mousy little kiss-ass, show some balls.*

Boticello shook his head. "Sometimes, I wonder, Johnstone, sometimes I wonder." He pointed at the door. "Now you two go out and get rid of that damned body. We've got a lot to do when you get back." He looked up at the clock. "Where in the hell is Bohlin? I should be getting a report from him by now. I want to hear *his* story about last night."

Wild Bill Bohlin awoke with his feet propped on an open desk drawer and covered by his lucky coat. He tossed it onto the desk, stretched, dropped his feet to the floor, and looked at the clock on the far wall. *Well, I timed that pretty good.* He lifted the telephone receiver and dialed a number.

"This is Boticello," a voice growled.

"Bohlin, here. The delivery's done and I'm loaded for the next drop."

"Everything go okay? Were the pickup men there? Anything strange or out of the usual happen?"

"The flight was smooth, but the pickup people from Helena hadn't arrived. The men were there to unload the plane and when I left, it was all stacked neatly in the snow. I'm sure it was handled well." *He's awfully curious about last night. I wonder if he's heard anything about what happened. His voice sounds a little tight. He knows something.*

"Funny, I haven't heard from them yet. Nothing unusual, huh?"

"Nope, smooth on my end. Maybe it was a slow trip back to Helena. It's a long way and I don't know how much snow they'd had over there."

Bohlin, you're a lying bastard. Boticello fought to keep his voice civil. "Yeah, you're right. Weather can be a big factor."

"Are you going to be there for a while, Mister Boticello?"

"Yeah, I'm sitting here with Thumper Moran discussing some minor collection problems, but I'm sure he can work them out. I had Johnstone go over and get us some lunch. He'll be back pretty soon. There should be enough for you to eat with us. We need to talk about a few things anyway. Come on over as soon as you can."

"Yeah, I was planning on that, but I've already eaten, so don't wait for me. I'll see you in a little while. Go ahead and eat." Bohlin hung up the receiver, shook his head, and smiled weakly. *This is gonna be the end of any work for these people, Bill,* he told himself as he stood, shrugged into his coat, patted the packets of money in the inside pockets, took a final look around his bare office, and pulled on his leather flight helmet. *It was great while it lasted.* He smiled slightly as he adjusted and buckled the helmet and worked his fingers into his gloves.

Boticello slammed the receiver into the hook so hard that the phone flipped through the air and off the secretary's desk.

Moran reached down, picked up the phone, and slid it back onto the desk. "Calm down, Boss. You'll give yourself a heart attack."

Boticello took a deep breath, let it out slowly, and nodded. "He'd better have some damned good answers for my questions when he gets here. I hope you're not too good a friend of that bastard because I may want you to work him over before I'm done with him."

Moran smiled, put his hands together, and cracked his knuckles. "Whatever you say, Boss."

CHAPTER FORTY-TWO

Benjamin Boticello, John Johnstone, and Thumper Moran sat at a table in the conference room, finishing their lunch.

"So where'd you guys say you put the truck and the body?" Boticello asked.

"Like I said, Boss, we drove it out of town a ways and stuck it in a snowbank," Moran answered.

"Then we shoveled a lot of snow over it, so it probably won't show up again until spring," Johnstone added.

Thumper Moran poured himself a cup of coffee and lit a cigarette. "That was quite a firepower gadget you had built in your desk, Boss. I never knew it was there."

Boticello chuckled. "You weren't *supposed* to know it was there. I had a man build that special desk a few years ago and I've always taken it with me. The barrels were tilted up behind a thin wooden panel to take a man full in the chest if I ever used it. A ten gauge with eighteen-inch barrels loaded with double-ought buck. We never had a way to test-fire it under the desk, so I had to trust his word. It has a pedal built into an opening in the back corner to fire it."

"What about the janitor?" Moran asked, and lit his cigarette with a heavy silver lighter. "Doesn't he mess with it?"

"There's a little, well-hidden, panel up under there that I open to get to the pedal. He'd have to know what he was look-ing for to find it and I don't think he works that hard in the first place. Hell, he only comes in one day a week anyway and he was in last night."

"Well, I gotta tell you, Boss, that's one hell of a mess you got in there," Moran said.

"We'll be putting in some mighty long hours for the next few days," Boticello agreed. "And I'm going to have to take that shotgun out to clean and reload it."

"You want me to clean it for you, Boss?" Moran volunteered.

"I'll think on it."

A growing, roaring sound made the three men look up at the ceiling.

"That sounds like a plane flying pretty low," Johnstone stated.

"Well, no shit," Boticello mumbled around a mouthful of corned beef. "He's coming in to talk to me. Why'n the hell didn't he just drive over?"

"I'd say Bohlin's showing off," Moran commented and chuckled. "He likes to let people know how good he really is."

The plane made another loud pass.

"Just what in the hell does he think he's doing?" Boticello yanked the napkin from his shirt collar, wiped his mouth, and got to his feet.

"I told you, Boss, he's showing off," Moran answered, as he stood and glanced at the ceiling again. "Maybe he's flying in to join us. He can land that thing in the open field to the south."

"Yeah," Boticello agreed. "I told him I wanted to talk to him, plus I've got some questions about something else Bianci told me about last night."

"What else did he say to you, Mister Boticello?" Johnstone asked, then cringed when the plane made another rattling pass that sounded like it was going to hit the roof of the one-story building.

"Son-of-a-bitch!" Boticello shouted, running out of the room and through the front doors. He was quickly joined by Moran and Johnstone.

"That's Bohlin, all right," Moran stated, shading his eyes with his hand and watching the red, white, and blue plane circle and begin another inbound approach.

Bohlin saw the three men standing in front of the building watching him.

Suddenly, a white plume of air-show smoke rushed out to trail behind the plane.

"What the hell's that all about?" Boticello shouted as the plane passed overhead, banked, and came towards them again.

Bohlin adjusted his goggles, took a deep breath, and banked the plane so it was almost knife-edge vertical, with the left wing pointing at the ground. "It's air-show time, folks, so now get ready to see the great Wild Bill Bohlin in action," he said softly as he grabbed the handle for the whiskey racks under the left wing and yanked it back. The plane responded hard to the right from the sudden loss of weight on the left side, and Bohlin quickly brought it level again as he passed over the front of the building.

Benjamin Boticello's mouth dropped open as a chain of wooden cases suddenly slid from under the wing of the plane and came marching across the parking lot towards them. On impact, each case disintegrated on the snow-covered asphalt, throwing up a cloud of snow, with a fan spread of splintered wood, shattered glass, and a halo-like fog of whiskey mist.

The three men dove for cover behind Boticello's shiny, black Packard parked at the curb. The train of cases sped towards them until a case smashed beside the grand automobile and the mist of whiskey gushed against, over, and under it to settle on the clothes of the men cowering on the far side. The following case hit the back side of the car to shatter the window, cave in the door, and rock the vehicle up on two wheels. A case glanced off the top of the wavering auto and shattered on the wall above the gold and black lettered window. The next one obliterated the window and the secretary's desk just inside. The remaining wooden boxes in the chain could be heard bouncing and crashing on the flat tin roof of the building. Boticello, Moran, and Johnstone quickly rose to their feet and looked at the destruction of the car and on the front of the building.

Boticello's face was bright red as he stood wiping at the whiskey on his clothes and stammering out a steady string of profanity. A shard of glass impaled in his clothes cut a gash in his finger when he tried to remove it and he screamed out in pain and frustration. The gangster looked at the wound and stuck his finger into his mouth as he walked around to survey the damage to his expensive automobile. Shaking his head, he spit a gob of blood into the snow and continued to swear at Bohlin.

Moran yanked his coat open and pulled his chrome-plated forty-fives from their holsters. "I used to like that bastard," he muttered as he cocked the pistols and looked up, waiting for a chance to shoot at the plane if it passed again. "But, not after he tried to kill me with a whiskey bomb."

Johnstone ran around the building and disappeared.

Bohlin smiled grimly as he made a wide, banking S-turn and looked back down at the building. *I couldn't see how much damage I did on that run because of the building, so I'd best go take another look.* He could see two men standing in the parking lot and a man running through the snow alongside several snow-covered cars parked next to a warehouse behind the building. A line of dark liquid circles and smears marked the lot in front of the office building and a crumpled auto sat at an odd angle in front of the large broken window. *Looks like a good hit on the car.* The snow on the roof showed several wet grooves and marks and there were rough holes in the snow banked behind the building. *Now I've got twelve more to deliver before I get the hell out of here.*

He lined up another bombing run, dropped the right wing, hit the throttle to maximum for more speed, and grabbed the release lever on the right side of the cockpit. *Here goes!*

Thumper Moran stood in the middle of the parking lot with his hands at his sides. His narrowed eyes were trained on *The French Wench* as she dropped a wing and sped towards the front of the building.

Bohlin saw the man standing in the middle of the parking lot. "How fast can you run, Thumper?" he shouted and laughed. "You sure as hell make a good target standing out there." He gave a quick yank on the release handle and leveled the plane.

Calmly, Thumper Moran raised both hands and began to alternately fire his silver pistols, right, left, right, left, right, left. As he fired, he suddenly saw the chain of boxes dropping from the lowered wing. The plane leveled off and the train of falling wooden whiskey cases filled the sky and began cratering the snow towards him. He cursed as he spun and bolted to one side.

Bohlin appeared to wave as he passed overhead and Moran continued to fire both pistols until they clicked on empty chambers. "Son-of-a-bitch." He pushed the buttons on the sides to drop the spent magazines and watch *The French Wench* making her smoky climb away from him.

Bohlin thought he felt something tug at the sleeve of his lucky coat as he banked left and pulled back hard on the stick to put the plane into a steep climb and then go into a roll with his end-of-show-smoke, corkscrew, barrel-roll maneuver.

CHAPTER FORTY-THREE

Wild Bill Bohlin circled again to get a look at the results of his final whiskey-crate bombing run. A second line of whiskey craters ran across the parking lot to the shiny black Packard, now turned to face into the front of the broken-windowed building. *I must've hit his fancy car again.* The front left fender was crushed inward and the hood ripped free and wedged against the bricks under the shattered window.

Benjamin, "The Little Barrel" Boticello stood beside his automobile shaking his fists and cursing at the plane passing higher overhead.

Bohlin waggled his wings, turned off the show smoke, pulled back on the stick, and headed straight up into the clouds. *That probably wasn't the smartest thing I've ever done, but boy, it sure felt good!* He remembered the tug at his sleeve earlier and turned it up to look at it. *I'll be damned, another bullet hole. This is my lucky coat!*

Thumper Moran worked his freshly loaded pistols into their holsters as he walked across the littered parking lot towards Boticello, who still stood shouting curses and shaking his fists at the clouds.

"Calm down, Boss. You're gonna have a heart attack," he shouted. "Let's go inside where it's warmer."

Boticello spun to face Moran. "Don't *you* tell *me* what to do!" he screamed. "Look . . . look . . . look at my car," he stuttered, waving his hands around at the parking lot. "Look at the front of my office. Look at all that expensive whiskey . . ." His voice trailed off and he began to cough.

Moran put his hand on the man's shoulder and gently pushed him towards the building. "C'mon, Boss, let's go inside."

Their shoes made crunching sounds in the glass littering the floor as they walked through the rubbled remains of the secretary's office. The painting of Benjamin Boticello hung at an angle, the oil-painted face, dotted with small tears and cuts from flying glass and rivulets of whiskey, now gazed thoughtfully at the floor.

Boticello attempted to straighten the painting, but finally shook his head, shrugged, and, stepping over a typewriter, walked slowly to his office. He opened the door and stood silently as his eyes wandered over the damage. He pointed at his desk. "Look at that," he said, his voice barely a whisper. Large drops of whiskey dripped from a broken section of the ceiling onto his desk, now littered with plaster. Sadly shaking his head, he walked to a cabinet, brought out a bottle of whiskey, and slammed it down on his desk. "I want the bastard *dead!*" His voice rose until the final word was a scream. "Do you hear me? *Dead!*" He fumbled for a chair, sat down, and pulled a tray with a crystal decanter and glasses across the desk. He twisted the cork free, poured a glass half-full, took a good drink, coughed, and wiped the back of his hand under his nose. "Go to his hangar and see what's left there." He took another drink. "Where'n the hell're Suberg and Herbell?"

"Remember, Boss, you sent them to Minneapolis yesterday for something."

"Oh, yeah . . . put out the word I'll pay ten grand for information that leads me to Bohlin and that damned plane of his. Got that? Call me and let me know what you find. See if his mechanic's there. He can probably tell us something."

Moran nodded. "I've got it, Boss. I'm going." *His mechanic isn't gonna be there. They were too close for him to stay behind and take the wrath of Boticello when Bohlin was done with his damned bombing runs. I wonder what in the hell got into him anyway? He was making damn good money for a small amount of work.*

John Johnstone, wearing his overcoat and hat, stood in the wreckage of the secretary's office and watched Thumper Moran's car disappear in a cloud of exhaust around a far corner. He cupped his hands in front of his mouth, blew into them and shoved them into his coat pockets. *Damn, it's cold in here.* He slowly turned and looked at the damage the falling cases of whiskey had done to the room. "Well, I've got work to do," he said quietly, as he stepped over to the dangling Boticello oil portrait, managed to lift it free, and turned it to the wall. "Sorry, sport."

Boticello looked up at Johnstone's knock on his open door. "What'n the hell do you want?" he asked.

Johnstone stepped into the office and looked around it. "It looks like you're having a rather bad day, Mister Boticello," he remarked, smiled, squared his shoulders, and stood straighter.

Boticello raised the glass, paused, set it back on the table, and his eyes narrowed as he looked Johnstone up and down. "What kind of a smart-assed remark was that, you shithead?" he growled.

Johnstone lifted his glasses from his face, thumbed his blue silk necktie free from his coat, and began to polish the lenses. "Now that's not a very nice way to talk to a man who's done all your financial work for over a year now, Mister Benjamin Boticello. I'm the man who knows more about your business than you do at this time." He held his glasses up to the light to examine them, smiled, put them on, and pushed his tie back inside his coat.

"Don't you be getting pompous with me, you . . . you . . .

overeducated *bookworm* turd."

Johnstone shook his head and chuckled. "My, my, what language. I talked to Moran when he was leaving and he told me he was going over to Bohlin's hangar to see how much whiskey's left. Ordinarily I could give you an exact count, but I'm not sure how much he dropped in here awhile ago. They were falling too fast for me to get an accurate count of what to take off the recently shipped inventory. You must've done *something* to really piss him off."

Boticello's face reddened and he rose slowly to his feet. "Just *who* in the hell do you think you are, talking to me like that?"

CHAPTER FORTY-FOUR

John Johnstone smiled, reached inside his coat, and brought out an engraved, nickel-plated Colt revolver with ivory grips. "Your day is about to get a lot worse, *Mister* Benjamin, Little Barrel, Boticello." He hefted the pistol and rolled it in his hand. "I'll bet you didn't know I carried one of these, did you?"

Boticello's eyes widened at the sight of the fancy pistol in Johnstone's hand. "What kind of shit is this?" he blustered, standing straighter.

Johnstone chuckled. "For over a year now I've been the brains of your operation. Oh, sure, you've done all the roaring and shouting and beating on your chest, but I've done all the *mental* work for you. Like I told you before, I know more about you than you do. You're the outdated Capone-style-gangster-gunslinger-rub-garlic-on-the-bullets-bootleg-boss. But now the time is here for brains to rule over brawn. The financial end of the bootleg business needs to have the control of it. You can only get so much done with fear and intimidation. There has to be brains to manage it. Loose cannons will eventually knock a hole in the side of the ship and let the water in to sink it. To me, it is best to control those cannons before they are fired. Tie them down and use them only when necessary."

Boticello raised his glass with a shaking hand, took a swallow, and began to cough.

"Your man, Thumper, is useful for what he does, but any muscle can do that job. He needs direction. He's like a good dog. Bite for me and I'll reward you with a bone, a cash bone."

"Are you done?" Boticello asked.

"Do you know how many cases of whiskey you have in your warehouse right now?"

"Of course I do."

"No, you don't. You believe you have what you read on those sheets I gave you this morning. What if I were to tell you there was no whiskey in your warehouse?"

Boticello cocked his head and looked at him. "Where's all this going?" he asked softly.

"This has been an interesting morning. In some ways it fits right in with my plans. Morgan and Turner were gunned down in a barn near Wolf Point. You sent Suberg and Herbell to Minneapolis yesterday. I had the four flunkies who do the heavy work for you in the warehouse clean all the whiskey out and move it to a new location three days ago. I paid them very well, laid them off, and promised them work later. You had me send Darla home, with pay, and I told her I'd call her when the time is right to come back to work. I didn't know about that show Wild Bill Bohlin was going to put on for us today, and I have no idea why he did it, but that's another thing that played into my hands well. He's pissed off about something and burning, no, I'd have to say *bombing* his bridges behind him." Johnstone chuckled and hefted the pistol in his hand again. "I thought Bohlin was a whore who'd work for anybody who paid him, but I guess I was wrong about him. Anyway, as of now your total army is made up of one lone soldier, Thumper Moran."

Boticello took another small sip of whiskey and shook his head. "I'm still not understanding any of this."

"That man you blew the hole in today is named Dominic Bianci. He was the leader of a gang that was supposed to steal the shipments of whiskey you had going to Wolf Point."

Boticello looked thoughtfully at Johnstone and nodded his

head. "I couldn't figure out what he was talking about, but now I think I understand . . . wait a minute. How'n the hell do you know about Bianci? He didn't talk to you this morning. He was already dead when you got here."

Johnstone chuckled and continued to heft the silver pistol. "That's not important right now. Mister Capone knows you've been skimming from the profits. He doesn't like things like that."

"You know better than that, Johnstone. I trusted you to keep my books. You know I'm not skimming anything."

Johnstone chuckled. "You know that and I know that, but Big Al Capone doesn't. He's like you, in that he only knows what I tell him. I showed him you were skimming. Do you think he sent me up here to work for you just because I'm a good book-keeper?"

Boticello sat down in his chair and slowly shook his head. "No, no, no . . ."

"You had the ruthlessness and organizational abilities he needed to set up and initially manage this operation, but he really never trusted you with the finances. At this point, according to the second set of books you were keeping on your own, you've got over twenty thousand dollars in Capone's money."

"I've never touched those books."

Johnstone shrugged. "So you say. This can be an excellent operation financially, if it's handled by the right person. Mister Boticello, you're not that person." He swung up the pistol, squeezed the trigger, and ended the life of Benjamin, "Little Barrel" Boticello. The impact of the bullet high on his chest flipped him and the chair over backward. Blood ran from the corners of his mouth; his eyes blinked once before becoming forever sightless as they stared at the damaged ceiling above his desk.

Johnstone lowered the pistol and slid it into his shoulder

holster. "That twenty thousand I reported to Capone is actually forty thousand, but I can give him that twenty and still be ahead." He walked over to grin down at Boticello's body. "Like I told you, it's time for brains to take over the brawn. The Stone Man has now officially taken over Little Barrel Boticello's liquor distribution operation and is moving it down to Wolf Point, Montana. It was a short war, Benjamin . . . one shot."

CHAPTER FORTY-FIVE

John Johnstone walked slowly down the hall to his office, opened the door, and looked around the room. *Well, let's see, there are a few things I've got to do before I get out of here. The way The Little Barrel's luck is running today, I wouldn't be surprised if there wasn't a fire in here at about any time now. Whiskey burns with a nice blue flame and God knows there's been enough whiskey spilled around here today.* He opened a closet door, pulled a coat aside, pushed on the wall, and a spring release opened a section of paneling above the shelves. He reached over, snapped on a light, pulled the candlestick phone forward, glanced at a sheet of paper, and dialed for the operator. He gave her a phone number in Wolf Point, Montana, and waited for her to complete the connection.

"Good morning, this is . . ."

"The keg's been tapped," Johnstone interrupted brusquely. "Call my line from a pay phone." He immediately hung up the receiver, lifted a large empty metal box from a shelf above him, and stepped back out of the closet. *It'll take him a few minutes to get to a pay phone,* he told himself as he slid open a drawer and began rummaging through the files. He lifted files out, glanced at the titles, and tossed them to scatter the contents over the floor. Certain files he quickly slid into the metal box. Satisfied, he pulled out other drawers, dumped them on the floor, and kicked the papers around the room. He moved to a shelf of ledgers, selected a few, and stacked them on his desk. A light flashed on his intercom and he returned to the closet and lifted the receiver of his secret telephone. "What the hell happened over there last night?"

"What are you talking about?" Wolf Point Police Chief Parker Dennison asked.

"I've been told that your sheriff *executed* a bunch of whiskey runners last night."

There was a long silence before Dennison sighed and spoke. "Where did you hear this?"

"A man, Dominic Bianci, told Boticello that story, accused him of being behind it, and then was blown to hell by a shotgun hidden in Boticello's desk."

"Okay."

"Bianci was holding a shotgun on Boticello and made the mistake of standing in front of his booby-trapped desk."

"You said Boticello was dead. Did this Bianci kill him?"

"No, I did."

"You killed Boticello?"

"I just told you that, didn't I?"

There was another long silence.

"Then is this the day you take over Boticello's operation for Mister Capone?"

"Yes, it is. It's a bit sooner than I'd planned, but things happened that made *this* the day and I'm bringing the operation down into Montana. What's the story on your new police force?"

"They're here now. They arrived last night and I had them put up in a hotel. The mayor will be swearing them in first thing tomorrow morning." Dennison chuckled. "They even have fresh cleaned and pressed uniforms. I gave them the official Wolf Point police brass so they'll look good tomorrow for the ceremony."

"All right, see what you can find out about that sheriff of yours gunning down the whiskey runners last night. I'm going to be low on men until I can get a few sent over from Chicago.

I'll need drivers to start moving *my* line of whiskey. I understand from some people in Chicago that *you* have some good whiskey for sale."

"Indeed I do. We'll discuss it when you get here. Prince of Wales Scotch. I'll pay the sheriff a visit right now."

"This phone will be out of operation in a while. Is my office down there ready?"

"It's been set up for almost a month now. It's a suite of offices over the bank in the middle of the block downtown, a couple of blocks from the police station. I took care of it the day you called. I spent your money and had a truckload of the best office furniture I could find in Helena sent over. There's all the items you need for a legitimate office setting. Your name is painted on the glass door downstairs. All you have to do is move in."

"Good, did you get me a decent safe?"

"Of course, it's the mate to the one I have in *my* office."

"I'll call you from a pay phone tomorrow afternoon with some dates and times." Johnstone hung up the receiver, walked back into his office, and continued his selection of the files and ledgers.

A short while later he slid the last box of paperwork and ledgers into the trunk of his car, lifted out a gas can, walked back into the building, and set the can behind the upset desk of the secretary. Shaking his head, he walked into Boticello's office and slowly looked the room over. A large, open-topped, alligator-skin satchel sat in front of the open door of the safe, and he could see Boticello's feet under the conference table. *And so your kingdom and reign of power has ended today.* He knelt in front of the safe and proceeded to lift out banded stacks of money and place them neatly in the satchel. *With this and the payment I got for the whiskey he thought he still had in the warehouse, I've got over a quarter-million dollar nest egg to work with.* He closed the door of the safe and gave the dial a quick spin. *They can try to open it if they want to.* He snapped the latches on the satchel and set it on Boticello's littered desk. He used a gloved hand to wipe the plaster and whiskey residue from an expensive brass and teak humidor, then lifted and tucked it under his arm. *This will look good in my office in Wolf Point,* he told himself as he hefted a heavy gold desk lighter and slid it into his coat pocket. *A good Cuban cigar should always be lit with a good gold lighter. Or at least that's what you always told me, Mister Boticello.* He lifted the satchel and swung it beside him as he walked across the room, opened the door to his office, and put the satchel on his desk.

John Johnstone sat with his feet up on the corner of his desk, blowing aromatic cigar smoke at the ceiling. With his mind racing, he tipped his head back and closed his eyes. *Life is good!* He heard footsteps in the broken glass on the floor of the front office.

"Hey, anybody here?" Thumper Moran called.

Johnstone dropped his feet to the floor, lifted the silver Colt free, and laid it behind the satchel. "I'm back here, Thumper," he called.

Moran appeared in the doorway, thumbed his hat back, rested his hands on the door frame beside his shoulders, and grinned. "Boticello's gonna be more pissed."

"Why's that?" Johnstone asked and took a drag of smoke from his cigar. "You think he's in a good mood now after all that's happened here today?"

"Bohlin's mechanic and good buddy, Charlie Marcum, is no longer with us."

Johnstone's brow wrinkled. "What do you mean? Did you shoot him?"

Moran laughed, stepped over to a chair, swiped plaster chunks from it with a gloved hand, and sat down. "Naw, he's gone and so is the truck and a lot of the tools and equipment that were in the hangar. I knew he wouldn't be there, but the boss told me to go. Where is he anyway?"

"The last time I saw him he was under his conference table." Johnstone smiled wryly.

"What the hell's he doing under there?"

"He's staring at the ceiling."

Moran's eyes narrowed. "You playing games with me? Trying to be funny?"

Johnstone shook his head and moved his hand up onto his pistol. "No, he's dead."

Moran closed his eyes and rubbed his hands over his face. "I never really liked the little asshole anyway." He finally reached forward, dragged the fancy humidor towards him, and grinned, in an understanding way. "Now that he's not the boss anymore, are we smoking *his* good Cuban cigars?"

Johnstone chuckled as he moved his hand from his gun to the gold lighter and slid it across the desk towards Moran. "Yes, Thumper, my man, I guess *we* are."

CHAPTER FORTY-SIX

The knock on the door startled Sheriff Andy Larson, who was engrossed in the pile of paperwork on his desk. "Yes?" he called out.

The door opened and Deputy John Mooney stepped in waving a handful of papers. "I just got back from the hospital, Andy, and they want to send Bob to the hospital in Helena. When we finally took him out of the barn last night, he really didn't know what was going on. He just kept looking off, mumbling things about dead men, the blood, the mud and gas in the trenches, and the shelling. He wasn't with us anymore."

Larson nodded as he shook out a Camel, thumb-nailed a flame onto a match, touched it to the cigarette, and took a deep breath. "Yeah, John, I saw that kind of faraway look in men's eyes in the war. They called it shell shock. They said it came from a shell going off or an explosion being close to a man and scrambling his brain," he stated in a long cloud of smoke. "Poor Sullivan." Larson took another drag from his cigarette. "He was a damned good man for office work and things like that, but I guess all the shooting and blood and killing last night brought back too many bad memories. I knew he'd gone through some hell in The War, but like so many others, he didn't want to talk about it. They'll probably send him to the Marines' Home in Chicago to see what they can do for him."

Mooney slid a chair up, sat down, and laid the papers on the desk. "Now that Bob's gone, you're gonna have to get somebody to help you with all that paperwork stuff, Andy."

"Yeah, I know, I know. This was his specialty." He glanced up at the clock on the wall. "Damn, it's after ten and I haven't made a dent in *this* pile of paper. Now what've *you* got for me there?"

"Everybody wrote up their version of what happened last night, but I don't think any of us got a passing grade in penmanship in school. These'll all have to be translated and typed by somebody. None of us can do that. I doubt that the people these go to will want to work with anything rough."

"Yeah," Larson agreed. "We might run it by the mayor, but some blue-suit up the line is gonna bounce them. I've been thinking about asking Becky to help after school for a while. I hate to, but . . ."

"I can go see if there's anybody with the right skills out there looking for work," Mooney volunteered.

"I'd considered that, but there's just too much that goes on in here that I don't want to get out on the streets and I don't know who we could trust."

"I understand."

"Becky can probably whip through this in a couple of hours. I'll ask her this afternoon when she gets back from school." The phone on the desk rang and he lifted the receiver. "Sheriff Larson, here." He listened, then spoke. "I'm not going to discuss this on the phone. Come over here and I'll tell you what happened." He hung up the receiver, took a long drag of smoke, and shook his head. "It was that little bastard Dennison. Somehow he found out about the shootings out at the Merkel farm and he's steamed because I hadn't notified him about it. He's on his way over."

Mooney's chair scraped as he stood up. "I'll go warn the others. The bodies from last night are all out in Bement's Mortuary cold storage, so maybe we should get them loaded and trucked to the crime lab over in Helena."

"That's a good idea. If Dennison asks, as far as I know they're already on the way. And be sure to see that Bob gets the best treatment possible. Keep me posted."

As the door closed, Andy Larson squared the papers on his desk, laid his pencil on top of them, sighed, lit a fresh cigarette from the butt in his hand, and leaned back in his chair. *This has made the mess over in Bismarck look like a walk in the park. I'm sure Becky'll be glad to help with this . . . Poor girl, she sure as hell didn't know what she was hooking up with when she married me. It's a good thing she's a strong woman.* He took another drag of cigarette smoke and waited for Dennison's knock on his door.

At the sound of the knock, Larson smiled slightly, sat forward, picked up his pencil, and put what he thought was a concerned look on his face. "Come in."

Parker Dennison pushed through the door, heeled it shut, and untied the belt on his camel-hair coat. "Why in the hell wasn't I apprised of the incident that transpired out at the Merkel farm last night, Sheriff?" he demanded as he lifted his hat and hung it on the back post of a chair.

Larson fought the urge to grin as he watched Dennison smooth his hair with the palms of his hand. "Would you like a cup of good jailhouse coffee, Chief?" he asked and motioned Dennison to sit down.

"No, I don't want a cup of *jailhouse* coffee," Dennison answered and sat down.

Damn, Chief, you're almost the same height sitting as you are standing. "I was going to call you when I got all the reports finished. I lost my typist so things don't move as fast as I'd like them to."

"That's no excuse for not calling me!"

"That was county business, *Chief,* so there was nothing you can officially do at this time anyway. You're short of men and I have a full force right now."

"My new men are here and the force will be sworn in tomorrow. At that point I'll have a full contingent of experienced police officers and we'll be more than willing to assist with any criminal investigation anywhere in the vicinity of Wolf Point. It would be a simple matter for you to swear my men in as temporary investigative officers."

Sheriff Larson tilted his head and smiled slightly. "I'm sure that'd be something for me to consider, Chief, but for right now I think I'll just stumble along with *my* band of country bumpkins."

Dennison's eyes narrowed. "Suit yourself, Sheriff, but I'm sure this shooting incident last night will be grounds for a full investigation, possibly as high as a state level."

A look of mock horror came onto Larson's face. "State level?" Suddenly the look of horror became a wide grin. "Do your best, *Chief,*" he challenged with a chuckle. "Now, if you don't mind, why in the hell don't you get out of here and let me do my reports? I'll have one of my men hand-carry a copy of the whole thing over to you when it's finished. One will go to the mayor and I'll see to it they go up the chain to the Governor's and Attorney General's offices." He took a drag from his cigarette and made a shooing motion with his hand. "Now git, I've got work to do."

CHAPTER FORTY-SEVEN

Sheriff Andy Larson stood, hat in hand, by the door at the back of the county courtroom as Wolf Point Mayor George Hauger finished swearing in the new members of the city police force.

". . . so help me God."

"So help me God," the new, smartly uniformed policemen echoed in unison and lowered their hands. A light smattering of applause came from the city and county employees spread thinly around the room.

Police Chief Parker Dennison's face beamed as he stepped forward to shake hands with the mayor and each of the policemen. He turned and raised his hand. "It gives me great pleasure now to introduce my new officers. The new Wolf Point police force. First, Patrolman Robert Lamey. He's an expert in all facets of investigative police work."

A plain-looking man of medium height stepped forward, raised his hand, nodded, and quickly stepped back into line.

You wouldn't notice him anyplace, Larson judged. *He's one I don't trust right off the bat.*

"Next we have Patrolman Thomas Peppin. Also a well-rounded, qualified, and experienced police officer."

A short, stocky, gray-haired man stepped forward and gave the people a roguish smile before stepping back into his place.

How much longer is this crap gonna go on? Larson asked himself as he patted his pockets for his Camels. *This is one hard-looking bunch coming in here to work for Dennison.* He let his mind wander as he looked at the soon-to-be-retired members of the current Wolf Point police force. *I wonder what those poor bastards are gonna do now? They've basically been forced into retirement by the fear factor. Dennison did a good job with that.* The next two men were introduced and he only heard their names as he continued to study the faces of the men who were leaving.

". . . Patrolman Daniel Gilliam . . ."

". . . Patrolman Basil Barqhart . . ."

"Captain Glenn Rossi is my new department commander."

The name of the final policeman caught Larson's attention and he immediately turned his full attention to Captain Glenn Rossi.

A tall, dark, impeccably uniformed man with narrow, piercing eyes and a pencil-thin mustache stepped forward and sharply saluted Dennison.

Dennison returned the salute and Rossi gave the room a hard smile as his eyes, shaded by the polished brim of his uniform cap, moved from face to face as if memorizing the people in attendance before stepping back into the line of uniformed officers.

Rossi, Glenn Rossi? That's the name Bianci gave me! Larson studied the neatly uniformed officer. *He's the man who was passing orders down from The Stone Man. Now he shows up here as one of Dennison's new cops. His new top cop. This is getting more interesting every minute. Can it be that Dennison is The Stone Man?* He studied the faces of each of the new men. *I wouldn't trust any of those men any more than I'd piss into a strong wind. The streets of Wolf Point are about to go through a big change. Parker Dennison is making his move, so I guess it's time for me to make mine.*

As the people filed out of the room Larson pulled a roll of papers from his coat pocket and flattened them as he walked across the room to where Parker Dennison stood talking to Mayor Hauger. He smiled and stuck out his hand to the mayor.

"Well, Mister Mayor," he began as he shook hands. "It looks like Chief Dennison has brought a fine group of men here to control the crime in the streets of Wolf Point."

Mayor Hauger and Chief Dennison looked at Larson as if trying to read sarcasm in his statement.

Larson kept a straight face as he shuffled through the papers in his hand, separated them into two groups, and handed one to each of them. "That's the final report on the incident out at the Merkels' farm two nights ago. I've hired my wife, Becky, as a temporary secretary and she's done a good job of preparing the final edition of this report. I'll be mailing a copy of it to the Attorney General's office as soon as I get out of here." He shot a quick look at Chief Dennison. "I want to keep all those above me in the know when things like this happen."

Dennison looked down at the papers, then up at Larson, and smiled. "That wife of yours is quite a woman, Sheriff. Teaching school and still finding time to do *your* office work for you."

Larson chose to ignore the jab. "Yes, she is."

"Who's been doing your paperwork up until now?" Mayor Hauger asked.

"Deputy Bob Sullivan was handling all the typing of the reports and other necessary office chores," Larson answered. "He's a veteran and all the shooting the other night got to him. He's in the hospital over in Helena for a couple of days."

"Is he all right?" the mayor asked.

Larson nodded. "Yeah, he'll be okay. He just needs a little rest."

"Surely you must have the funds to hire a secretary," the mayor suggested.

"It's not really necessary right now. We can handle the usual daily paperwork okay."

"I'll have a word with the County Commission members for you, Sheriff," the mayor said. "I'm sure it will all work out fine."

Larson nodded. "Yeah, I'm sure it will. Hey, Chief, how about introducing me to your new police force?"

Dennison nodded and led him to the group of uniformed men involved in a quiet discussion. "Gentlemen, this is Roosevelt County Sheriff Andy Larson." One by one he introduced Larson to each of the men and they shook hands. The last man in the line was Captain Rossi. Their hands clasped and Larson felt the man begin to apply pressure.

This must be my first test, Larson told himself as he matched the grip. Their eyes locked and Larson began to smile. *Is this all you've got?* He slowly applied more pressure with his thumb into the space between the bones on the back of Rossi's hand and saw anger and pain begin to show in his narrowing eyes. *That's enough.* He released his grip, pulled his hand free, and glanced down as Rossi dropped his hand to his side and began to flex his fingers. *I think I passed the first test and probably even won it. I got those powerful thumbs from milking cows when I was a kid, city boy.*

"I'm glad to meet you, Captain," Larson said, smiling. *He's not going to let that little hand-crushing incident slide.*

"It's my pleasure, Sheriff," Rossi answered graciously, but there was no mistaking the anger in his eyes. "If I can ever do anything for you, please feel free to just ask."

"This is probably going to be pretty tame, easy work for you men coming out here to the wilderness from a big city back east," Larson said.

Rossi looked down at Chief Dennison, then back up at Larson, and shook his head. "Oh, I'm not too sure about that. After all the things we've been told about the shootings and robberies out here in Wolf Point, it would seem to be a little bit like the old Wild West."

Larson chuckled as he put his battered, stained black cowboy hat on his head and adjusted it to his liking. "Yes, to some of us it is like the old Wild West, but the firepower and speed of our guns is a lot heavier and faster."

"I'd say we had a prime example of that out at the Merkel farm the other night," Dennison said.

Larson nodded. "I've still got a lot of work to do. It was a pleasure meeting all of you men. Especially you, Captain."

CHAPTER FORTY-EIGHT

That afternoon Sheriff Andy Larson drove a borrowed pickup truck back into Wolf Point from a long session of investigative and cleanup work at the Merkel farm. He and his deputies had loaded the remaining cases of whiskey into the booze runner's truck to be driven back to town to be locked in a garage behind the jail.

"Hey, look here, Sheriff," Chief Deputy Dusty Durbin had called as he walked out of one of the stalls swinging a pint bottle of whiskey in front of him. "Everything's loaded and locked in the truck and I found this remaining bottle of evidence lying over there in the hay. It'll be a lotta work to unlock the truck for just this little bottle. There's cases of whiskey in there and nobody'd know the difference if this bottle wasn't in there, would they? Huh?"

"No, I don't guess anybody'd know the difference. 'Sides, far as I'm concerned you boys have earned a drink or two. Crack it open and let's all have a snort."

When the others had driven off to town, Larson wandered around the barn pondering the events of the past few days and looking for anything that may have been overlooked. Satisfied, he'd nailed boards across the doors and posted "no trespassing, crime scene" posters in several places on the outside of the barn. He drove in the last nail and stepped back to admire his work. *Damn, I shoulda done this before, but it's worked out well for me anyway.* Someone had left the remaining evidence pint bottle standing on the hood of his truck with a good swallow of whiskey left in the bottom of it. He chuckled, drained the bottle, and tossed it into the snow-filled box of his truck.

As Larson turned onto the main street of Wolf Point, he noticed the big, new Dodge police cruiser that had been purchased to replace the one shot up and destroyed by fire a few weeks before. *Parker didn't spare any expense when it came to replacing the old one,* he told himself as he braked at a stop sign and turned onto the street behind the jail. *I'd best check the doors of the garage before I go in for the day.* He noticed the new police car had turned in behind him. As he watched in the rearview mirror, the headlights began flashing and the siren gave a short roar. *What the hell's this all about?* He pulled his truck off to the snow-banked side of the street, stopped, put the transmission in neutral, and pulled on the hand brake. He watched in the side mirror as the big car pulled in behind him and the front doors opened. Two uniformed men stepped out and adjusted their blue coats and gun belts as they walked up on both sides of his truck. *I got a gut feeling this ain't gonna be pleasant.* He heard the siren dying as he rolled down his window and looked up at Captain Rossi. "You got a problem?" he asked.

Rossi squared his cap, smiled evilly, nodded, and put his foot up on the running board. "Could I see your driver's license, please?"

"What for?"

"You failed to come to a complete stop at that stop sign back there at the corner."

"Bullshit. I stopped."

Rossi leaned down and looked across at the policeman standing on the other side. "Patrolman Gilliam, didn't you see this vehicle fail to come to a halt at that stop sign back there?"

"Yes, sir, Captain," Gilliam agreed and frowned. "That was definitely a rolling violation of the Wolf Point city driving code."

"Okay, this isn't funny anymore," Larson stated and released the hand brake. "I've got work to do. I'm on official business."

Rossi's hand shot into the truck and gripped the steering wheel. "Leave it out of gear, put the brake back on, and show me your driver's license."

Larson did as he was told, rolled his eyes up at Rossi, shook his head, and muttered as he unbuttoned his coat to get his wallet.

"Did you say something?" Rossi demanded and leaned down closer to Larson.

"It doesn't matter," Larson answered as he thumbed through his wallet.

"Have you been drinking?" Rossi asked, sniffing inside the truck.

"No, that's my aftershave lotion," Larson answered sarcastically and chuckled as he pulled out his license and held it up to Rossi.

Gilliam looked in the box of the truck; his hand disappeared into a hole in the snow, and he brought out an empty pint bottle. "Look at this, Captain," he said, triumphantly. "It looks like you can add drunken driving to the citation."

Rossi looked across the truck and smiled. "Yes, indeed," he agreed as he snatched Larson's driver's license and, without looking at it, slid it into his pocket. "Step from the vehicle."

"What?"

"You heard me, step from the vehicle," Rossi stated, tersely.

"This is so much bullshit," Larson said, releasing the hand brake, wiggling the shift knob, and pushing in the clutch pedal. "I've got work to do and I'm not gonna spend time playing stupid, big-town-cop games with the likes of you assholes." He raised his hand out the window and flexed his fingers. "Now gimme my license back and get your damned foot off my running board."

The side of Andy Larson's head cracked, his ear rang, his eyes filled with stars, and his hat slid down over his face as he sagged back against the seat.

Captain Rossi yanked the door open, and waved a heavy, black leather sap in front of him. "Don't *ever* attempt to resist arrest with me, mister," he growled, as he reached across and turned off the ignition. "Gilliam, relieve him of his sidearm."

Larson shook his head as his hand dropped to the butt of his pistol. "Somebody's about to get hurt here," he snarled as he yanked his old Colt revolver free, shoved it against Rossi's chest, and thumbed back the hammer. "Captain, you just made the biggest mistake of your life! This gun's got a hair trigger and it doesn't take much to make it go off."

On the other side of the truck Gilliam clawed at his holster.

"You tell that bastard if I see his gun, I'll put a hole in you he can walk through!" Larson shouted and emphasized it with a sharp jab of his pistol into Rossi's chest. "Now, both of you put your damned hands up." He was fighting very hard to keep control of his temper.

Rossi's eyes narrowed to slits of anger as he slowly raised his hands. "What we have here right now, Sheriff, is a classic standoff. There's no way you can take both of us."

Larson gripped Rossi's gun belt and pulled him up close. "Are you willing to die for something this stupid, Rossi?"

"Are you, Sheriff?" Rossi asked, looking across at Gilliam who was slowly lowering his hands.

Larson shook his head. "No, not really, but I'm not gonna be buffaloed by the likes of you two. Chief Dennison's not gonna look very kindly at one or two of his new officers being shot down on their first full day on the job now, is he?"

"Probably not."

"You tell your man on the other side that if his hands get any lower, I'm gonna pull the trigger. Tell him to unbuckle his gun belt and throw it in the back of my truck."

"Kiss my ass."

Larson pulled Rossi's belt tighter, moved the barrel of his pistol slightly, and squeezed the trigger. The gun roared and the flame belching from the barrel set fire to the front of Rossi's coat and the slug punched a small hole in the snowbank behind him.

"Son-of-a-bitch!" Rossi screamed, looking down and beating at the burning cloth with his gloved hands. "You've shot me!"

Now you can add discharging a firearm in the city limits. Larson shoved Rossi backward to fall in the snow, leaped out, and leveled his smoking pistol across the hood at Gilliam. "You're next," he snarled as he thumbed back the hammer. "And I've had about all this shit I'm gonna take!"

Gilliam's eyes were wide with fear, his head shaking and his hands stretched high. "No, no, no," he said, his voice barely a whisper as he backed up, twisted off balance, and fell facedown into the snow.

"Keep your face down, put your hands out to your side, and stay there," Larson ordered, glancing over his shoulder to see Rossi slamming handfuls of snow against his smoldering uniform coat. He stepped back to stand beside Rossi, pointing his pistol down at him as he continued to pat snow on the smoking fabric.

"I think the standoff is over, *Captain,*" he said, sarcastically and smiled. *Damn, my ears are ringing.* "You're gonna have to learn that I may be a plain old country boy, but I'm a damned mean and *smart* old country boy. You've pushed my temper to the limit here today. You came damn close to getting shot for stupidity. How about if I made you two take off your gun belts and throw 'em in the back of my truck? Then I took them to the chief and let you try to explain that to the top dog."

Larson saw something in the snow beside his truck. "Stay

real still," he said as he reached down and brought up Rossi's black leather sap. He chuckled as he stepped back, knelt beside Rossi, and laid the sap on the officer's burned jacket. Without taking his eyes from Rossi's frightened face he reached up and tenderly explored the lump beside his eye with his fingers. "I'll bet this is gonna be a beauty of a shiner in a day or two. Now if I was a vengeful man," he said, lifting the sap from Rossi's chest. "I'd take this leather and lead toy of yours and make a real mess out of your face . . . What do you think I should do?"

Rossi rolled his head back and forth in the snow, a gloved hand over one ear. "I think that shot might've busted an eardrum," he muttered. "Please, now don't do anything foolish with that sap."

Larson tapped the black leather surface several times on Rossi's forehead. "Foolish, foolish? It seems to me that you already did something damned foolish today, didn't you, Captain?" He smacked the sap harder on the man's forehead. "Open your eyes and look at me when I'm talking you."

Tears ran from the corners of his eyes and down his cheeks as Rossi opened them.

"That was a bit hard that time, wasn't it?" Larson said and tucked the sap into his coat pocket. "I guess I should apologize for that, huh? Tough shit. Oh, yeah, while I'm thinking of it, give me back my damned driver's license."

Rossi reached into his pocket, brought out Larson's license, and held it up to him.

Larson took the license, glanced at it, nodded, and tucked it in with the sap. "That's better."

Rossi ran his fingers under his watery eyes. "What're you going to do now?"

"I'll tell you what I'm gonna do," Larson said, standing up, lowering the hammer on his pistol, and slipping it into his holster. "I figure you've learned one hell of a lesson today and you're gonna give me a wide berth when you see me coming. That goes for me, and all of my men. I don't know what you and the chief are up to, but I've got my suspicions. If you wanna make out an official report on this incident, you go right ahead. But I don't think you should show the chief that burn on your nice uniform coat, because it'll take a lot of explaining and he won't be very happy. Now you good police officers stay here and calm down while I go on about my business. Rossi, roll over on your belly and put your hands out to your side, like your partner over there. That'll help cool off the burned spot." He nudged Rossi's leg with his boot. "You can keep your guns because I don't want to have to go through all the work of taking them to Dennison and hearing a bunch of bullshit from his over-educated mouth. Remember, you give me and my boys a wide berth or this little fracas today will seem like grade school recess."

Larson walked to the truck and turned. "You don't wanna get on my bad side any more than you are already, *Captain*. Trust me on that."

Rossi turned his head up and glared at Larson.

Sheriff Andy Larson raised his hand in the shape of a gun, cocked his thumb, and let it drop. "Bang!"

CHAPTER FORTY-NINE

Sheriff Andy Larson stood outside the door to his office, straightened his coat, thumbed his hat back, gently explored the lump beside his partially closed eye, and took a deep breath. *Remember, this ain't no big deal,* he told himself, as he slowly let his breath out and opened the door.

His wife, Becky, sat at his desk heavily engrossed in a stack of papers laid out in front of her. She glanced up, smiled, and looked back down at the papers. "This paperwork is really a mess, Andy . . ." Suddenly her head shot up; she gasped, leaped to her feet, and rushed to stand in front of her husband. "Oh, Andy," she said softly as she tentatively raised her fingers to his injured face. "What happened?"

"Oh, nothing really, dear. I bumped my face on a door out at the barn that swung open when I wasn't expecting it," he lied, taking her hand and kissing her palm.

"Andy, I was thinking all day at school and when I was here this afternoon, about how dangerous this job has gotten. It's as bad, if not worse, than North Dakota."

Larson sighed. "I know, Becky."

"Look at poor Bobby Sullivan, what's to become of him now?"

"Oh, he'll get good care. They do a lot of good things for veterans in those hospitals."

"What if something like that happened to you, Andy?" she asked, reaching out again to touch his face. "Or, what if you were machine-gunned down like so many other men have been here lately. Andy, this is turning into another war. A bootleg war!"

Larson looked at her beautiful face, felt tightness in his throat, and nodded. "You're right, Becky. It's time for us to move out of here. Do you think your father is still willing to have me come back to Devils Lake and work on his farm?"

She leaned up, kissed him, and broke into a wide smile. "Now that's a stupid question, *Sheriff*," she said, as tears welled up in her eyes. "He *wants* you to go back there and work for him. In a letter we got today he told me Bradley had taken a job with the National Guard out at Camp Grafton. He'll have to hire a hand to help with the plowing and planting in the spring anyway."

"What's Brad doing that for?"

"He's at that age now when he wants to jump out of the nest and see if he can fly on his own."

Larson nodded. "Yeah, I can understand that. Since you're so good with words, why don't you start working on paperwork for my resignation? I know Dusty'll make a good sheriff, so while you're doing official things, make out a letter of recommendation for him. I'll talk this over with all of the guys in the next day or two."

"Are you sure about this, Andy?"

Andy nodded. "It's a matter of time before I'll have problems with Dennison's new police force. Write up something for me and I'll make a final decision. I'm sure Dusty and the boys can take good care of Wolf Point."

"I want you to give this some serious thought now."

"I will. Oh, hell, I have to be honest with you, Becky. I got this black eye from a run-in with Captain Rossi and another one of those new goons on Dennison's police force."

Becky put her hand to her mouth. "Oh, no," she said softly,

and then suddenly she stamped her foot. "You lied to me, Andy?"

Larson stepped back and raised his hands. "Now, Becky, I didn't exactly lie to you. I just didn't tell you the whole story."

"You told me you got the black eye from bumping into something out at that barn."

"Okay," he said, resignedly. "That *was* a lie."

Becky's eyes narrowed and she again stamped her foot. "All right then, Andy, I want the *truth.*"

Larson quickly related most of the story about the incident with Captain Rossi. He managed to leave out the part about setting fire to Rossi's coat. *I don't think it's gonna be reported 'cause he's too embarrassed. She's gonna worry enough the way it is. It's not a lie. It's just something I forgot to tell her.*

CHAPTER FIFTY

Sheriff Andy Larson sat on the front edge of his desk, sipping from a mug of steaming coffee and waiting for his deputies to get their coffee and pull up chairs.

"Where'd you get that shiner, Andy?" Chief Deputy Dusty Durbin asked, with a slight smile.

"I ran into a door."

"I kinda figured Becky had a good left hook," John Mooney joked.

"Okay," Larson said, gently touching his finger to his bruised face. "Let's get all the smart remarks out and over with."

The men looked at each other, shrugged, and shook their heads.

"What, no fun if you know it doesn't bother me?" Larson asked. "Okay, here's what I've got for today. I'm considering resigning and moving back to North Dakota to work on Becky's family farm."

The men again all looked around at each other and then back at Larson.

"Is this a little humor to start off the day, Andy?" Durbin asked.

Larson shook his head. "No, I'm serious. I'm having Becky write me a resignation letter."

The room was silent.

"Damn, Andy, I don't know what to say," Durbin said, slowly getting to his feet. "Who's gonna replace you then?"

"I'm recommending you for the job, Dusty."

"Well, that's bullshit! What if I don't want the job?"

Larson waved his hands. "All right, calm down. It's not like I'm packing my bags and leaving on the train tonight. We have a few things to clear up before I leave. To be honest . . . Hell, I just wanna keep Becky happy. Last night I tried to talk her into letting me send her back to North Dakota, but she wouldn't go for that. She said if I wasn't going right away, she wasn't either and besides she couldn't leave until the school year's over. So, I guess that means you're stuck with me as sheriff until at least June."

The four deputies in the room all nodded.

"Okay, now that I've got that out of the way, I'm going to brief you on something I probably should have told you about awhile back. It's about Chief Dennison's new police department. I'd heard the name Rossi before. I got it from that fella, Bianci, the night of the shootings out at the Merkel place. He told me this Rossi was a main connection to someone called The Stone Man and he was the power behind this bootleg control war we've got going on here. Then he managed to escape, so I didn't get anything else from him."

"You sure it's the same Rossi, Andy?" John Mooney asked.

"Bianci told me he was a tall, good-looking man, with piercing eyes and a pencil mustache. His nickname back east is Tiny. I'm sure he told me his real name, and Rossi isn't that common a name. At this point, I'm saying he's our man." Larson pulled Rossi's black leather sap out of his back pocket, slapped it on the palm of his hand, and gave them a quick rundown on how he'd gotten his black eye. "Don't underestimate how mean and ruthless those guys might be. If in question, you act first, got that?"

The men nodded in agreement.

"You really set fire to his coat with your pistol?" Mooney

chuckled. "Damn, *that's* funny."

"I did," Larson answered and nodded. "Remember: always expect the worse from these thugs."

"A known bootlegger is now the head of Dennison's police department?" Bernie Ward asked. "Can't we do something about that?"

"We're the county law," Larson answered. "I got that information from a man who's long gone now. We can't do a thing without something concrete to work with. We'll start watching them for anything we can use. It's gonna cut down on the amount of sleep we'll be getting, but I think we can come up with what we need. I see this as a big move for bringing in an army to control the booze being run through Roosevelt County, and, boys, it's up to us to stop it."

"I'll work out a schedule," Durbin volunteered. "We should be able to start today. After all, we've gotta lotta work to do between now and the first of June."

The men in the room laughed.

"I wanna warn you of something," Larson said. "There is no love lost between me and Captain Rossi, but I don't think we're gonna find them doing anything illegal during the daytime. Those are the kind of thugs who do their best work after dark."

"We ain't too bad after dark ourselves," Mooney added.

"We're short one man now, Andy," Durbin stated. "You got somebody to fill that space?"

"Does anybody know if Mike Goetz is still in town?" Larson asked. "He was the assistant chief and he'd know some of the inside workings of the department. Of course, I don't know how much Dennison has changed things to suit his programs."

"I heard he already got hired on in Denver," Bernie Ward volunteered.

"Anybody got any suggestions?" Larson asked.

The men in the room shook their heads.

"Well, think on it and if you come up with somebody, let me know. Right now, it looks like we're outmanned . . . and *out-gunned.*"

CHAPTER FIFTY-ONE

John Mooney sat slouched down in the cab of his truck, bundled in a buffalo robe and fighting to stay awake. Another buffalo robe was wrapped around his legs. It was seven o'clock and very dark. "I sure wish they'd do something," he mumbled, pulling the thick, brown hair up tighter onto his neck.

The door of the police station suddenly threw a fan of light out onto the street and Chief Parker Dennison was outlined as he stepped out onto the snowy sidewalk. The light quickly disappeared when he pulled the door shut.

Mooney wiggled down until he could just see over the dash. *No doubt who that little man is.* Mooney watched the chief push his collar up against the cold and stride off down the street. "Shit, now I guess I'll have to get out and follow him," he mumbled, as he freed himself from his buffalo robes. He waited until Dennison rounded the corner, then stepped out into the street and quietly pushed the door shut. "Damn, this cold ain't good for my old bones and joints," he complained to himself as he hobbled a few steps until he loosened up and was able to walk quickly to the corner. He peered around the building and saw Dennison standing in light coming from a glassed door. He pulled his head back as the chief cautiously looked both ways before opening the door and disappearing inside. He could see Dennison's shadow on the snowy street and guessed from his movements that he was locking the door.

Mooney walked to the door and looked through the glass in

time to see Dennison's feet disappear around a corner at the top of the stairs. He leaned back and looked at the name painted on the glass; JOHN J. JOHNSTONE, Certified Public Accountant. *Odd time to be seeing a CPA.* Mooney tried the door and found it locked. *I's right; he was locking the door. They must not want any company.* He turned and walked across the street to look up at the lighted, upstairs windows. He could see the torso of a large man with folded arms, leaning against a door frame. His head was tipped slightly and he appeared to be listening intently to someone, or something, that Mooney couldn't see from below.

John Johnstone sat at his desk. Chief Dennison was seated across from him while Thumper Moran watched and listened intently.

"So, how many cases of whiskey do you have for me right now?" Johnstone asked.

"I've got fifteen-hundred and eighty-five cases of good 'Prince of Wales' blended Scotch whiskey under guard and lock and key. Canadian priced for you at one hundred and ten dollars a case."

"I'll take it *all* for one-hundred dollars a case."

"Cash?"

Johnstone looked intently at Dennison and nodded. "Cash, but it'll take me two, maybe three days to get the money sent in."

Dennison smiled. "I can work with that."

"I want to see the product and get a sample case. I pick the case."

"Don't you trust me?"

"At that price I want to make sure it's the *good* stuff. I know for a fact the Bronfman Brothers are now making all their bootleg booze in thousand-gallon redwood vats and aging it anywhere from five to ten days before they bottle it up in Yorkton. They've got a machine that can bottle and label a thousand quart bottles an hour."

Dennison shrugged his shoulders. "So? It's now the machine age."

"Don't be a smart-ass with me, Parker," Johnstone warned. "I have it from a good source that it all comes out of the same vat. They vary the price by the label, 'Blarney Fiddler' being the cheaper, lower grade, and 'Prince of Wales' is the top of the line. I'm told 'Blarney Fiddler' is one step above goat piss. I've got a dealer in Denver who'll take it all, providing it's good whiskey. *I* want to know it's quality Scotch."

Dennison nodded. "I've had this whiskey for over a year. According to the code on the label, this was produced and aged before the machine age took over the bottling industry up in Canada. Besides that, it wasn't made by the Bronfmans."

"You know bottled liquor doesn't age, don't you? It might get older, but it doesn't *age*. It only *ages* in the barrel."

"I know that," Dennison answered indignantly. "I've been in this business for a few years. Do you want to see it and take your samples tonight?"

"Night's the best, fewer snoopy people around. Let's get it over with. How far away is it?"

"It's a couple of miles out of town."

"Thumper, go get the car and pick us up around in front."

"Gotcha, Boss."

From below, Deputy Mooney saw the big man put on his hat and start shrugging into his coat.

It looks like somebody's moving, he told himself. *Time to get back to my truck.*

CHAPTER FIFTY-TWO

Deputy John Mooney trotted back to his truck. "I hope this damned thing hasn't been sitting in the cold too long and doesn't wanna start for me," he mumbled, as he turned on the key and pushed his foot on the starter. *C'mon, baby, talk to me.* The engine groaned several times, backfired, and chugged to life. "Whew," he breathed softly, as he pulled the buffalo robe up over his shoulders and drove slowly to a point where he could see the front of the building he had been watching.

The upstairs office window went dark and a minute later Police Chief Parker Dennison and John Johnstone stepped out of the door. As Johnstone checked the door, headlights appeared in the alley and a black Packard touring car pulled around the corner. Thumper jumped out and opened the back door. Dennison and Johnstone climbed inside. The big man shut the door, hopped back into the front seat, and the vehicle pulled away from the curb.

Mooney watched the car until it rounded a corner and disappeared from his sight. *Let's go see where they're headed.* Keeping his distance and driving slow in the dark night without headlights, he followed the Packard as it drove aimlessly on the streets of Wolf Point for a few minutes and then turned off the city streets and onto a country road. *The only thing out here these days is the old railroad yard.*

The Packard stopped at the gate of the railroad yard and soon an old man, bundled up in a heavy coat and hat, walked out of a nearby building waving his arms at the car. Mooney picked up the field glasses from the seat and quickly brought the scene into view. *There's Ole Guttormson, they must've honked the horn to get him out there.*

The old man unlocked the gate, walked out to the car, and spoke to someone through an open window. He nodded, smiled, raised his hand into the car, quickly withdrew it, and brought his hand close to his glasses. His smile widened and the bill disappeared into a coat pocket. The old man hobbled quickly to the gate and swung it wide to let the car enter. When the vehicle was clear, he closed the gate, went into the guard shack, and snapped on the lights as the car drove off across the railroad yard.

John Mooney watched until the car disappeared behind the roundhouse. *Maybe I can see them from farther down the road.* He drove slowly up the road until he saw the headlights reappear on the far side of the large block building and finally come to a stop not far from a lone boxcar. He coasted to a stop and brought up the field glasses again.

"All right, stop here at the side of the loop," Dennison ordered and pointed as the headlights lit up the boxcar. "We'll have to walk into it."

"This is where you've got the *whiskey*?" Johnstone asked.

"They think this is full of my furniture and books. The cold can't hurt it. It's a very safe place. And, I've even got a guard." He brought out a long, tin flashlight and switched it on. "Dark out there tonight, and even darker in my boxcar."

"Okay," Johnstone said, stepping out into the snow. "Let's go take a look."

The three men walked up alongside the boxcar and Dennison handed Thumper Moran a ring of keys. "The big silver one is for that lock."

Moran shook out the right key and looked questioningly up at the lock.

Dennison laughed, bent down, reached under the wheel, and dragged out the ladder. "This is an important item for me when *I* have to check the locks."

Moran leaned the ladder beside the door, climbed up, worked the lock open, and swung the hasp free. "Ready, Boss?"

"Just open the damned door," Johnstone answered.

Moran climbed down, put a gloved hand and his shoulder to the door, and slowly rolled it open.

Dennison shined his flashlight beam up on row upon row of wooden whiskey cases stacked all the way to the ceiling of the car. The end of each case bore a black stencil: **PRINCE OF WALES, Special Blend, Scotch Whiskey, Baird and Company, Inverness, Scotland.** "It didn't really come from Inverness, Scotland," Dennison confessed. "But it's some of the best Scotch whiskey made in Canada. This was barrel-aged for about six months. Not five to ten days like the Bronfmans are doing now. This *is* good whiskey."

"Would you drink it?" Johnstone asked.

"I've tasted it."

"That's not what I asked you."

"I'm not a Scotch drinker."

Johnstone rolled his eyes down at the little man. "Are my Denver customers going to be satisfied?"

"Definitely. I have no doubt that this is decent booze. I never had a complaint about it when I was running it into Chicago."

"All right, Thumper get up in there and pick out a case for us."

Moran sidestepped along inside the door, worked his gloved fingers into the cut-out handle of a wooden case at his shoulder height, and began to try to wiggle it. "There's too damned much weight on top of this, Boss," he grunted. "How about I

241

break open the end of it and pull out the bottles from there?"

"No, don't do that," Dennison called. "Get up higher. There's less weight on the upper cases."

"Here, let me move the ladder," Johnstone said, lifting it across and leaning it on the wooden cases. "You should be able to get one of those from the top rows."

Moran nodded and stepped onto the ladder to where he could reach the higher cases. With a little wiggling, he managed to get one moving and soon it came free. "I got one, Boss," he said, and pulled it out. The cases above it instantly dropped down and filled the space.

"Careful, now," Dennison instructed.

"I got it." Moran swung the wooden box onto his shoulder and slowly stepped down the ladder.

"I can reach it now," Johnstone said, holding up his arms. "Give it to me."

Moran swung the case around and dropped it into Johnstone's hands. "Here you go, Boss."

Johnstone lowered it to the snow, worked the metal latch, opened the lid, and lifted out a bottle.

Dennison moved the beam of the flashlight to the label and smiled. "There it is, John. Good premium, Prince of Wales, Scotch whiskey."

"Should we taste it here, Boss?" Moran asked, as he dropped to the snow.

"Be serious. Let's get this car locked up and out of this damned cold," Johnstone answered.

"How are *you* going to test that, John?" Dennison asked.

"I've got some good quality Scotch back at my office. I guess we'll do some comparison tasting."

"That'll be good, Boss." Moran put his shoulder to the door and rolled it shut.

★ ★ ★ ★ ★

John Mooney dropped the field glasses to the seat and drove back towards town. *Time to go give Andy a little rundown on what I've seen tonight. I'm sure he'll be interested in this.*

CHAPTER FIFTY-THREE

Andy Larson looked up at the sound of Mooney's knock. "Come on in." He pushed the pile of papers away from him and leaned back in his chair.

John Mooney opened the door and pulled off his fur cap as he walked into the office.

"Damn, John, from that grin on your face, I'd say you must've had an interesting night."

Mooney nodded, walked to the coffee pot, selected a mug, wiped the inside with his fingers, and poured it full of steaming coffee. "Andy, I got a story that'll make your day. Maybe your whole week," Mooney stated as he pulled up a chair and sat down.

"I was freezing my ass off and watching the police station like I was s'posed to, when Chief Dennison came walking out into the cold night air."

A smile turned up the corners of Larson's mouth as he stuck a cigarette in the corner of it, snapped a flame onto a match with his thumbnail, and lit it. "So, go on."

"He walked down around the corner and went upstairs to those offices above the bank. He locked the door behind him, so I had to stand across the street and see what I could from down there. All I could see was a big fella standing in a doorway, but he was sure as hell listening to someone talking." He paused and took a sip from his coffee. "Oh, yeah, the name, fresh-painted on the glass door downstairs, is John Johnstone, Certified Public Accountant. I thought it a bit odd the chief going to an accountant this time of night, so I hung around. Pretty soon, I see the lights go out up there so I headed back to my truck. A big fancy car comes out of the alley and picks up the chief and this taller fella I took to be Johnstone, the CPA. They drove out to the old railroad yard and Guttormson let 'em in. They rode around behind the old roundhouse and parked near a boxcar setting off by itself. I drove up to where I could see 'em through my field glasses and watched 'em open that boxcar. Now, Andy, what do you guess they had in that boxcar?"

Larson shrugged and blew a cloud of smoke. "I don't know, *potatoes?*"

Mooney laughed. "No, it was full of boxes. Wooden boxes with writing on the ends."

"Writing that said what?"

"I couldn't tell from where I was, but they had handles cut out on the ends of the boxes like wooden booze cases. Then they got one case out of the boxcar and opened it. Guess what they pulled out?"

Larson looked thoughtful. "A potato?"

Mooney grimaced at his attempted humor. "Stop it now, Andy. It was a bottle of booze!"

Larson broke into a great grin. "Now, *that's* some interesting news! A boxcar loaded with liquor, right here under our noses in the railroad yard of Wolf Point, Montana. Damn fine work, John."

"What're we gonna do, Andy?"

Larson took another drag of smoke, closed his eyes, and tipped his head back. "Don't we have some dynamite around here someplace?" he asked, through a cloud of smoke.

"Hot damn, now that's an idea!" Mooney exclaimed, with glee. "We got four or five cases in that old root cellar out at the property yard on the edge of town."

"Who's got experience with dynamite?"

"That'd be Dusty. He and his brother worked in the mines over around Butte for a few years, before they came over here and got in the bar business . . . I mean *before* prohibition set in."

Larson chuckled. "I know what you mean. Who seemed to be in charge? In other words, who probably owns the whiskey?"

"Dennison had the keys and did a lot of pointing and gesturing. I'd say it belongs to the chief."

"That's good, John. Now go get some sleep. I've got to work a few things out in my mind. We'll discuss this at the meeting first thing in the morning."

Sheriff Larson looked at his deputies sitting around the table in his office, listening intently to Deputy Mooney relate his adventure the night before.

Mooney suddenly paused and looked at Larson. "It's all right if I tell them this, isn't it, Andy?"

Larson nodded. "It's not a secret. Well, not amongst us, anyway. Dusty, hang around when the others leave. I wanna talk over a couple of things with you. I'll brief the rest of you later. Get out there and make life miserable for the bad guys. Business as usual. Make sure people see you out and about checking the roads. Stay away from the rail yard. Don't piss off the local cops. Now, get going."

Chief Deputy Dusty Durbin poured himself fresh coffee, pushed a fresh unlit cigar into the corner of his mouth, and pulled up a chair. "Let me make a guess from John's story that you wanna blow up that boxcar of booze."

"Exactly. I figure in the long run it'll save me a lot of paperwork. You figure out how much dynamite we're gonna need and get it out of the root cellar in the property yard. We'll meet about four o'clock and go over the fine details. I want this to be something to impress a few people. Got it?"

Durbin smiled as he got to his feet. "Got it, Andy. I damn well guarantee it'll be impressive. And I've always had a hankering to blow up a boxcar."

Sheriff Larson drove up to the gate of the railroad yard, honked his horn, and shut off the engine before walking to the guard shack to be greeted by Ole Guttormson.

"Well, by golly, it's gute to see ya, Sheriff," Guttormson said, as he swung open the door and stuck out his hand.

"How are you, Ole? You're looking pretty good these days. You got the coffee on?"

"Ya, sure, I always got the coffee on. Come on in an' sit a spell."

The two men sat, drank coffee, and talked over things going on in the world. "I'll tell you why I'm here, Ole. Don't you have a daughter over in Helena or someplace?"

"Ya, Helga lifs over in Helena. She's got seven kids now, you know. Chust had a new boy a couple a veeks ago."

"Ole, I want you to do me a favor and go visit her for a week. I'm sure she'd like to see you."

"Ya, und I'd like to see that new little one, Lars. He vus named after my pa, but, I gotta vurk, ya know."

"The county is going to pay for your train ticket, Ole."

"By damn, vhy are dey doin' dat?"

"All right, let me explain some things to you."

Minutes later Larson stopped talking and shook out a new Camel. "That's the whole, honest story, Ole. I'd just like you to not be here for a week or so."

Ole poked his finger down into his pipe and looked up grimly at Larson. "So dat bastard, Dennison, vas playin' me fer a fool, huh? He tol' me dat boxcar was full of his furniture an' books an' personal stuff. Plowin' my roads und all dat crap to git on my good side. Pshaw. Vus I stoopid or vhat?"

Larson nodded. "You call Dennison and tell him you have an emergency at your daughter's, and you'll be back in about a week. Since this is out in the county, you'll wanna leave the keys with me, so my men can check the gates from time to time. It'll be interesting to see how often he visits his boxcar when he thinks I have the keys. Why don't you go get packed, give him a call, and we'll put you on the two o'clock train. Now I've got more things to tell you. First off, we never had this conversation."

"Ya, ve've never talked."

"Okay, now listen carefully to this . . ." When Larson finished, he smiled at Guttormson, who broke into a wide grin and nodded. "Ya, you betcha, Sheriff. Dat'll vurk fer me. Ha, ha. It von't take me long an' Helga's sure gonna be surprised vhen I knock on her door."

Sheriff Larson returned from the railroad station to join Chief Deputy Durbin standing in the garage behind the jail with rows of dynamite sticks laid out on the workbench.

"You get Ole on the train okay?" Durbin asked, rolling a red, paper-wrapped tube under his hand.

Larson glanced at his moving hand and nodded. "Damn, should you be doing that?" he asked, nervously.

Durbin laughed as he picked up the stick of dynamite and tossed it from hand to hand. "Did you know that I got the nickname, Dusty, because of all the dust I made in the mines when I was younger?"

"No . . . no, I didn't. Will you please stop doing that?"

Durbin juggled the dynamite like he was about to drop it and laughed again at the look on Larson's face. "Okay, okay," he said, laying it on the workbench. "It's safe at this point. Now, let's go over the plan."

"Okay, I want to go out there tonight, cut through the fence, and make a big mess with Dennison's whiskey. How'll we do it?"

"I've been thinking about it and here's how it'll go. We'll put four sticks of dynamite on top of each wheel and four in the springs beside the wheels. That's a total of thirty-two sticks of dynamite."

"Damn, that sounds like a lot of explosions. Why on the tops of the wheels? Can't you just stick 'em on the ground under the car?"

"If they're stacked parallel on top of the wheel, that gives a solid base and the blast goes up directly into the bottom of the car. The same for those on the springs. If it's on the ground, the blast will spread and lose a lot of its power before it reaches the bottom of the car. You want to tear through the bottom of the car, don't you? I can do this so the only thing left is the wheels and the steel frame and that'll probably be bent up a little."

"Okay, how do you balance them on top of the wheel?"

"You'll like this one. We wrap the dynamite in a strip of wet burlap. As cold as it is, the minute the wet burlap hits the metal of those wheels, it freezes and sticks in place. Just like when you were a kid and put your tongue on a pump handle in the winter."

"Yeah, I remember that. I only had to do it once to learn my lesson."

"Right. I've got some good blasting caps." He lifted a coil of heavy gray cord. "This fuse was sealed in a can, so it's still nice and dry. Fuse out in the open will absorb moisture and it's hard to judge burning time. Good fuse burns at a rate of forty-five seconds per foot. I tested some of this; it's still good and I can figure it pretty close. How many of us are going on this little caper tonight?"

"Just you and me to do the work. I'm gonna have John drive and keep a lookout for us."

"All right."

"Do you need me to help you with this?" Larson asked hesitantly, pointing at the dynamite sticks.

"No, I'd rather do it myself. You get some old burlap bags and cut 'em into strips about six inches wide and about two feet long. We'll wire 'em into bundles of four sticks, so we need to wrap it around the middle of the bundle at least a couple times. We'll wet 'em out there. A dynamite stick is eight inches long, so it'll leave the ends open and I can put the blasting caps in place. The cap only goes into one stick and it takes all the others with it. One big bang! I'll cut all the fuse so we've got about ten minutes. That gives us plenty of time to get clear and watch from a distance. Now leave me alone so I can get this done. Scram!"

Chapter Fifty-Four

Deputy John Mooney drove slowly past the chain-link boundary of the old railroad yard, randomly lit by bulbs under round enamel shades on buildings, wires above intersections and atop wooden poles. Sheriff Larson and Deputy Durbin, large canvas bags on their laps, were crowded on the seat with him.

"That's it back there," Larson said, pointing to a boxcar behind the old roundhouse. "If someone goes through the gate, it looks like an inside job. If someone cuts through the fence, it makes it look like someone with no contacts. When this thing blows up, I want all parties concerned to be suspicious of each other," Larson answered. "And possibly want to go to war."

"Okay, John, drive down here a ways, turn around, and drop us off. You can park on that side road about a half mile back there. If need be, you can get to us in a hurry. We'll signal you when we're ready to be picked up. It's almost midnight, so I doubt there'll be any traffic."

"We'll have about ten minutes when we light the fuses," Durbin added. "Plenty of time to get a ways off and watch the blasts. When the fuses are lit, we'll hold them up in the air and you should be able to see at least one of us. That'll be the signal. Burning fuses."

"Seems to me we should get a few cases of that stuff in there before you blow it all up," Mooney said, as he turned the truck and headed back towards the railroad yard.

"There might be a few unbroken bottles lying out when the

snow melts in the spring," Durbin answered. "You just have to be here when the snow starts to go."

"This is good right here, John," Larson said. "Watch for the burning fuses."

Larson and Durbin quickly floundered through the snow, stopped, and knelt by the fence. Durbin brought out a pair of wire cutters, looked up at the "GREAT NORTHERN RAILROAD PROPERTY, NO TRESPASSING" sign, and began to snip at the chain-link wires.

"That should be big enough," Larson said, folding back the mesh. "Let's go in there and do it."

They slowly walked on the trail in the snow around the boxcar, looking it over closely in the dark.

"It'd be great if there was a moon out tonight," Larson commented, as he set his bag on the snow and gingerly lifted out the first bundle of dynamite.

"Damn, Andy, relax. This stuff is safe until the lit fuse gets into the blasting cap," Durbin said, pulling the cork out of a gallon jug. "Here, gimme that thing."

"Yeah, I know," Larson said, handing him the dynamite. "The stuff still makes me a bit nervous, but I'm okay."

Durbin quickly poured water over the burlap wrapping and handed it back to Larson. "By the time you get under there, it'll be soaked in and ready to put up on the wheel. I'll wet 'em down and hand 'em under for you to put in place. When they're set, I'll put in the blasting caps and fuses. You just do what I tell you and we'll be out of here in quick time."

"You're the boss."

Fifteen minutes later Durbin crawled from under the boxcar, clapped his gloved hands together, walked around the front of the boxcar, and gathered up six fuses from the snow. "They weren't in the snow long enough to do any damage," he said, twisting the ends together and holding them out to Larson.

"Here, hold onto these and get out four or five matches. Light 'em all at once 'cause I want a good blaze when we touch 'em off. We want John to see 'em burning." Durbin turned and disappeared around the end of the boxcar. "Listen up and I'll tell you when."

Larson dug in a jacket pocket and brought out four stick matches. He stepped closer to the boxcar and rested the hand with the matches against the metal edge.

"Ready?" Durbin called.

"Say the word."

"Fire in the hole!"

Larson scratched the matches down the side of the boxcar and watched the flame flare and become steady. He held the wad of fuses up, put the matches under it, and it immediately began to spark, spit, and sputter. He gave it a quick wave over his head, hung it over the car hitch, and started walking down the trail towards the fence. He heard Durbin walking behind him and lengthened his stride. "That was like clockwork," he said, over his shoulder.

"A very smooth operation," Durbin agreed.

They ducked through the hole in the fence and stepped out on the road in time to meet Mooney's truck. Larson pulled open the door and they climbed into the slow-rolling vehicle.

Durbin pulled the door shut and began to laugh, joined quickly by Larson and then Mooney.

"How much time we got?" Mooney asked.

"I don't know," Durbin answered. "Four or five minutes. You like driving with no headlights?"

"Anybody else out here will have theirs on," Mooney stated. "About time to turn around and see what happens, isn't it?"

"Do it," Larson said.

Mooney turned into a side road, backed out, and turned the truck to face the railroad yard. "It should be about time. Wish we had a drink to help celebrate this, if it works," he said.

"If it works?" Durbin said, incredulously. "This job was handled by probably one of the finest powder monkeys in the state of Montana and you say *if it works.*"

"Hell, we can't even see the damned thing," Larson said. "We know about where it is, but that's a long way off from here."

Suddenly, a bright flash lit up and lifted a corner of the boxcar. It was followed immediately by a single, gigantic, brilliant explosion that shredded the sides, blew off the top, and lifted the metal-framed wooden box off the wheels. A massive ball of red and blue flame burst upwards, spewing blue-flame-roman-candle-like projectiles and chunks of burning wood hundreds of feet into the air to fly out over a wide area and drop, hissing, into the snow as the shock wave of sound from the explosion rattled the windows and rocked the truck.

Larson raised his hand and squinted at the bright flash. "Damn, that whiskey makes a purty blue flame. You sure we couldn't have used a little more dynamite, Dusty?" he asked with a wide grin.

Durbin put his hands to his ears. "Boy, I do nice work," he chortled.

"That was flat-assed beautiful," Mooney said, softly. "It's too bad Dennison wasn't here to see it."

"C'mon, John, let's get back to the jail. I figure the phone's gonna start ringing and as soon as it does, we'll have to come back out here to investigate." Larson pulled a silver flask from his pocket, unscrewed the cap, and lifted it in a toast towards the burning remains of the boxcar. "And we'll have a victory snort or two on the way back to the jail."

CHAPTER FIFTY-FIVE

Police Chief Parker Dennison was awakened by the telephone ringing across the room. *I've really got to move that damned phone.* He snapped on the lamp, looked at the clock, struggled from his quilts, yawned and mumbled as he hobbled across the chilly room, cleared his throat, and lifted the receiver of the candlestick phone. "This is Chief Dennison."

"Do you know what just happened?" a voice shouted.

"Who is this?" Dennison demanded.

"This is Johnstone!"

"John, it's after midnight. What's so damned important you have to call . . . ?"

"Somebody blew up my . . . no, *your* boxcar of Scotch whiskey!" Johnstone yelled.

Dennison was suddenly fully awake. "What did you just say?" he demanded.

"Hell, half the town heard the blast," Johnstone answered.

"Slow down, slow down. Are you sure it's *my* whiskey? How long ago did this happen?"

"There was a hell of an explosion out in the country about a half-hour ago. It must have rattled every window on this side of town. It woke me up and I called down to the hotel front desk to see what they knew. They said somebody was using the lobby phone to call the police and he told them it was out at the old railroad yard. I called Moran's room and sent him to take a look. He came back and said it looked like it was what's left of

255

your boxcar burning. The only real light in there was from the fire and it was about where your boxcar was sitting. He tried to roust the old man at the gate, but couldn't get him."

"He's gone for a week. He called me and told me his daughter over in Helena had an emergency and he had to get over there. Since the yards are out in the county, he took the keys to the sheriff's office. Let me call the station and find out what they know. I've got your number here someplace. I'll phone you back." He dialed the police station. Before the man answering could say anything, Dennison identified himself with a shout, "This is Chief Dennison, who's this?"

"This is Gilliam, Chief."

"Why wasn't I notified about the explosion out at the old rail yards?"

"It ain't in town, Chief, so I didn't see any reason to get hold of you. That's county business."

"Yes, you're correct, Gilliam. Send a car to get Captain Rossi and then you two come by and pick me up. I want to go out and see what this is all about."

"Yes, Chief."

Dennison looked at the list of phone numbers beside his phone and dialed the sheriff's office, but got no response. *Maybe they're already out there.*

Sheriff Andy Larson nudged Deputy Dusty Durbin, who was leaning on the fender of the official sheriff's car, and thumped the hood to wake up Deputy John Mooney, dozing behind the steering wheel inside. "Looks like we've got more company," he said, and smiled. There were five other vehicles parked in a line along the road with people looking out at the smoldering boxcar residue through field glasses. Several men had walked to the boundary fence and were trying to make out the smoking wreckage.

In the distance they could see a vehicle coming down the snow-banked road with the headlights flashing. "Must be somebody important," Durbin joked around his unlit cigar as the sound of the siren reached them.

"Yeah, I'd better get ready," Larson said, straightening his coat and squaring his hat. "This'll sure be interesting."

The police car slid to a halt on the snowy road. Captain Rossi leaped out, opened the back door, and Chief Dennison jumped down to the snow.

"What the hell are you doing standing *out here*?" Dennison demanded, as the siren ground to a whimper.

Larson glanced at Durbin, stepped forward, put on a concerned face, looked down at Dennison, and shrugged. "That's private property, Chief," he said, pointing at the fence. "We can't go in there until we get permission from the railroad."

"What . . . what do you mean by that, Sheriff?" Dennison sputtered, glancing at the rail yard. "Gottormson told me you have the yard keys."

Larson gave him a questioning look. "I'm sorry, but I don't have the keys."

"He called my office and told one of my men that he'd leave the keys with you."

Larson looked at Durbin. "You know anything about those keys?"

Durbin shook his head. "First I've heard about 'em."

Mooney rolled his car window down farther. "I don't know anything about any keys."

"There's a crime in there," Dennison sputtered. "We have to investigate it."

"There appears to have been some sort of an explosion in the railroad yards. To me, until I know better, that's an accident, not a crime." He lifted a pair of binoculars from the hood of the truck and held them towards Dennison. "Here, take a look."

Dennison's eyes blinked rapidly as he lowered the binoculars and stared up at Larson. "Well, what if someone's been injured in there?" he finally asked, handing them back to Larson.

"In his hurry to get to his daughter's, Ole must've forgotten to drop them off. Old people are like that you know. He'll probably get there and find them in his coat pocket and be embarrassed as hell."

Dennison kept looking over his shoulder at the columns of smoke and steam coming up from the remains of the boxcar.

"I doubt that there's anybody in there, so we'll wait until morning when we get permission from the railroad to go in."

Larson noticed Durbin and Rossi appeared to be sizing each other up. *This'll be interesting.*

Durbin's eyes were narrowed and his cigar rolled in the sly smile, partially hidden by his great, red beard. *It's just a matter of time, isn't it?*

Rossi returned the stare of the big deputy. *Country boy, you're gonna regret it if we tangle.*

"You wanna go in there, Chief, we'll go as soon as we get railroad permission." Larson's voice trailed off. *He must be sweating bullets under that fancy coat of his.*

Dennison sighed and shook his head dejectedly. "I guess you're right. Please try to make contact with the railroad and get permission for us to go in there and look around tomorrow. There's not much we can do tonight and I'm sure that if there's anybody in there . . . Call me in the morning." Dennison turned and walked back to his car and waited for Rossi to open the door for him. "Good night, Sheriff."

Dennison sat at his desk, numbly staring at the telephone in front of him. *What in the hell happened?* he kept repeating to himself. *Fifteen-hundred and eighty-five . . . no, fifteen-hundred and eighty-four cases of whiskey gone . . . Now I have no whiskey and very little money.* He finally, slowly, reached up, lifted the receiver, dialed the phone, and waited for Johnstone to answer.

CHAPTER FIFTY-SIX

"John, this is Parker. I have no idea what happened out there tonight. I can't get in to the yards until the railroad people arrive sometime tomorrow." He held the receiver away from his ear and waited until he could no longer hear Johnstone shouting. "I'll see what I can through the fence as soon as it's light and give you a call." Without waiting for an answer, mumbling a string of curses, he hung up the receiver and sat staring at the phone.

Would Johnstone have blown up that boxcar full of whiskey? Is this a move on his part to take over? He was buying that whiskey from me to sell and now he doesn't have it. If he has more whiskey, he can peddle it. I have no whiskey, therefore, for all practical purposes, at this point in time I'm out of the whiskey market. He's got Boticello's stock and that has to be a good-sized stash. He could have destroyed mine . . . Dennison pushed up from the chair and began to pace his office. *Like a dumb ass, I showed him what I had and where it was. Now I have nothing.*

Sheriff Andy Larson walked into his office yawning, stretching, and scratching. "Did you get hold of the railroad?" he asked Deputy Bernie Ward.

"They're sending someone out from Helena as soon as they can. I hear I missed a little fun last night."

Larson chuckled as he poured himself a mug of coffee. "No, Bernie, you missed *a lotta* fun. Guess I won't need these now," he said and tossed a ring of keys to Ward.

"Mooney told me all about it before he headed out to the rail yard this morning to see what he can through the fence as soon as it gets light enough. Must've been one hell of an explosion out there. Got any idea what could've caused it?" he asked, sarcastically, and held up the ring of keys. "Lost and found?"

Larson shrugged and nodded. "I'll tell you what I'm going to tell the railroad investigators," he said as he put a somber look on his face and took a sip of his coffee. "No, sir, I really have no idea what could have happened out there. I understand they leave a lot of stuff lying around when they close places like that. From what I could see through the fence, it might've been a carload of explosives. I know they did a lot of blasting to level some of those grades in and out of here. My guess is old dynamite. I understand the nitroglycerin crystallizes and can be mighty unstable. I'm sure your railroad people will be able to tell us more after a thorough investigation." He grinned at Ward, finished his coffee, shrugged into his coat, and pulled on his old cowboy hat. "It's almost eight o'clock and starting to get light. I'm gonna go over and introduce myself to this new accountant above the bank, if he's open this early. A man named Johnstone, or at least that's what's painted on his door. I'll be back in a little while."

"You are one hell of a fine liar, Andy," Ward stated. "But are you making so much money you need an accountant now?"

Larson heard him chuckle as he closed the door without giving him an answer.

Sheriff Larson glanced up at the lighted windows above and tried the windowed door with Johnstone's name painted on it. It was locked. Larson stepped back and looked up again at the lit windows. He could see a shadow move in the front office. *Well, let's see if the back door is locked.* He walked to the back of the building, tried the door, and found it would not open. He studied the lock, glanced both ways in the alley, dug out a pocket knife, crouched, worked the blade into the space against the lock bolt, and wiggled it several times. He felt the bolt slide back slightly and repeated the process several times until the bolt was clear and the door opened. *Maybe I should've been a crook,* he told himself as he stepped into the hallway and pushed the door shut. He glanced up at the light at the top of the stairs and began to walk quietly up the steps.

Thumper Moran sat at his desk in the outer office of John Johnstone, CPA, reading an old copy of *Western Stories Magazine.* His lips moved silently as he eagerly read about the execution of five Mexican banditos. He heard a knock and waved at the partially open door without looking up from his story. "C'mon in," he called. "I'll be with you in a minute." He finished the page and looked up to see a man dressed in a blue corduroy, sheepskin-lined coat and an old black cowboy hat standing in the doorway, smiling at him. Moran's face had a startled look as he jerked upright and his hands crossed to his armpits inside his coat. He smiled warily as he looked Larson up and down and slowly brought his hands out and laid them on the magazine. "Well, I'll be damned, Wild Bill's old cowboy friend. What's your name, Andy something or other? You wouldn't happen to know where that bastard Bohlin is, do you? I've got a little score to settle with him." His eyes narrowed and he rubbed his jaw. "And that pop you gave on my jaw doesn't put you too high on my *buddy* list. Hey, how'd you get in here?"

Larson shrugged and shook his head. "Cheap locks. It's Andy Larson, and no, Thumper, I don't know where Bohlin is. As for that pop on the jaw, that'll teach you never to try and take a gun away from someone when you're standing that close to him."

"I'll remember that, but from the looks of that mouse on

your eye, I'd say you might've forgotten one of your own rules."

Larson raised his hand and gingerly touched the swollen area by his eye. "I ran into a door the other day. You sure seem to get around, Thumper. Last time I saw you, I believe you were in the liquor business. You in that same line of work now?"

Moran smiled and shook his head.

"Is your boss in? I'd like to introduce myself to him."

"I don't think Mister Johnstone is interested in some local cowboy," Moran said, getting to his feet and opening his coat so the silver pistols in his armpits were revealed. "He's a busy man."

"Impressive hardware there, Thumper, let me show you mine." Larson slowly unbuttoned his coat and spread it open to show *his* gun belt and pistol. He smiled and pulled the other side back to reveal a silver star. "Please, tell Mister Johnstone that *Sheriff* Andy Larson would like to meet him."

Moran's eyes narrowed as they focused on Larson's badge. "You're shittin' me, aren't you?"

Larson's smile widened and he shook his head. "No, Thumper, I'm not. I *am* the sheriff of Roosevelt County, Montana."

"Why'd you tell Bohlin you were just a cowboy?"

Larson shrugged. "It seemed right at the time."

The door to the inner office was thrown open and John Johnstone stepped through it. "Something going on out here, Moran?" he asked, then turned to Larson and saw the badge. "Ah, the local law."

"This is the sheriff, Mister Johnstone," Moran said motioning with his hand. "I thought the downstairs doors were locked."

"I can see that. Is there something I can do for you, Sheriff . . ?"

"Larson, Andy Larson. I like to introduce myself to new people here in Wolf Point and let them know that, as the law in the county, I'm always willing to help the citizens when I'm needed." Larson closed his coat, stepped forward, and stuck out his hand.

Johnstone gripped his hand firmly and gave it a single shake. "Well, thank you, Sheriff, and I'll be sure to keep that in mind if I'm ever in need of the law."

"I'm the law out in the county. The enforcement of the law here in Wolf Point is under the control of Chief Parker Dennison. Have you met him yet?" Larson asked, looking Johnstone up and down. *He dresses almost as good as Parker.*

"No, I've only been in town for three days now, so I haven't had a chance to meet many people."

That's lie number one. "What brings you to a wide spot in the road like Wolf Point, Montana, Mister Johnstone?"

"I'd heard that Wolf Point might be in need of a good CPA," Johnstone answered and smiled.

"Where'd you come in from?"

"I was working for a man up in Estevan, Saskatchewan. He moved to Chicago and I didn't want to go back there, so I looked around and decided on Wolf Point."

"Ah, Estevan, whiskey-making country. I've had some trouble with people trying to run whiskey into Roosevelt County, but I'm bringing it under control. I don't like people who try to bring illegal liquor into what I consider *my* territory. You're not a whiskey man, are you Mister Johnstone?"

"Sheriff, do I look like a whiskey runner?"

"Does Al Capone look like a whiskey runner?"

"Good point."

"Now, I know that Mister Moran here was in the illegal booze business awhile back. Are you still in the whiskey business, *Mister* Moran? Oh, that's right, I already asked you that, didn't I?"

Moran glanced at Johnstone and shook his head. "No, Sheriff,

I'm not in the liquor business. I was never really in it. I was the muscle for the organization your buddy, Wild Bill Bohlin, was flying for. I can be the muscle for anybody who needs it, but I don't deal in illegal liquor."

Larson looked at Moran thoughtfully, thumbed his mustache, nodded, and smiled. "Muscle with a glass jaw, huh? Do you have a city permit for that muscle you carry under your arms, *Thumper*?"

"I didn't know I needed a permit for tools necessary to protect Mister Johnstone."

"Now that is a crock of shit," Larson stated. "Why does a CPA need a bodyguard?" He looked over at Johnstone. "You carry a gun?"

Johnstone smiled, unbuttoned his expensive, blue, wool, double-breasted, pinstriped suit coat, and spread it to show his blue shirt, suspenders, and wide, silk tie. "I keep my heat in my desk drawer," he joked as he rebuttoned his coat.

Larson nodded. "I'll remember that. You really should go over and introduce yourself to Chief Dennison. Especially if you're doing work that requires a bodyguard. Check and see if he needs permits for his fancy silver *tools*." Larson turned, paused at the door, and leaned back into the room. "It's nice to meet you Johnstone. Thumper, you be careful with those things under your arms. Some of these old country boys might not understand your cross-arm actions and bust you on the jaw. Nice meeting you, Mister Johnstone. You really should go meet Chief Dennison. You both dress *real* good. Oh, and one more thing, if I were you I'd get that lock downstairs upgraded. It wasn't that hard to get past."

CHAPTER FIFTY-SEVEN

John Johnstone stepped to the window and watched Sheriff Andy Larson walk down the street. *Dennison wouldn't blow up his own whiskey. Maybe after I paid him for it, he'd do something that stupid, but why . . . ?* "Where'n the hell's Dennison? He should have something for me by now. Get him on the phone and tell him to get over here with a report now," he told Moran, as he returned to his office. *He'd better have a damned good story about last night.*

Moran reached for his candlestick phone. "Gotcha, Boss," he said. "And then I'll go down and make sure the front door is open. He probably can't pick a lock like the sheriff."

Johnstone grimaced and shook his head. "See which one he picked and get it replaced. As a matter of fact, get them all replaced. If the sheriff can get in, I'd hate to think what a real crook could do."

Moran nodded. "I'll take care of it, Boss."

His hands clutched behind his back, Police Chief Parker Dennison paced in his office mulling the loss of his whiskey. "Over a hundred and fifty-eight thousand dollars' worth of whiskey blown to hell . . . ," he muttered over and over to himself. "Who would do that? Johnstone? Why would he do it? He was standing to make some damned good money from that transaction. Whiskey doesn't blow itself up! There's got to be an answer. Who else, besides the three of us who were out there that night, knew about it? The old man on the gate? I never had a problem like this until I showed the whiskey to Johnstone and he agreed to buy it. I don't understand . . ." The ringing of his phone broke into his thoughts.

A sharp knocking on the outer office door startled Thumper Moran, who was again deeply engrossed in his western pulp magazine. Before he could respond, the door opened and Chief Parker Dennison stepped in. Moran stood up as Captain Glenn Rossi, with a hard look on his face, filled the door behind the chief. Rossi's badge could be seen over the top of Dennison's hat. *Damn, I know that man from someplace.*

"I'm here to see Johnstone," Dennison said, as he strode across the office.

Moran stood, shrugged, and pointed at the door across the room just as Johnstone opened it.

"I'm here," he said. "Come on in, Chief, we've got to talk. You two stay out here."

Thumper Moran looked carefully at the tall policeman. "Don't I know you from someplace?"

Rossi smiled slightly. "Yeah, you do, *Thumper,*" he answered. "You did a job on a friend of mine back in Chicago a few years ago. Does Boner Matacotti ring a bell?"

Moran shook his head and a shiver ran up his spine. "No, can't say that it does," he answered, keeping his voice steady. *Shit, I killed him for Capone with a baseball bat. Matacotti put out the word that he was gunning for Capone, so Al had me beat him to the punch.*

Rossi's eyes narrowed and his face hardened. "You think on it, *Thumper,*" he said, pulling up a chair and swinging his feet up onto the desk. Without taking his eyes off Moran's face, he shook out a cigarette and lit it with a silver lighter. "Someone caved his head in with a baseball bat, *Thumper,*" he said, through a cloud of smoke. "Boner Matacotti."

Johnstone ushered Dennison into his office and closed the door. He sat at his desk and pointed to the chair in front of it. "Sit down, Parker. Do you have anything new to tell me?"

"I drove out there again when it was light enough to see and used binoculars. I can't get inside there until I get permission and the damned railroad unlocks it. There's a big melted circle and all I could see were the black wheels and some twisted metal. Do you know what's going on? What happened? I'm out over a hundred and fifty-eight thousand dollars and a boxcar of quality Scotch whiskey. Sheriff Larson said something to me awhile back about a whiskey war here in Roosevelt County. Is this the opening shot of that war?"

Johnstone shrugged and leaned forward onto his elbows. "Let me tell you something I found out this morning about your boxcar of Prince of Wales Scotch whiskey. I remembered a story about a stolen load of liquor awhile ago and made a couple of phone calls back east before you got here. About a year and a half ago, just this side of Minneapolis, there was a train that had the wheels of ten freight cars all freeze up. It seems somebody had poured sand into the gear boxes and the train had to be sidetracked for repairs out in the middle of nowhere. The first night, there were no guards on the train and someone broke into it and stole a lot of good Scotch whiskey. *Prince of Wales Scotch whiskey.* Somewhere around thirty-five-hundred cases. A full boxcar will carry sixteen-hundred cases . . . but you knew that didn't you? That's a lot of trucks and cars needed to move all that liquor. They did a good job for a one night heist. Someone had the inside track and knew what that train was carrying from Canada down to Minneapolis. It was a very smooth, well-thought-out operation. They knew exactly when and where to put the sand in the gear boxes to stop the train where it had to be sidetracked. Pretty smart people put that operation together."

Dennison, blank-faced, returned Johnstone's stare.

"You don't have anything to say?" Johnstone asked.

"No."

"Where'd you get that boxcar load of Scotch?"

"I bought it."

"Who from?"

"It was over a year ago."

"What did you pay for it?"

Dennison grinned. "That's none of your business, but I gave you a good additional discount so you would have gotten a nice profit."

"I don't think you paid anything for that whiskey, Parker," Johnstone said, slowly. "I think *you* were the brains behind that train heist. You're a smooth, smart man with good contacts. I don't know how you did it, but I'm sure that whiskey I looked at last night was from the Minnesota train heist. Being the brains, you kept half the take."

Dennison was expressionless, but his eyes began to blink rapidly and he shook his head.

Johnstone sat back. "There's still a sizeable reward for information on that stolen whiskey."

Dennison laughed. "What whiskey?" His face was immediately sober again. "This isn't funny. I lost a lot of money last night."

"Do you have any more whiskey?"

Dennison shook his head. "Not that quality." His eyes hardened. "No, John, to tell you the truth, I *don't* have any liquor remaining. That was my nest egg. With the cash I'd have made from that carload, I'd have been able to buy more . . ."

"And been in competition with me," Johnstone interrupted.

"No, there's enough business going through Roosevelt County for both of us." Dennison raised his hand and tapped a finger as he rattled off cities. "Billings, Kansas City, Seattle, Portland, Omaha, Denver, Phoenix, Tucson. Hell, we can control the whole western half of the country if we play it right."

Johnstone laughed, stood, and pointed at the door. "Parker, you're out of chips and out of the game. Now get the hell out of my office. You're finished in the liquor business!"

Parker Dennison's face hardened as he slowly rose to his feet and shook his fist at Johnstone. "Don't forget who's the law here in Wolf Point."

Johnstone grinned and pointed at the door again. "Don't force me to bring out Boticello's files, *Chief.* He kept meticulous records of his liquor transactions and other things . . . Things like installing a police chief in Wolf Point who would give him free reign on liquor distribution. Liquor brought in, and stored in the county for disbursement to points west and south. Just before his buildings in Estevan were destroyed by that big fire, I went through his files and records and secured papers that may be very incriminating to certain people. Do you understand me, Parker? Do *you* understand me?"

Dennison stood, his eyes slits of anger and his lower lip stretched tight against his teeth. "You bastard," he hissed and jabbed a finger at Johnstone. "You did this, didn't you?"

Johnstone grinned at the angry little man. "You're out of the game, Parker." He shrugged. "It's your call, *Chief.*"

Dennison walked slowly to the door. He turned and stabbed a finger at Johnstone. His voice was only a whisper, *"You will regret this. Trust me, you will regret this."*

CHAPTER FIFTY-EIGHT

Sheriff Larson lit a fresh Camel from the butt in his fingers and blew smoke out across his desk. *So Thumper Moran is back with Wolf Point's new certified public accountant. He was the big man driving Johnstone's car last night. Now we've blown up a boxcar of whiskey that his boss, who's not in the whiskey business, was looking at. I'll bet there's a lot of tension in those offices right now.* He glanced up at the clock. *It's been almost three hours since I was there. I wonder if Johnstone's talked to Dennison.*

"Hey, Thumper," John Johnstone called out from his office. "Is the Packard gas tank full?"

Thumper Moran stepped into the doorway and nodded. "Ah, I think it's about half-full, Boss. We going someplace?"

"I've got a few more phone calls to make on these transactions. I've got all of Boticello's old contacts. We're going to drive up to Estevan tomorrow and pay cash for several truckloads of liquor. We'll be gone three or four days."

"Gotcha, Boss. You gonna replace the booze that was blown up last night, huh?"

"Yes, I've made a number of very good buys this morning. Cash always makes dealing faster and easier. I've got fifty cases of decent Scotch in the warehouse across town that'll help keep the customers satisfied until we get the bigger shipments. We'll be a little late with large deliveries, but it'll work out."

271

★ ★ ★ ★ ★

Parker Dennison paced his office, a steady string of mumbled curses flowing from his mouth. He pulled himself up onto his elevated desk chair, leaned back, and pressed his fingers against his aching head. *Nobody does something like this to me! Why would he have done that? He had nothing to gain by blowing up the whiskey. He was going to make a good profit on what he bought from me. If this is his first shot in a whiskey war . . . It's time for me to return fire. I'll show the bastard that I'm nobody to be fooled with!* He pushed the button on his intercom. "Captain Rossi, I need to talk to you."

Rossi pulled a chair up to Dennison's desk. "What's up, Chief?"

"Someone from the Butte railroad office is on their way here with the keys and permission to let us in there. I want you to take everyone out there and scour the area around the remains of that boxcar. Look for anything that might give us a clue as to who blew that damned thing up.

"I told you I brought you out here to go into the whiskey running business."

"Yeah, we knew that."

"Well, that boxcar blown up last night was full of whiskey. *My* whiskey. I'd made a deal to sell it and the cash was going to be my stake in what promised to eventually become one of the largest, most profitable liquor operations in the nation. It had all been very carefully planned for a long time and I had the contacts ready to go after I had the cash for the whiskey in the yard last night."

"Damn!"

"I'm trying to raise more money now, but I'll have to go back east and do it face to face."

"I understand. We'll go out and scour the area. I'll leave Peppin here to manage the office . . ."

"No," Dennison interrupted. "I'll be here to take care of the office. I want you men to go over that area with a fine-tooth comb. Understand?"

"I do," Rossi answered and stood up. "We'll be waiting at the gate."

"Nobody treats Parker Dennison like that," he mumbled as he walked to the door and snapped the lock. He crossed the room to a closet and unlocked the door. "Nobody, nobody . . ." He brought out an olive drab canvas haversack with US ARMY printed on the side. He laid it on his desk, pulled it open, and from the top pocket removed the barrel and action of his favorite weapon, a Thompson machine gun. He hefted the gun and smiled as he gripped the wooden handle and worked the action several times, enjoying the solid slam of the actuator against the receiver. "John Johnstone, nobody crosses me like you did . . ." He lowered the weapon and made shooting noises as the gun bucked up and down in front of him. He felt the goose bumps rise on his forearms as he remembered the sound and feel of the Thompson as it spewed death and destruction. He laid the weapon back on the desk and dug three loaded twenty-shot magazines from other pockets in the canvas bag. "Time to go calling . . ."

"Hey, Boss, I gotta go down the hall and take a crap," Thumper Moran called as he picked up his western pulp magazine and walked to the door.

"Are the downstairs doors locked?" Johnstone shouted.

"Yeah, Boss, I checked them again after the chief and his head dog left. They're tight against anybody except maybe the sheriff." Moran chuckled at his humor as he stepped off down the hall to the restroom. "Oh, hell, I'd best go find out which one the sheriff picked this morning and give it another check." He snapped on the light for the stairs and walked down to the back door. *Nice work, Sheriff. I'll have to put a drop bar across this door when we get back.* He worked the lock several times, and rattled the knob. "It'll do for now," he muttered as he started back up the stairs. He stopped at the top, looked back down, and snapped off the light. *Yeah, it's okay for now.*

John Johnstone looked at the bound packets of money carefully laid out in rows on his desk and smiled. "Like I said," he said softly as he riffled a stack of hundred-dollar bills. "Cash talks and bullshit walks. We're about to get back into the whiskey business in a big way." He moved the packets of money into stacks, keeping careful count, writing figures on a pad, and punching keys and racking the side handle on his adding machine. He lifted an alligator skin valise to his desk, intently recounted bundles of bills, placed them in it, and marked numbers on his pad. "That's two-hundred thousand in hard cash," he told himself as he closed the leather case and shut the hasps. "I should be able to double that in a short period and it just keeps adding up from then on." He tore the curl of paper from the top of the adding machine, smoothed it, and tucked it into the pad. "Damn, I like cash money!"

Chief Parker Dennison stepped out of the door of the police station, bundled against the cold wind in his camel-hair topcoat. He pulled the door shut, glanced both ways, squared his hat, and adjusted his blue woolen muffler with a gloved hand. His other hand was shoved in a pocket gripping the machine gun hanging vertically on a canvas strap under his arm inside his coat. It was beginning to snow and he tipped his head slightly against the wind-driven snow. He stopped in the alley across the street from the bank, looked up, and saw Johnstone's back at the window. *He's there.* He crossed the street and glanced at the closed sign on the door of the darkened bank as he passed. *It's a good thing it's Saturday and too cold for many people to be out on the streets.* He stopped and checked the John Johnstone glass-fronted door. It was locked. *There's going to be a lot of noise upstairs in a few minutes and if people were in there they might wonder what's going on.* He looked both ways and walked non-chalantly to disappear into the alley. He turned and watched the street for a minute before continuing down to the back doors of the bank and the upstairs offices. The bank door was clearly marked and Dennison tried to turn the knob on the door beside it. He glanced down. *Simple deadbolt, I was doing locks tougher than this when I was ten years old*

A minute later, Dennison stepped inside, quietly closed the door, and waited for his eyes to adjust to the dark staircase. He opened his coat, slid the Thompson up to hang across his chest, snapped a clip in, and, with experienced hands, worked a shell into the chamber. *I'll have to take out the guard and then blow through his office door before he realizes what's happening.* He thumbed off the safety and felt the other clips to reassure himself he would be able to get one out for a quick reload. He took a deep breath, let it out slowly, and, with the machine gun pointed ahead of him, began to cautiously walk up the stairs. When he could see over the top step, he stopped and scanned the empty hallway. *Easy now, easy.* Satisfied, he continued up onto the landing and, knowing the boards in the center of the hall were more liable to squeak, pressed his back to the wall and began to slowly sidestep down the hall towards the door at the end. He stopped and listened at a door marked RESTROOM, heard nothing, and continued to move down the hall. *Smells like that place could use a good cleaning.* He returned his attention to the door ajar at the end of the hall. *This is where his bodyguard sits so it can all start right here.*

Parker Dennison stopped, leaned out, took a quick peek into the partially open doorway, and saw an empty desk. He took a deep breath, slid the barrel of the machine gun through the door, stepped in behind it, and glanced around. *Nobody here.* He looked at the door to Johnstone's office. *I wonder if he's still in there.* He walked quietly over and pressed his ear to the door and heard humming. "This is it," he told himself as he thumb-checked the safety on the machine gun, took a deep breath, and put his hand down onto the doorknob.

CHAPTER FIFTY-NINE

John Johnstone hummed contentedly as he opened his ornate humidor, chose a fat Cuban cigar, and dropped the lid. He prepared the cigar, picked up a heavy gold desk lighter, and snapped a flame onto it. He rolled the end of the cigar across the flame, stuck it in his mouth, took a deep drag of aromatic smoke, and set the lighter on the desk. *Life is good,* he thought as he stepped to the window and looked out at the falling snow. *And about to get a lot better.* He blew a smoke ring against the glass and watched it spread and dissipate. *We'd best get out of here before the full storm sets in or else leave later.* "Hey, Thumper, you out there?" he called.

Dennison swung the Thompson towards the hall door. *I wonder where in the hell Thumper is?*

"See if you can find out how long this snow is supposed to last and if it's okay to head out for Estevan tomorrow."

Dennison heard the knob on Johnstone's door rattle, swung the barrel of the gun up, and flattened against the wall behind it.

Johnstone's head appeared around the door and he looked out at Moran's desk. He muttered something as he stepped back and pulled the door shut.

Dennison's heartbeat sounded to him like a bass drum as he lowered the barrel of the gun and tried to get a deep breath. "Damn," he whispered, as he glanced at the hall door, walked back over and closed it, but found the lock didn't work. "Oh, hell," he muttered. "This'll be fast." He stepped to Johnstone's office, turned the knob, and jerked it open.

Johnstone was standing again looking out the window. "Where in the hell were you . . . ?" He saw the reflection in the window was not Moran and spun around, making a dive for his desk drawer.

The Thompson in Dennison's hands cut a short swath of noise, fire, smoke, and lead over the top of the desk. The first two slugs caught the alligator skin valise, sending it spinning through the air. The next three slugs snapped into the open doors of the safe, making gray, mushroom patterns of flattened lead on the back wall and kicking banded stacks of money off the shelves and out onto the floor. Four balls of hot lead caught John Johnstone across the chest and for a millisecond his forward motion was stopped as his sightless eyes closed and he dropped heavily to the floor. A slug hit the side of the adding machine, sending it spinning off the desk. Three more slugs chewed chunks out of the wall before Dennison was able to let up on the trigger and raise the smoking machine-gun barrel up onto his trembling shoulder. He coughed, his eyes blinked rapidly in the smoky air, and he used a hand to fan the smoke away from his face.

He stood motionless, the hair on the back of his neck bristled, and he had that inner feeling that he was not alone. He slowly turned enough to see over his shoulder.

Thumper Moran, hat tipped back on his head, stood in the open doorway of the outer office, his twin silver forty-fives held straight out from his shoulders. "Hello, *Shorty*," he said softly and smiled.

Dennison spun, but the strap hung the barrel of the Thompson up on his shoulder as the automatic pistol in Moran's right hand blew out a ball of flame and the slug punched through the scarf wrapped around Dennison's throat, blowing a cloud of red mist into the air behind his backward falling body. His hand cramped in a death grip and he fired the rest of the clip into the ceiling as he crashed onto his back and the red mist settled, coloring his face. His eyes blinked rapidly and then remained open, staring at the ceiling as if he were trying to comprehend what had just happened. His head dropped off to the side at an unnatural angle, a trickle of blood ran from his lips, and his glazed eyes stared at a packet of hundred-dollar bills not far away. Smoke trickled out of the barrel of the machine gun still held to his shoulder by the canvas strap.

Thumper Moran holstered his pistols as he walked across the room and looked down at Chief Dennison. "Well, Shorty, it looks like Wolf Point will be wanting a new police chief again." He fanned his hat at the lingering smoke as he continued on into the inner office. "Damn, this place is a mess," he said as he stepped around the room and stopped to look at Johnstone's body lying facedown behind his desk. "It looks like more than one person made a mistake up here today," he said, kicking a bundle of bills in front of his foot and using his heel to grind out Johnstone's cigar. He picked up the alligator skin valise, turned it to examine the two small holes in one side and the larger holes with bits of shredded money sticking out of them on the other side, set it on the desk, pushed the hasps open, and looked inside. "I think this is still usable and nobody'll care about a few torn bills."

He swept a clear space on the desk with his hands and began to pick up bound packets of bills from the floor. He finished his money cleanup by carrying the remaining money from the safe and adding it to the stacks on the desk. He noticed the pad with the rows of figures lying on the floor and picked it up. The number two-hundred thousand was written at the bottom of the columns. "I'd make a guess this is how much was in the case to take to Estevan," he told himself, looking down at

Johnstone's bloody body and over his shoulder at Dennison's blank eyes. "The two other men in this room are dead, so the way I figure it, all this money is mine. Now I can go to Estevan, make one hell of a booze buy, and continue in the business, or I can go to Florida and live damned good for a long time," he muttered to himself as he looked at the numbers again. "A very *safe*, easy life."

Moran put the rest of the money in the valise, closed the lids, pushed the hasps closed, tapped the top, and told himself, "There's gotta be at least a half million bucks in here." *Time to roll. Oh, yeah, Johnstone has that fancy silver pistol in his desk drawer, doesn't he?* He pulled open the center drawer, lifted out Johnstone's engraved, ivory-gripped, silver-plated revolver, carefully examined it, smiled, and laid it on the desk.

"Tell you what I'm gonna do, *Stone Man*," he told the body on the floor. "I'm gonna trade this gun for one of mine. Not exactly the same quality, but it's the one that killed the chief." He brought the pistol from under his left arm, wiped it with his coattail, knelt, pressed it into Johnstone's cold hand, and wiped it again. "Now it looks like *you* put that slug through the chief's throat." He picked up the pistol from the desk and pushed it into the empty holster under his arm. "There, now wasn't that easy? Not a matched set anymore, but what the hell . . . ?" He turned slightly and glanced out the window to see a group of people standing across the street looking up and pointing at the window. He spun away from the window. "Damn, time to get my ass outta here!"

Thumper Moran gave the room a cursory look, opened the ornate humidor, pulled out a handful of cigars, and stuffed them into an inside coat pocket. *I can afford to smoke these things now.* He grabbed the handles of the alligator valise and strode out of the room, slamming the door behind him. As he shrugged into his topcoat in the outer office his mind was already working on a plan to go to the hotel for his clothes, fill the Packard with gas, stop by the warehouse to pick up a few cases of Scotch, drive east for a day or two, then head south to Florida to begin his new life of leisure and wealth.

CHAPTER SIXTY

Thumper Moran went down the stairs three at a time, stopped at the door, and listened. Cautiously he opened it, looked both ways, stepped out, pulled it shut, and darted to the garage doors across the alley. He pulled the doors open and was hit with a wave of warmth from the three electric heaters in the room. Even in the cold Montana winters a car will start in a heated garage. He opened the door, tossed the valise on the seat, slid in, turned the key, and pushed his foot down on the starter switch. The engine roared to life; he drove slowly into the alley, then turned and headed into the street. He waved at the growing crowd of people who were pointing at the upstairs window. His smile turned to a chuckle and then a deep belly laugh as he drove to the hotel to pick up his belongings.

Police Captain Glenn Rossi stood looking across the wide, melted, burned crater and the blackened steel remains of the frame of the boxcar and the two sets of blackened wheels that had been rolled down the tracks by the explosion. "This isn't good," he muttered to himself as he watched his men wandering around and looking down in the snow beyond the crater.

Peppin suddenly knelt, shoved his hand into the snow, and leaped up, swinging a bottle above his head. "I found another one!" he shouted.

"Okay, that's enough," Rossi shouted and waved his hands. "C'mon in, so we can have a talk."

Gilliam, Barqhart, Lamey, and Peppin slowly walked back to him, constantly looking down at the snow. Each carried three unbroken quart whiskey bottles with remains of charred labels on them.

"Wait'll the chief sees these," Gilliam said, proudly.

"Okay," Rossi said, holding up his hand. "I wanna tell you something before we take these in and show them to the chief. I'm sure this won't be a surprise, but the chief's not gonna be too happy about this blown-up whiskey business."

"What do you mean?" Barqhart asked. "We got twelve bottles of drinkable evidence here."

"You know we came out here to pose as cops and run liquor," Rossi said.

All four of the uniformed men nodded.

"That boxcar of liquor *belonged* to the chief. That whiskey was the initial stock for this whole liquor operation. He took me out here the first day and showed it to me. He said he might have someone who was willing to buy the whole carload and that would be a big start. That's all I know up to now. We'll have to show him this, tell him what we've seen, and see what he does."

"He's got a damned mean temper," Peppin said. "It ain't gonna be nice."

"All right, when we get back, you men come into the squad room, but keep it down. Let me go in and tell him first. I'm sure he already knows what it was that got blown up." Rossi motioned towards the car. "Let's go back to the station and get it over with."

As the police car neared the station the men inside could see several people milling around in front of the door.

"I wonder what this is all about?" Rossi said, as Barqhart pulled the car up to the curb.

Rossi stepped from the vehicle and raised his hands towards

the people, who were all talking at once. "All right, *one* person tell me what's going on."

A man stepped forward. "There's been some kind of a shooting at the offices over the bank," he said, pointing down the street.

"What do you mean, some kind of a shooting?" Rossi asked.

"A couple of people were walking across the street when they heard a bunch of fast gunshots and saw flashes in the upstairs window. They think they saw a man fall, but it was so quick they aren't sure."

"Okay, did you go in and tell the chief?" Rossi asked, motioning towards the station door.

"We went in, but there's nobody around," another man volunteered.

Rossi turned to his men. "The chief should be here. Let's go in and see if we can find him."

The men filed silently into the squad room, put their charred evidence on the booking bench, and stood looking at each other as Rossi walked across and knocked on their boss's door. "Chief Dennison, we're back," Rossi said. He knocked again. "Hey, Chief." There was no response, so he opened the door, looked inside, and turned back. "He's not here. I wonder where in the hell he went?"

The men seemed to relax and began to talk to each other.

Chief Deputy Dusty Durbin hung up the phone and walked into Sheriff Larson's office. "I just got a phone call, Andy, from Stillings over at the Texaco station and he said somebody came in and told him people were standing in the street downtown claiming they'd heard shooting upstairs over the bank."

"Didn't anybody call the police?"

"He said the guy told him there was nobody in the police station."

"That's odd. I wonder where Parker and his band of merry men are? Those offices up above the bank are where I talked to that phony CPA Johnstone awhile ago. He had my old pal, Thumper Moran, up there with him. Maybe we better go over there and see what's happening. Did he say how much shooting there was?"

"Nope, somebody just heard shooting."

"Okay, let's you and I wander over there and see who got shot. I can use the exercise."

CHAPTER SIXTY-ONE

Sheriff Andy Larson and Chief Deputy Durbin turned the corner in time to see the police car stop and Captain Rossi and the other four cops climb out and walk up to the growing crowd on the sidewalk, talking and pointing at the window across the street.

"All right," Rossi began. "Who saw the shooting?"

Larson and Durbin trotted up and joined the crowd.

An older couple stepped forward and raised their hands. "We did, Officer," the man volunteered.

"Tell me about it," Rossi ordered.

The man cleared his throat and pointed up at the window. "My name is Vince Tidball. Agnes and I were walking along, minding our own business, when we heard this bunch of fast shots and looked up to see a couple of flashes in that window . . . It was like *ratatatatat.*"

"I'm sure I saw a man fall," Agnes interrupted.

"We were looking up and there was one more flash and the sound of a shot, *bang,*" Tidball continued. "And exactly after that shot there's another bunch of shots and flashes, *ratatatatat.* We just stood here with our mouths open, listening to the shots and looking up at the flashes in the window. That whole thing didn't take but a minute, probably less. It got real quiet, and then we could see the shadow of someone moving up there and then we saw this fella come around and stand with his back to the window for a minute."

"He was a big man, with a hat on," Agnes said.

"Could you see his face?" Rossi asked. *It had to be that bastard Moran. I wouldn't put it past him to kill a few more people.*

They both shook their heads.

Rossi looked over their shoulders at the crowd. "What do you think, *Sheriff?*" he asked.

Larson glanced at Durbin, smiled, turned back to Rossi, and shrugged. "That's up to Chief Dennison, isn't it? This appears to be city business."

The other policemen moved up into a line behind Rossi.

Hmmm, this could get interesting, Larson told himself. "By the way, where is Chief Dennison?"

Rossi bit his lip and tilted his head. "Ah . . . he'll be here in a few minutes."

"Then I guess we'll all just stand here and wait for the chief to arrive and take command of the operation," Larson stated and smiled.

"How long are you gonna wait?" someone in the crowd called out.

"Yeah," another chimed in. "What if there's been a killin' an' the killer's gettin' away, huh?"

Rossi was beginning to show signs of nervousness. "All right, all right," he said. "I'll send one of my men to go find the keys. Who knows where the banker lives? He should have the keys."

Several people raised their hands.

"Why don't ya just smash the glass in the door?" someone in the crowd suggested.

Larson nudged Durbin. "C'mon, I know the back way." He stopped and motioned to the policeman. "Hey, Rossi, go over to the fancy painted glass door and I'll let you in."

Rossi looked at him questioningly. "Have you got a key, Sheriff?"

"No, I just said I'd let you in. Go to the door and I'll be right there." Larson, followed closely by Durbin, crossed the street and disappeared down the alley where they saw the open garage door.

"It ain't cheap to heat a garage like that," Durbin stated, trotting over, walking around and unplugging the three glowing heaters. "Someone must've left in a hell of a hurry. They didn't even bother to turn these things off and that could've started a fire in here."

Larson dug out his knife, quickly opened the door, and beckoned Durbin to join him. "Let's get around in front and let the cops in."

Durbin looked at the door as he walked through. "How'd you unlock . . . ? Oh, never mind."

They opened the inside door and saw Rossi, the policemen, and a wall of people standing at the glass door at the end of the hall.

Larson strode down the hall, turned the latch, and pushed the door open. "There you go, Captain. We'll wait down here for the chief to arrive. You folks stay out there, please." He pulled the door shut and Rossi and the other uniformed men pushed past him and started up the stairs.

"Smells like gun smoke, doesn't it, Dusty," Sheriff Larson said as he leaned back and watched the last of the cops disappear upstairs.

"Holy shit!" someone shouted from upstairs.

Larson locked the door and started up the stairs three at a time. "Let's go, Dusty!"

They charged into the outer office to find the policemen filling the door to Johnstone's office. None of them were speaking as Larson and Durbin pushed through to see what they were looking at.

The first thing they saw was Chief Dennison's body lying on the floor, his head in a pool of blood and his unseeing eyes staring across the floor at their feet.

"I guess we know where the chief is now," Durbin said softly and chuckled.

"Geez, Dusty," Larson mumbled, elbowed him in the ribs, and frowned at him.

Durbin made a face and shrugged.

Rossi, standing in the center of the room, spun and glared.

Gilliam, Barqhart, Peppin, and Lamey stood with looks of disbelief and shock on their faces.

Rossi rubbed his thumb on his chin and his lips moved as if trying to say something, but no words came out. "There's another one over here," he finally said, pointing behind the desk.

Larson and Durbin walked to where they could see Johnstone lying by his desk.

"Yeah, that's Johnstone, all right," Larson said, turning back to Rossi. "And he's really been chewed up. I'd say it was by that chopper the chief's got clutched in his hand. Well, what're you gonna do now, *Captain*? You've got one hell of a battle scene here in this room."

Rossi shrugged and rubbed his hands together nervously. "I really don't know," he said softly. "I've never had to handle anything like this before."

"Are you guys really cops?" Larson asked, exasperation in his voice. "Or just part of Dennison's grand scheme to own the booze market running through Roosevelt County?"

"We were cops," Peppin volunteered. "But, we were traffic cops, not homicide. We gave out tickets and stuff like that."

Larson made a sweeping motion with his hand. "So you've never handled anything like this?"

Rossi shook his head. "No, we've never worked a murder scene. Look, here's the chief, dead on the floor and another guy over there probably gunned down with that Thompson on the chief's chest. Ah, hell . . . we've seen shooting before, but we never had to investigate them. Shit, we're traffic cops."

"All right," Larson said, shaking a Camel from the pack in his hand. "Somebody go down and tell those people everything's under control, but we can't release anything right now."

Rossi snapped his fingers. "Gilliam, go down and take care of that."

"Don't anybody touch anything," Larson ordered. "Dusty, use the phone in the outer office and get someone in our office to bring the camera over and start taking pictures. You've got to have cameras over at your office, Rossi. Does anybody know how to use them?"

Rossi shook his head. "No."

Larson gave a snort of disgust. "Why don't all of you go back to the station for now? Make some calls to Helena and see if you can get hold of somebody from the State Crime Bureau or the Federal Marshal's office. Go out the back door so nobody sees you leave. Go on, get out of here. Go to the station and wait for me."

Rossi suddenly straightened up and glared at Larson. "How in the hell do you . . . ? What makes you think . . . ? We're the official law enforcement here in Wolf Point and we don't take orders from some backwoods lawman."

Larson's eyes hardened; he crossed the room in two steps and stood toe to toe with Rossi. "Listen, Rossi, you asshole," he hissed. "I'm not in the mood for any of your shit. As of right now I'm officially heading this investigation until someone from a higher office gets here and takes it over from me. Either get your people out of here, or you're gonna end up on the floor with those other two!"

Rossi glanced at the other three policemen standing by the door watching him. "You can't . . ."

Larson's fist caught him on the point of the jaw; Rossi's eyes rolled up, he rocked back onto his heels and then crumpled like a wet sock.

Durbin pounced through the door and grabbed Barqhart and Lamey by the nape of the necks with a crusher grip that made both men stand on their toes as he dragged them backward into the outer office. "I'll smack your heads together like a couple of melons," he threatened, around his unlit cigar. "That'll bring the floor count up to five." He looked down at Rossi lying on the floor and chuckled. "Damn, Andy, I wanted to do that!"

Peppin shook his head as his hands shot up into the air. "Hey, easy, easy. I'll do whatever you say. Just . . . you tell me what you want me to do."

Larson stood looking down at Rossi and rubbing his hand. "Damn, that hurt," he muttered. "All right, when I tell you, I want you all to put your guns on the floor real slow, then get your captain on his feet and go back to your station. I'll be over there in a while to discuss what's gonna happen next."

Durbin released his grip on the men, shoved them forward, and quickly stepped back, drawing his pistol, but letting it hang down at his side. "Put your hands up 'til we tell you to move."

Barqhart and Lamey glanced at each other questioningly as if looking for direction, then at the pistol in Durbin's hand, and quickly raised their hands.

"Don't be stupid," Durbin warned. "Keep your hands up . . ."

Gilliam clumped up the stairs and stopped when he saw the men with their hands in the air looking bewildered and Captain Rossi laid out on the floor in the next room. "What's going on?"

"Just do what they say," Peppin said meekly.

Gilliam nodded and raised his hands.

"Now," Larson ordered, continuing to rub his hand. "Very slowly, one at a time, lift your pistols out and put them on the floor. Do the captain's last and then get him on his feet."

The uniformed men carefully unholstered their pistols and put them on the floor.

Larson pointed at Rossi, who was beginning to stir. "Get him up and take him to the station. I should go over there and lock you bastards up right now. Get him out the back door."

Rossi was rapidly blinking his eyes and rubbing his chin as they silently helped him stand. He jerked his arms free, coughed, and cleared his throat. "Sheriff, you are a dead man," he said, his voice barely a whisper. "You *are* a dead man."

Larson walked over and again stood toe to toe with Rossi. His eyes narrowed and a muscle on the side of his face twitched as he spoke through clenched teeth. "This is about the third time you and I've tangled." He put his finger on the tip of Rossi's nose. "You've pushed your luck with me for the last time and now you are about to find out just what a mean bastard I can be!"

Barqhart and Lamey grabbed Rossi's arms and pulled him backward through the door. "We're leaving, Sheriff. We've had enough. We'll be at the station."

Durbin holstered his pistol as he watched the five men crowd into the hall and disappear down the stairs. He turned back to Larson, "I don't think that's the smartest thing you've ever done, Andy."

Larson shrugged and began to walk slowly around the office. "We'll see. Maybe, with any luck they'll make a run for it and we won't have to mess with them anymore. Where's Mooney with the camera?"

CHAPTER SIXTY-TWO

Larson stepped to the window in time to see the five uniformed men cross the street and crowd into the police car. Rossi glared and shook his hand back up at the window before ducking in and slamming his door. "That man is dangerous," Larson told himself, turning back to look at the room.

Deputy John Mooney came into the outer office and prepared to take pictures. "The back door was open," he said as he walked into Johnstone's office. "Damn, look at this mess," he stated and set off the first flashbulb.

Larson knelt, lifted a spent cartridge from the floor, and carefully turned it as he examined it. "Hey, Dusty," he said as he held out the cartridge. "Look at this. Remember the thing we noticed about all the empty shell casings we recovered after Chief Grubb and Billy Hollis were gunned down?"

Durbin nodded as he took the empty cartridge; he looked at it carefully and his cigar bobbed as he broke into a big grin. "I'll be damned. This is from the same gun."

"How can you tell that?" Mooney asked, looking at the cartridge between Durbin's fingers.

"Look at the base, John," Durbin said, turning it towards Mooney. "See how that firing pin barely hits the edge of the primer and the ejector paw tears the rim of the shell."

Mooney adjusted his glasses and leaned closer. "Damn, it hardly does touch the primer and that is a deep ejector mark."

"If the firing pin was any more off center, it wouldn't hit the

293

primer hard enough to fire it," Larson said, taking the empty shell casing from Durbin. "And that is a very distinctive ejector dig. I'm sure when we do the comparison we'll find all three sets of these casings are identical and that tells me this Thompson was used in all three of the shootings. In other words, the *chief* did all three killings."

"He must've had a powerful master plan," Mooney said. "Do you think he just slipped into town, gunned down his target, and left?"

Larson nodded. "I don't see why not. He's a cop, so he knew what he was doing. Cops make the most dangerous criminals because they think they have all the answers. No one saw him in town at night. He did what he was here for and disappeared. It would seem he had it all worked out a long time ago. To him it was just a matter of taking it one step at a time."

Deputy Bernie Ward walked into the office and stood looking around. "Damn . . . look at this . . . Oh, yeah, we got a call from Helena that there'll be a Federal Marshal and some State Crime Bureau people over here sometime Monday morning. Where're the cops?"

"They're back at the station," Durbin answered.

"Locked up?"

"No, we sent them back over there to wait."

"Wait for what?"

"For us to come lock them up," Larson answered and laughed. "God, this day has turned into a hell of a mess, hasn't it?" He leaned over to look at Johnstone's body. "Johnstone's got a forty-five auto in his hand and I'd guess that's what took out Dennison's Adam's apple."

"You think they shot each other?" Durbin asked. "Where's that muscle of Johnstone's?"

"Thumper Moran," Larson said. "Hey, Dusty, remember the open garage door across the alley?"

"Yeah."

"I'd bet Thumper left that door open when he was getting the hell out of town."

"That open door on the safe makes me wonder how much money he got out of here with. I have no doubt Johnstone had plenty of cash on hand. Especially if he was looking to buy Dennison's whiskey."

As the five policemen climbed out of the car in the station garage they were all angrily talking and pulling off their uniforms.

"Shut the hell up for a minute!" Rossi shouted as he unbuttoned his uniform coat and loosened his tie. "You'll take our car to the hotel, pack what's necessary, and we'll get the hell out of here as fast as we can. I can't believe that jerk sheriff trusted us to come back here and wait for him to come and lock us up. Peppin, you get my stuff I told you about and bring it when you come to pick me up. Got that?"

"What're you gonna do right now?" Lamey asked, dropping his pistol belt to the floor and kicking it away.

"I've got a couple of things to take care of in here," Rossi answered. "Now go get changed and packed and come back here to pick me up. Be back in an hour."

The others piled into the vehicle they had originally driven to Wolf Point and Rossi opened the door to the station and disappeared inside. Muttering to himself, he got out the ring of all the station keys and walked to the arms room. He unlocked a padlock on a gun rack and pulled the end of a chain that ran through the trigger guards of all the weapons. He lifted a scoped M1903A Springfield sniper rifle free and worked the bolt several times. "This'll do fine," he told himself as he unlocked an ammunition drawer, selected a box of cartridges, and one-by-one pushed five cartridges down into the magazine. "I know the bastard will walk in front of that window upstairs sooner or later and when he does . . ." He chambered a round and snapped on the safety. "Time to go hunting." He buttoned up his coat, squared his hat, pulled on his gloves, slung the rifle over his shoulder, and headed for the door.

CHAPTER SIXTY-THREE

Thumper Moran slid a fourth case of Scotch whiskey into the trunk of the Packard and stood back to look at his work. He had packed his clothes from the hotel room, filled the gas tank, and was now loading what he considered the last of his traveling necessities. "Six more cases and it's time to hit the road. There's a nice profit margin on ten cases of whiskey, especially when I didn't pay anything for them in the first place. Maybe I should take more . . . No, just get the last six loaded and hit the road."

"One last spin through Wolf Point," he told himself as he turned onto the road that would take him down the main street of town. In the distance, walking towards him on the side of the snow-banked street, was a tall man in a police uniform. *Damn, that's Rossi.* Moran turned the car onto a side street and turned to watch out the rear window.

Rossi stopped on the corner and looked both ways. *The alley across the street from the bank would be the best place to see that window and I can brace this rifle against the wall to shoot.*

Moran sat very still when Rossi appeared to be staring at his car. *He can't see me in here. Damn, he's got a rifle slung over his shoulder. Where in the hell is he going with that?* He watched as Rossi continued up the street and disappeared around a corner. "This really isn't any of my business," he told himself as he put the car in gear and drove slowly up the street. *What the hell is he gonna do with that rifle?* His curiosity got the better of him and he circled the block to see where Rossi was going. He pulled the car over to the curb, put it in neutral and pulled on the hand brake, and stepped out of the car. *It'll stay warm.*

Standing behind a telephone pole at the mouth of the alley, Rossi nervously rubbed his gloved hand on the rifle sling as he looked at the upstairs window across the street. He could see shadows of people moving. The big deputy walked across, stopped, and, with his back to the window, appeared to be examining the ceiling. Rossi slid the rifle free and held it vertically behind the pole as he watched the window. "C'mon, Sheriff," he muttered, as he slowly positioned and repositioned the rifle so he could lower and fire it quickly. "One shot, just give me one shot."

Thumper Moran stood peering around the side of the building on the corner across the street. *He's gonna try to shoot somebody in that window up there,* he thought as he watched Rossi repositioning the rifle. *Is it Sheriff Larson or one of the deputies? Where are the rest of the cops? Do you suppose he thinks I'm up there? I know he wants revenge for his buddy, Boner Matacotti.* Moran leaned back against the building and blew into his cupped hands as he looked for people walking in the area. *Too damned cold for people to be out if they don't have to.* He took another quick peek around the corner, shoved his hands into his pockets, put his head down, and walked briskly across the street and out of sight from the alley. He stopped, leaned his back against the building, and shivered. *Why'd I leave my damned gloves in the car?* He took a deep breath, dug an expensive cigar out of his pocket, put it between his teeth, and rolled his tongue on the tobacco as he looked back at the cloud of exhaust surrounding the back of the Packard with the engine running. *All right, I don't think this is any of my business. I've got a case full of money, a fancy car loaded with gas and booze over there, and I'm chewing on a dollar cigar. Just get back in the car and go.* He unbuttoned his coat, crossed his arms inside, felt the warm silver pistols, and again glanced at the big car. *But,* he argued, *I got Rossi down there in the alley and he wants revenge for me thumping his buddy, Boner. He won't give up on it very easy. I'll always have to be looking out for him getting behind my back.* "Oh, hell, just do it," he told himself softly as he brought out the silver pistols and pushed them down into his outside coat pockets. He looked both ways, saw no people on the cold streets, lowered his head, stepped round the corner, and walked, almost casually, down the sidewalk towards the alley where Rossi stood watching the upstairs window.

Rossi tensed when he saw the reflection of the man walking towards him in the bank window across the street.

The man stopped and looked in a store window two doors down from the alley as he dug a lighter out of an inside pocket and lit the end of the cigar in his mouth. He blew several clouds of smoke against the glass, shoved his hands down into his coat pockets, turned, and head down, continued his walk.

"C'mon, get the hell outta here," Rossi muttered to the man as he quickly glanced back up at the window and saw a man's back framed in it. *That looks like Larson.* He leaned out for a clear look at the man walking towards him. There was something familiar about the big man as he approached. Rossi realized who it was and spun to bring the rifle down to bear on him.

But unexpectedly the man had a fancy silver revolver in his hand that belched fire and smoke three times.

The trio of slugs punched through Rossi's uniformed chest and slammed him back against the alley wall. The sounds of the shots echoed off buildings and the rifle clattered to the frozen alley dirt as Rossi toppled forward to lay facedown beside it.

"That was because of your buddy, Boner, and my need for peace of mind," Moran said, shoving Johnstone's ornate pistol into his pocket, lowering his head, and running straight back across the street.

The sound of the shots made Andy Larson spin and look down in time to see a man run towards him and out of sight at the front of the building.

Moran rounded the corner to yank open the Packard door, release the hand brake, shove the transmission in gear, stomp on the gas, and steer the swerving car off down the street.

CHAPTER SIXTY-FOUR

Sheriff Larson burst out the glass front door and looked both ways for the shooter. "He's gone," he said to Durbin as he shoved out behind him.

"I'll go down to the corner," Durbin volunteered and turned to run.

Larson grabbed his elbow. "Which one? He could have gone either way, even down the alley, and he's got a good lead by now. We won't catch him. Let's go see who's lying over there in the alley."

They crossed the street and looked down at the man with his face pressed into the frozen dirt.

"That's Rossi," Durbin stated.

"No shit," Larson answered. "Look at that rifle." He turned and looked up at the office window he had been standing in minutes before. "He was in here to shoot somebody." Larson dug out his Camels. "I'd say it was probably me."

Durbin nodded. "There's no doubt in my mind about that. I wonder who shot him?"

I know that was Thumper Moran running across the street. "I really didn't get a look at the shooter," Larson stated, in a cloud of smoke.

"What about the other cops?"

Larson chuckled and shook his head. "I really was hoping the whole bunch of them would make a run for it and save me a lot of paperwork," Larson confessed. "That's the reason I sent them back to the station on their own. But that's city work so whoever comes over from the state offices will have to handle it anyway."

Durbin pointed down at Rossi's body. "What about him?"

"We'll find something to cover him up with for now. Bring the rifle. I don't want somebody to wander by and pick it up. Let's get back upstairs and try to wrap that up enough to give a report to the state people when they get here Monday."

Gilliam, Lamey, Barqhart, and Peppin, dressed in civilian clothes, got out of the car, walked to the station door, and found it locked.

Peppin chose a key from the ring on his belt and the four of them crowded through the door into the booking room.

"Hey, Rossi," Peppin shouted. "I got your clothes here so you can change and we can get on the road."

Lamey pointed at the burned-label bottles on the booking bench. "We better take those with us. Just 'cause the labels burned off doesn't mean there's anything wrong with the booze in the bottle."

Gilliam walked around the office, opening doors and calling for Rossi. "He ain't here," he finally decided. "Anybody got any ideas?"

"You don't suppose he went back to get the sheriff, do you?" Peppin asked.

"Naw," Barqhart answered. "He ain't that stupid, is he? What d'ya think?"

The four ex-cops stood looking at each other.

"We could go back to the shot-up offices and see if he's there," Peppin suggested.

"Yeah," Lamey agreed. "Maybe he went an' gave himself up." Everyone laughed.

"I say let's hit the road," Barqhart volunteered.

"If Rossi's in town and we leave him, the bastard'll hunt us down and that ain't gonna be good," Lamey stated. "We can't just drive off and leave his ass here in Wolf Point."

"Okay," Peppin said, "we'll get in the car and drive by the shootout. Nobody knows anything about the car we got now, so if we put our hats on and sit low, we can at least take a look."

"Oh, I don't know," Lamey argued. "What if one of us bundles up like we're trying to stay nice an' warm an' just walks by the place? Ain't nobody gonna pay any attention to some guy walkin', mindin' his own business, are they?"

"Are you gonna do the walking?" Gilliam asked.

"Okay, yeah, I'll do the walkin'. We can drive up around the corner an' I'll walk. Let's lock the place up an' git the hell outta here."

The three ex-cops sat in the car and watched as Lamey, bundled against the cold and a scarf covering the bottom half of his face, started down the sidewalk across from the bank building.

"I hope this don't take too long," Gilliam said. "I'd like to be a few miles down the road before it gets dark."

"We got a full tank of gas," Barqhart said. "I say we go all the way to Williston. It's about a hundred miles and if the roads are clear, it's an easy drive."

"You're driving," Gilliam said.

Lamey saw three men standing, talking, and pointing at something in the entrance of the alley ahead. He pushed the scarf up a bit higher as he stepped up to see what they were interested in. A tarp-covered body lay in the frozen dirt and Lamey immediately recognized the boots sticking out from one edge. *Those are Rossi's fancy, expensive boots he was always so damned proud of.* "What happened?" he asked with a muffled voice.

One of the men turned and looked over at him and Lamey

saw the badge on his coat. He recognized him as a deputy sheriff, but he couldn't remember his name.

"Somebody shot him," Mooney answered, almost casually.

"You know who shot him?" Lamey asked.

"Nope," Mooney replied.

"Got any idea why they shot him?"

Mooney shrugged. "He had a rifle, and right now that's about all we know. He was the captain of the police force here in Wolf Point."

"Where are the cops anyway?" one of the men asked, looking at the others.

Mooney chuckled. "What's the old line about where's a cop when you need one?"

Lamey joined the others in their laughter, then turned and slowly walked back down the street, stopping from time to time to look in windows. He turned the corner, trotted to the waiting car, and jumped in. "Let's get the hell outta here. That's Rossi lyin' back there in the alley under a tarp. He ain't gonna be hunting for us any time soon."

CHAPTER SIXTY-FIVE

One Month Later

Sheriff Andy Larson looked up from his mail. "Hey, Dusty, I got a letter today from the Mounties up in Estevan telling me they found my truck."

Durbin came and stood in the doorway. "I guess that's good news."

"A road crew found it in a snowbank with a frozen, shot-up body in the back end. According to his papers it's Dominic Bianci, the guy who told me about Rossi and then escaped during all the shooting. He'd been shotgunned."

"I wonder what he was doing up there?"

"Hard to tell, but no doubt it had to do with illegal booze."

"When do you get your truck back?"

"According to this letter, it's going to need a new radiator and probably a few more things done to it. Everything's froze solid so I guess I should've put some of that seized liquor in the radiator."

Both men laughed.

"They'll let me know when I can come and get it."

"What happened over at the mayor's office last night?"

"About three weeks ago the town fathers agreed to give all the former cops a five-dollar-a-week pay raise if they'll come back to Wolf Point. They offered Mike Goetz ten more a week if he'd be the chief and he agreed. He should be here in the next day or two. Graves's talked to all the others and he's pretty sure they'll be coming back. They really didn't want to leave, but the killings drove them out. They've all got homes here that haven't sold and it looks like it's going back to pre-liquor days."

"Yeah, I'd say Wolf Point is going to be the same dull place it used to be," Durbin stated. "We haven't seen any sign of traffic on the back roads, so if they're still running booze through here, they're staying on the main roads and aren't slowing down or stopping."

"The newspapers did a pretty good job with the stories about what a badass, no-nonsense sheriff we have here in Roosevelt County and I think that made a big impression on the bootleg people. They may like the big-city, shoot 'em up stuff in Chicago and places like that, but it's not going to work out here. The profit isn't worth the price."

"I'd say the state crime boys will be glad to get out of here and back to Helena."

"Like you said, Wolf Point's turning into a pretty dull place again."

EPILOGUE

May 1924

Andy and Becky Larson stood with a group of friends on the courthouse lawn in Wolf Point, Montana. Andy's Model A pickup truck stood at the curb, the back piled high with well-tied-down boxes.

"Well, *Sheriff* Durbin," Andy said, holding out his hand. "I'm sure you'll do a hell of a job keeping the county peaceful and safe from the bad guys."

Dusty Durbin's face was shaved for the summer and the constant unlit cigar was more prominent as it rolled back and forth in his grinning mouth. "You sure you don't wanna change your mind, Andy? I'll make you *my* chief deputy."

Larson, glancing out of the corner of his eye at Becky, who was holding onto his arm, just smiled and shook his head. "No, Dusty, I'm looking forward to going to Devils Lake, North Dakota, and just being a farmer for a while. Becky's dad has got to have help with the plowing and it's been too wet to plant anything yet, so the timing is working out good."

Police Chief Mike Goetz stepped up and offered his hand to Larson. "Andy, I want to tell you that you did a hell of a job. We're going to miss you. If you ever want to be a cop again, just send me a letter and I'll see what I can do for you."

"I already told him that last night," Sheriff Durbin said.

Mayor George Hauger clapped his hands for attention. "Miss Becky, you were a terrific schoolteacher and all the kids are going to miss you. Andy, we have a little something for you as a remembrance of the time you were here in Wolf Point, Montana. Dusty, if you'd be so kind."

Sheriff Dusty Durbin's grin got bigger as he stepped forward, dug in his shirt pocket, brought out a leather case, and flipped it open to reveal a beautiful gold star badge. "It says on this fancy thing: Andy Larson, Honorary Sheriff, Roosevelt County, Montana. Oh, yeah, and one more thing. That badge is solid gold."

Larson's eyes blinked rapidly and he wiped a finger across his mustache as he took the cased gold badge from Sheriff Durbin and held it up for the people to see. "I'm gonna tell you all thanks one more time and then Becky and I've got to get on the road. Becky."

Becky Larson dabbed at the corner of her eye and she smiled at the people gathered around. "I'm sure Andy and I thanked all of you individually last night, but once again, thank you all so much for a truly memorable time in our lives."

The women lined up and began to hug Becky and the men stepped up to shake Andy Larson's hand one last time.

"Okay, folks, we gotta go," Larson called as he took Becky's hand and began to walk towards the truck, waving his new gold badge case in the air. "Goodbye and thanks again for everything!"

As the truck pulled away from the curb, Andy reached in his shirt pocket, brought out a postcard and handed it to Becky. "This was in the office mail today and Dusty gave it to me awhile ago."

Becky looked at the picture of *The French Wench* and turned the card over.

Andy: I still have a few of these cards left so I figured I'd use them up. Charlie and I are living well out here in

California. We ran into another old Army buddy who's making movies. Look for me in the westerns. I still wear my spurs, but I've got a bigger mustache. Thanks for everything!

Wild Bill

ABOUT THE AUTHOR

Mike Thompson is an award-winning writer and photographer. He and his wife, Ruthie, live with two cats, Daisy and Molly, on the Laughing Horse Ranch, Land and Cattle Company in San Angelo, Texas. He retired from the government, where he tested explosives and was founder and curator of an army museum, the Yuma Proving Ground Heritage Center. He is a Vietnam veteran (1966–67). In Vietnam he was a field medic and a medical research specialist. His military career includes the U.S. Air Force, Army National Guard, and Reserves. He has owned several businesses; worked as a stage and screen actor, carpenter, bartender, and oil landman; raised horses; and done many other things while trying to decide if he'll grow up.